A Secret
at the
Cottage
by the
Loch

BOOKS BY KENNEDY KERR

LOCH CAMERON

The Cottage by the Loch

MAGPIE COVE

The House at Magpie Cove

Secrets of Magpie Cove

Daughters of Magpie Cove

Dreams of Magpie Cove

A Spell of Murder

Kennedy Kerr

A Secret
at the
Cottage
by the
Loch

bookouture

Published by Bookouture in 2023

An imprint of Storyfire Ltd.
Carmelite House
50 Victoria Embankment
London EC4Y 0DZ

www.bookouture.com

ISBN: 978-1-83790-378-8
eBook ISBN: 978-1-83790-377-1

For all the romantics

PROLOGUE

I just don't want a baby this much, Paul had said to her. *I want you, Liz. But I can't do this anymore.*

What? She hadn't believed it, at first. But, as she looked in his eyes, she could see he was speaking from the heart.

But I thought you wanted a baby, she'd said, not believing what was happening.

I did. I do. But not like this. The arguments. The silences. I constantly feel like I've... failed. Because I can't give you what you want, he'd answered, dully.

She had tried to wrap his arms around her, the way she used to. But he'd pulled away. *Don't. I can't.*

It's the hormones, she'd said, starting to cry. *I'm not myself. I know I've put on weight, and...* The tears started rolling down her face. *Please. Please don't leave me. And, it's not you. It's me. I'm the infertile one.*

Yeah, but it's both of us that are in this. And it's nothing to do with your weight, Paul had said with a sigh. *I love you whatever size you are. And I love you when you're moody and snappy and when you cry. But I can't live with seeing what this is doing to you anymore. You're suffering too much, and I just don't think it's worth it. And... and I can't take it anymore. If we knew for sure it would work this time...* He trailed off.

But we can't know that, Liz finished his sentence, and he nodded.

Yeah.

She and Paul had been about to start a fourth round of IVF, and Liz's doctor had put the decision in their hands. Many people conceived in the first two or three rounds, she had said, but there was still a good chance that you could have a baby on your sixth or seventh round.

That had been the day before. She and Paul had signed the paperwork in the doctor's office: as far as Liz knew, Paul was as committed as she was to another round.

Until today.

The doctor said IVF could still be effective between six to nine rounds, Liz had reminded him, knowing from Paul's face that he had already made his mind up.

I can't do this another six times, Paul had replied, tiredly. *I can't do another one. And we can't afford another three or four times, Liz. The money is ridiculous. It's too much.*

Money doesn't mean anything to me, she'd argued, stubbornly. *This is a child we're talking about. You can't put a price on life.*

Paul had said, *Why don't we use that money for a really great holiday instead? We could both do with a break: let's relax, get away, and see what happens.*

Liz had got up and paced around the room. *I'm so far beyond 'let's relax and see what happens'. Can't you see that?* she'd argued. *You're a man. You can be relaxed about being a father. I can't.*

We have a few years left. You're only thirty-seven, he'd argued back.

You just don't get it, she'd shouted.

No, I guess I don't.

There were things that Liz felt that she knew Paul wouldn't understand if she told him. She had felt, for the past few years, that she was on some kind of baby countdown game show, where the top prize was a child: previous winners would be paraded in front of the players in every episode, complete with their buggies and prams and chubby babies. This was what it was like, going about her life in the world every day: at the supermarket, on the street, on buses and trains, Liz saw women with children everywhere, and her heart sank every time. Not because she begrudged those women their children. Because she wanted her own baby, so very much.

Those women had played the game, and won.

She could see, in her mind's eye, her own particular prize at the top of a brightly lit board: a photograph of herself being a mother. She had visualised it so hard that she knew every detail: a stray wisp of her own hair on her cheek, the flush on her face, a background of trees in the evening light, and her daughter in the foreground: a little girl with her brown hair in wonky pigtails, wearing red corduroy overalls.

But that photo, of Liz cuddling her daughter-to-be, seemed to get more out of reach every day. Every time she began a new cycle of IVF, she imagined herself on the game show, answering questions, passing ridiculous tasks, being injected and poked and prodded, all in the name of motherhood. All to reach that glowing photograph, ringed with flashing pink lights.

Watch as Liz Parsons from Glasgow competes to win her perfect life. Will she win the jackpot? She imagined the smooth voice of a gameshow host narrating her life.

Was she good enough to play the game? Would she win, this time?

She couldn't explain any of that to Paul. She couldn't explain how important it was to rig the game in your favour, any way that you could. Because the torture of thinking that she might never have her own child was more than she could cope with.

Paul moved out the next day. Liz had sat on the sofa, watching Paul pack his clothes into suitcases.

Please don't go, she'd begged him. *I love you. Don't you love me anymore?*

He had refused to answer. He couldn't even look her in the eye.

He had left her there, on the sofa, sobbing her heart out and feeling that her heart had broken forever. As he'd closed the door he'd repeated, *I'm sorry. I just can't do this anymore. I can't handle the heartbreak. It's too much.*

And so, now, Liz was alone. And the photograph in the game show of her life as a mother – the little girl with her hair in corduroy overalls and wonky pigtails, and Liz next to her – was ripped into tiny pieces.

ONE

Liz Parsons stood outside the door to the distillery for a moment before she stepped inside.

Today, she was beginning again, and though she had made many brave new starts in her life, they never got any easier. Yet, this was a *good* new start: a new job as Sales Director at a family-owned whisky distillery, in a tiny little village called Loch Cameron.

Liz had experienced too many failures in the past few years; she had built her hopes up again and again, only to have them dashed when her fertility treatment didn't work. So, now, she hoped that this job – which had meant she'd had to move her whole life away from Glasgow to a tiny Highlands village – was something new that she could hold onto.

The job offer couldn't have come at a better time. She had wanted a child so much. But it hadn't happened. And it wasn't going to happen with Paul, now.

Liz felt tears well up inside her and fought them down. She couldn't start her new job crying: what would they think of her?

This isn't the time, she told herself firmly. *Of all the times, this is definitely not it.*

But it was all still so raw. Even though Liz wasn't on IVF's punishing schedule anymore – taking hormones, having scans, having the eggs extracted, fertilised and transferred – she still felt hyper emotional. She missed Paul. But he had made it perfectly clear that he wanted out.

Ironically, that meant that Liz had not gone forward with the fourth round of IVF, which was what Paul had wanted.

But, right now, she had to focus on her first day at Loch Cameron Distillery.

She pushed the old wooden door, noticing that the paint was flaking off a little and the hinges were beginning to rust.

That's something that needs repair, she thought. *Can't have the entrance to your business looking anything other than perfect.*

The building itself was a long, whitewashed Scottish farm-house with the name of the distillery painted in huge block white letters on its black slate roof. Liz was going in at the main entrance which had huge wooden double doors, painted black apart from where it needed a touch up. To the side of the main building, there were a number of matching white outbuildings with black window frames and doors, and a tall red brick building that stood alone in the middle. Liz guessed that was the main distilling area.

Liz walked inside, into an open reception area where a woman sat at an old-fashioned wooden desk, in front of a glass floor-to-ceiling panel that displayed the logo of the distillery: LOCH CAMERON DISTILLERY, EST. 1785 against the image of a castle. That would be Loch Cameron Castle, she imagined; she'd seen it from afar, a brooding grey stone struc-ture on one side of the loch.

'Hi. I'm Liz Parsons. I'm starting as Sales Director today.' Liz held out her hand to the woman, trying to ignore the flut-tering feeling of nerves in her stomach.

'Ah, great. We're expectin' ye, of course.' The woman stood

up and took Liz's hand, shaking it vigorously. 'Welcome tae Loch Cameron Distillery!'

'Thank you.' Liz gave the receptionist a firm handshake in return.

'I'm Carol. I've been on reception fer twenty years,' the woman explained. 'No' without a break, mind! Haha. Would ye like a tea or coffee? I dinnae think they're ready fer ye just yet.'

'Oh, that's okay, I can make myself a coffee.' Liz looked over at the clunky self-service drinks machine that stood in one corner. 'No trouble.'

'Pffft. You will not.' Carol looked scandalised. 'Let me make ye a proper one. That's just fer ordinary visitors.' She bustled into a kitchen off the side of the reception area, beckoning Liz to follow her. 'We've got a proper Italian machine in here,' she explained. 'Ben insisted.'

'Ben Douglas?' Liz knew he was the owner and CEO of the distillery, a family business. He'd interviewed her online, though their talk had been pretty brief. Frankly, Liz had been amazed when she'd been offered the job.

'Aye. He likes gadgets.' Carol sailed into the small but cosy kitchen that adjoined the reception. She was probably coming up to sixty, though Liz was terrible at guessing people's ages. She was tanned and slim, and dressed nicely in a skirt suit with a pale blue blouse underneath the jacket: Liz thought that she looked like someone who enjoyed her holiday in the sun every year, and kept busy.

'How is he as a boss?' Liz asked, following her. The little kitchen was very well appointed, with a gleaming silver espresso machine which sat proudly on top of a white marble worktop. The kitchen units were also white, in a cottage style which fitted the feel of the white distillery buildings outside with their black trim.

To one side of the coffee machine, which Carol started operating expertly, there was a smart, glass-fronted wine fridge, full of champagne and white wine. Next to that was a shelf displaying a row of Loch Cameron Distillery twenty-year-old whisky.

'Ach, he's fine, bless him,' Carol trilled as she flicked switches and steamed milk. 'Sweet boy, nothin' like his faither. Mind ye, not really a boy anymore, but that's me showin' ma age. Now. Espresso, cappuccino, americano? I'm havin' a cappuccino.'

'Sounds great. I'll have the same.' Liz smiled.

Liz had been grateful to have the opportunity to have an online interview rather than come to the distillery in person. It had been a tough couple of months, with Paul moving out and her old firm squeezing every last bit of work out of her before she finished up her notice period. The distillery was a good couple of hours' drive from Glasgow and, if she was honest, she hadn't felt up to attending in person at the time.

So, when Ben had offered a live online call, she'd accepted.

However, that did mean that she'd accepted the job without ever seeing the distillery, or meeting Ben or anyone else in person. Usually, Liz would never have done that. She liked to get the feel of a workplace, and the people in it. She had received a lot of praise in her career for her sales instincts – a nebulous quality that some people seemed to have, and some people just didn't. What most people thought it meant was that Liz was very good at finding the right people and the right opportunities to sell her products, but, as far as she was concerned, it was about building relationships and listening to your gut.

Liz's gut was telling her right now that Carol was an important person to be friends with at the distillery, and also that she liked her a lot.

'So, where were ye before comin' tae join us?' Carol enquired. 'Ben was very excited when ye accepted the job; he's been singin' yer praises in meetin's for weeks. Top Sales

Director o' the Year, five years runnin'. You won some awards, too, he says.' The receptionist shot her a curious look.

'Oh. A hospitality company in Glasgow. I was there for ten years.' Liz named probably the biggest company in the industry, and Carol whistled.

'I'm not sure Ben could compete with whatever ye must've got paid there.' She shot Liz a curious look. 'Why'd ye want tae give that up and come up here? I got a friend that works there, and she says they've got fridges ye can help yerself from all day. Beer, chocolates, the whole kit and caboodle, aye. Plus, a gym, big pension, all that. Why give that up? If ye dinnae mind me askin'.'

It was a good question, but Liz wasn't about to spill the real reason she'd taken a pay cut to come and work in a remote lochside village.

'Just fancied a change,' she said, noncommittally. That wasn't a lie in itself. She had needed a change. She'd needed to get away from everything that reminded her of Paul, and of their past few years of disappointment after disappointment. And, though she'd loved her job, it demanded so much from her. Frankly, she wasn't sure that she could do the late nights, the stress and the travelling anymore.

Feeling tears threatening to overwhelm her again and not wanting Carol to see, Liz turned away and pretended to look for something in her handbag. She took some deep breaths, trying to compose herself, and pulled out a tissue to blow her nose.

'One cappuccino.' Carol handed her a white mug with an expertly-made coffee in it. 'I didnae put any sugar in, but we have it, if you'd like?'

'Oh, no, I'm fine. Thank you so much for this.'

'Ach, it's nae bother,' Carol assured her.

In an ideal world, Loch Cameron Distillery wouldn't have been Liz's first choice in finding a new job. If anyone had asked her a year ago if she would have wanted to move to a tiny village with questionable internet connection and nothing more than a quaint high street for miles around, she would have laughed at them. She loved her job. She loved heading up a big sales team for the world's industry leading hospitality company – which, also, provided excellent maternity benefits. She would be a fool to give all that up.

But now, there was more at stake than just her career. Liz had genuinely felt that if she stayed in Glasgow for one day longer than she had, and if she had had to drive from her flat to her job, past the hospital that she had spent so much time in, then she might go mad. She had spent so much time in the hospital. She knew its car parks and corridors and cafés as well as she knew her childhood home. She couldn't bear to see it every day any more.

And, every time she walked past the door to the spare room in her flat – the one she had imagined as a nursery, so many times – she was reminded of that last day with Paul. Of begging him not to go. Trying to persuade him to try with her, one last time, to have a family.

Liz couldn't face living in that flat any more. It was as if the empty spare room taunted her. The family she could have had. The baby she could have loved. The future that had been taken away for what seemed like forever.

However, Loch Cameron was a new start. The change would be good for her; the job was a new challenge, the air in the village was fresh and clean, and just breathing it in made her feel better.

'Ah, hello, Liz. Sorry to keep you. I'm Sally Burns.' A woman poked her head around the door of the kitchen and knocked on the wooden doorframe. 'I heard voices out here, so I thought I'd come and see if it was you.'

Liz looked around, hoping her face wasn't flushed and her eyes were clear.

'Yes, hello, Sally.' She was tall, dark skinned, looked like she worked out and was impeccably dressed in a well-cut grey trouser suit and a crisp white shirt. Liz liked her soft brown eyes, which held a curious, friendly look.

'I'm the Finance Director here, so we'll likely be working together pretty closely,' Sally explained, walking in and extending her hand to Liz who shook it.

'Ben's asked me to convey his apologies. He was supposed to be here today to welcome you and do your induction, but something unavoidable's come up. I'm so sorry. But I'm happy to show you around, if that's all right?'

Liz felt a twang of irritation at the fact that the owner of the company – her new boss – wasn't there on her first day and wondered what was so unavoidable.

'Follow me. Bring your coffee, and I'll show you your office.'

'Lovely. Thanks.' Liz picked up her bag. 'Lovely to meet you, Carol. I'll see you later, no doubt.'

'Aye, you will. Ask me if you need anythin' – I'm happy to help.' Carol beamed.

'It's great you were able to join us so soon,' Sally said as they passed through reception and walked into a glass corridor that joined one part of the building to another. Liz guessed it was a modern addition, and she liked how it complemented the older buildings, allowing you to see them ahead of you as you walked along.

Fortunately, Liz had had some holiday owing to her, so she'd left her job a couple of weeks before the end of her three-months' notice. Surprisingly, there had been no stipulations from her old firm as there sometimes were if you left a sales job: her old boss, Sharon, had told her that she wasn't particularly worried about Loch Cameron Distillery being serious competition.

I will miss you, Liz, Sharon had said, giving her a hug. They were friends as well as colleagues, and Liz had felt guilty for leaving, if only because Sharon had been so supportive throughout her IVF. *But I get it.*

'Glad to be here.' Liz followed Sally into a corridor with a series of offices.

'Okay. Well, Ben and Eva – she's the Operations Director – will join us tomorrow, so you'll meet them soon. But here's your office,' she said, stepping in front of Liz and opening a door. 'If you want to leave your stuff here you can, and I'll take you on a tour of the distillery, and bring you up to date on where we are.'

'Great.' Liz liked her office immediately. Rather than a slightly soulless corporate block, Loch Cameron Distillery's offices had been built into the old distillery buildings and styled with exposed brick and a window out onto a circular garden filled with wild flowers. She had a desk and a comfortable-looking leather chair that looked out onto the garden, but her office also had an old fireplace, a cabinet filled with antique-looking glassware and decanters – some of which were full of an amber liquid Liz assumed was some of the distillery's own – and, unexpectedly, a rather aged-looking black and tan dachshund in a tartan dog bed.

'Oh! Who are you?' Liz bent down immediately and reached out her hand to the dog, who sniffed it and licked her fingers tiredly.

'Ah. That's Henry. I forgot he had a bed in here. I can move it, if you like,' Sally offered. 'He's Ben's dog, but he kind of lives here most of the time. He's pretty quiet, but he does like a scratch behind the ears, and...' Sally opened the top drawer of the desk, and took out a bag of dog treats. 'He'll be your friend forever if you give him one of these.'

'Oh, yes, of course, he must have one!' Liz took the bag from Sally and took out a bone-shaped biscuit. Henry sat up, suddenly interested. 'Do you want a biscuit? Do you, widdle Henry? I bet you do. Yes, you do.' Liz realised she was doing her 'talking to animals' voice, and cleared her throat. 'Sorry. Not very professional.' She fed the biscuit to Henry, who was most appreciative.

'Don't apologise. Henry's a fixture around here. More or less the fifth member of the Directorate,' Sally told her with a grin. 'Ready for a tour?'

'I am.' Liz dropped her handbag on the leather chair and gave Henry a last ear scratch. 'Let's do it.'

TWO

'As you'll see, it all started in 1785.' Sally pointed up at the company name that arched above her head in huge black letters, painted on the whitewashed wall of the main distillery shed. 'Ben's ancestor started it; legend has it that he was taught by a local monk.'

'The monks were the ones who spread knowledge about how to distil alcohol after Henry VIII closed all the monasteries down,' Liz commented. 'So, that doesn't surprise me.'

They walked into a cobbled courtyard, circular like the wild garden Liz had glimpsed through her office window. Pathways led off it in different directions, following their way past buildings that looked as old as the rest of the complex. All of them bore whitewashed walls and black tiled roofs. Against the dark green of the pine trees that surrounded the distillery, the whole place had a slightly otherworldly feeling.

'Ah, of course. You probably know more than me about that.' Sally smiled, opening the door into the main shed. 'After you.'

Liz stepped through the glossy black wooden door and into a high-ceilinged hangar filled with huge gleaming copper stills.

Each one was roughly the length of a car, and the shape of an oversized genie's lamp: bulbous at the bottom and tapering into a copper chimney at the top.

Of course, every distillery was different, but she'd seen many over her years working in the beverage industry, and so this sight was reasonably familiar for Liz. The smell of the fermented mash liquid being boiled in these huge copper cauldrons was also familiar, and somewhat reassuring too.

'The mash tuns are still in their original positions, as is the waterwheel which once powered the whole distillery,' Sally added as they walked through. 'You'll see it when we walk out.'

'It's beautiful,' Liz said, taking it all in. 'Very traditional.'

'Yes, it's been this way pretty much since the 1780s, as I understand it.' Sally pointed to some framed black and white photos on the wall behind them that showed the copper stills in the same position, tended by men in suits from a bygone age.

'I love those. It's so nice when distilleries have that long history. That's partly what drew me here,' Liz said, peering at the picture. *And the chance to escape,* she thought. Somewhere that didn't constantly remind her of Paul, and of the dreams for a family that she'd had to start to try and forget about.

Liz knew, rationally, that she couldn't just forget her dream of being a mother. It had been something she'd always wanted. More than that: it was something she needed. Even though she loved her work – she always would – she had also known she was meant to be a mother. She had spent so long fantasising about having a child, had spent so long visualising all those happy times together, that it would be almost impossible to let her dreams go.

But she had to try. Because, now, she was thirty-seven, single, and had already failed three rounds of IVF. According to urban myth, she was now more likely to be abducted by aliens and struck by lightning at the same time than to meet someone new and have a baby with them. As much as it broke her heart, she had to step down as a contestant in the baby game show, and admit that she was never going to win.

'Not goin' tae introduce me?' A man wearing a baseball cap and a striped apron over his checked shirt and jeans tapped Liz on the shoulder and laughed at her surprised expression. She had been temporarily immersed in her own thoughts, and almost jumped out of her skin at the sudden touch.

'Ah, sorry. Ye must be Liz. I'm Simon, the Master Distiller. Welcome.'

'Oh, hi, Simon.' Liz shook his hand. 'Nice to meet you.' She hoped she didn't look too much like a space cadet, standing in the distillery shed, clearly away in her own world.

'What d'you think, then?' He held out his arms, indicating the space.

'It's beautiful,' she said, honestly. 'And everything looks very spic and span. It looks like you're running a tight ship here.' Liz knew that the role of Master Distiller was important; Simon was the person who oversaw the production of the whisky at all stages. If there was a problem with the whisky, then it would be Simon who had to answer for it. In the trade, Master Distillers held a lot of status and had often spent their entire careers learning the whisky process in forensic detail.

'I hope so,' Simon said, smiling warmly. 'I try my best, anyway. Ben not here tae show ye around, eh?' He raised an eyebrow. 'No' that Sally isnae wonderful, o' course. I'm always tellin' her she should run the place,' he added, doffing an imaginary cap to the Finance Director, who rolled her eyes.

'Simon. You know he was called away unexpectedly,' she replied, clearly refusing to return his more playful tone. Liz wondered if Sally was just a very serious person, or if she found Simon's irreverence irritating. Liz liked him instinctively; she generally warmed to big characters and vivacious personalities. It probably came from working in sales most of her life: a lot of the people she met were like that.

'I think I'll meet Ben tomorrow,' Liz replied. There was no way she was going to show that she was, actually, a little annoyed about the fact that Ben wasn't here on her first day.

'Well, if ye want any info, ye can always come tae me,' Simon assured her. 'I've been workin' here since I was sixteen. I learned the craft from my dad. He was Master Distiller before me, aye.' He pointed to a number of framed awards on the wall: Guild of Whisky Makers, Master Distiller Award, 2015. 2012. 2007. And, above those was a longer row of awards with dates from the 80s and 90s.

'Those older ones belonged to your dad?' Liz walked over and looked at the certificates.

'Aye.' Simon came to stand next to her. 'He passed ten years back. Worked until the day he died.'

'That's quite something,' Liz remarked. 'And I'm sorry for your loss,' she added.

'Thanks. But he died doin' what he loved.' Simon touched the nearest frame to him softly. 'It's an art. Not everyone appreciates that.'

'Oh, I certainly do. I've worked in the beverage industry most of my life. Distilleries are like home to me.' It was more than Liz had intended to say, but it was true. She realised, as she stood among the gleaming copper stills, that she had missed these places. Yes, she loved her Sales job. She was great at presentations and conferences, and great at thinking outside the box when it came to new and better ways to get the brand out there.

But part of the reason she'd applied for the job at Loch Cameron Distillery was that it reminded her of her first job at the distillery in Auchentoshan, the rural village where she had grown up. It had been at that first job, where she worked as a general helper, doing everything from sweeping up in the barn to answering the phone, where she had found some autonomy, and a place to go away from her constantly arguing parents.

Like the Loch Cameron distillery, Auchentoshan was a place full of these copper monsters, and the round mash tuns like huge alien saucers, parked in a barn. This was a place that smelt like home, where she could retreat from the world.

'Ah. All the more welcome tae ye, then.' Simon met her eyes, and they shared a look of... what? Fellowship, perhaps, or knowing. 'No' like some people, who swan intae the business after university, not knowin' barley from grass.'

'Not now, Simon,' Sally said, in a low voice.

'Ah, I'm just messin' with ye. Ye'll get used tae me, Liz.' Simon gave her a friendly grin. 'Anyway, I better get back tae it. See ye anon.'

'Nice to meet you, Simon.' Liz nodded. She wasn't building a great image in her mind of Ben Douglas, the owner: she assumed that was who Simon's last comment had been aimed at.

'Well, that was... interesting,' she said, as they walked out of the other side of the main shed and found themselves outside again. 'The university comment. I assume that was about Ben?'

'Hmm. Simon's very talented, but he's got a chip on his shoulder,' Sally said, shortly. 'He resents Ben because he inherited the business. Probably thinks he could run it better himself.'

'Could he?' Liz asked. 'I mean, I looked at the accounts. I assume that's why I'm here – to improve sales? Business hasn't been so great over the past few years.' She remembered that Sally was Finance Director, and therefore responsible for the accounts she had just mentioned. 'I'm not saying anything about your side of things, obviously. But you can only do what you can when the income's so low.'

'No, I don't think Simon could do a better job,' Sally replied, just as shortly as before. 'And, don't apologise. I understand, and I agree. Ben loves this place. But, yes, we do need help.'

'Hmm.' Liz was noncommittal: until she had the full picture

of what was going on at the distillery, she wasn't going to draw any firm conclusions. 'So, tell me more about the history of the place.'

'All right. Well, there are rumours that there was an illegal operation happening on the site before the Douglases started the company as it is now, but that's hearsay. It received an official license to produce and sell whisky in 1785, making it Scotland's oldest whisky distillery. Prohibition meant that it was mothballed from 1921 until 1959, though. That was because its main business at that point was making whisky for one of the big imported blends. It always made a single malt, but that wasn't enough to keep the business going during those years.'

'I didn't know that.' Liz followed Sally around a corner and came upon a huge water wheel attached to the side of one of the buildings and sitting in the low water of a wide stream, leading into the loch in front of them. 'Ah. The waterwheel! It's huge. Always find these things a bit forbidding.' She shivered. 'I think there must have been a horror film I saw when I was a kid, where a woman was tied to one of them and drowned.'

'Well, nothing of that nature happened here, as far as I know.' Sally stopped with her and gazed up at the cast iron wheel: even its spokes were as thick as a tennis player's thighs.

'Good. Go on, tell me more about the distillery,' Liz prompted. 'It's good to know the story of the place. Story is important. That's how you sell something. You tell the story of the brand.'

'Right. Well, let's see, what else can I tell you? We've got an annual capacity of 1,000,000 litres, but we produce less than half of that. Simon will tell you that we could definitely produce more.'

'Interesting.' Liz made a mental note. 'Why don't you?'

'Ask Ben.' Sally gave her a smile that implied she didn't agree with whatever the reason was.

'All right.' They walked on.

'Well, I guess another thing to say is that our vault is Scotland's oldest,' Sally added.

'I'd love to see it,' Liz said. 'I guess I'm interested in the story of the distillery, though. So, it closed during the Prohibition years, but then it opened again in 1959? Then what? Any stories after that? Any points of interest?'

'Hmm. I don't really know,' Sally mulled as they approached another glossy painted wood door; this one was titled VAULT. 'Here we are, as if by magic.'

Liz stepped into a hallway with stairs that led down into darkness. It was much cooler in here, and she shivered involuntarily. Sally tapped a switch, and the stairs were bathed in light.

'I'll go down first. Watch your step; the treads are a little old,' she cautioned. Liz rested her hand on a wooden banister as they made their way down, cautiously.

'I hadn't realised that monasteries were the ones that really developed alcohol production,' Sally commented as they reached the bottom of the stairs. 'I just knew that Ben's ancestor learnt it from a monk. I just kind of had an idea he was a rogue agent or something.'

'Oh, no. The first records of people fermenting grain was found in the archaeological digs of Babylon and Mesopotamia. Then, the European Christian monasteries got hold of the idea. They needed to produce several types of alcoholic beverages to be used in ceremony, so, kind of ironically, the Church preserved the process of fermentation and distillation during the Dark and Middle Ages.' Liz blushed, thankful it was dark in the vault. 'Sorry. I'm just kind of a nerd about this stuff.'

'Not at all. It's fascinating. I've picked up quite a lot of whisky information since I've worked here, but it's not my area of interest.'

'How long have you been here?' Liz asked.

'Five years.' Sally flicked another switch and dim lighting

glowed the vault to life, highlighting a space that stretched into distant corridors, lined with barrels.

'Wow,' Liz breathed, looking around her. 'This is amazing. It looks like it goes on for miles. What's the oldest cask you have down here?'

'Oh, gosh. I think there's an 1810 down here somewhere. But, yeah. Some really vintage ones, for sure.' Sally frowned. 'You'd have to ask Ben.'

'I will.' Liz already had a few things to mention to the distillery owner – when he chose to show up.

'And... are they ever sold? The market for vintage whisky from niche distilleries like this is very active.' Liz traced her finger in the dust covering a row of oak casks, stamped with the Loch Cameron Distillery name.

'Not as far as I know.' Sally raised an eyebrow. 'So, you were saying,' Sally prompted her. 'My distillery history lesson.'

'Oh. Stop it,' Liz snorted. 'You know all this. You don't have to humour me.'

'Actually, I don't. I'm a finance person, remember. I mean, I like whisky. But I'm more of an enthusiastic amateur.' Sally shrugged.

Liz smiled. Now that she was at the distillery, she was in her element, and any first day nerves or anxiety had melted away.

'Okay. Well, what else...? Okay, well, although we can probably thank the monks for their sterling work in perfecting the art of distilling, some records show that the ancient Celts practiced distillation during the production of their *uisgebeatha*. That means *water of life* in Gaelic,' she added. 'It wasn't what we think of as whisky now, but it was a kind of alcohol made from the plants that were available. Whisky – and beer – came about from grain because grapes don't grow in these kinds of cold climates. In Italy, France, Spain – those hot countries – they had grapes, so they made wine. We had rain, farmers growing grains, peat and clean spring water, so we made whisky.'

'I see. So the rain was good for something, then?'

'Yeah.' Liz laughed. 'Only that, though.'

'Right. The rain does get a bit relentless,' Sally chuckled. 'Fortunately, me and my partner live in the next village. It's a lot more hilly there, so at least we're not in danger of getting flooded anytime soon. Which has happened in Loch Cameron before.'

'Really? I didn't know that.'

'Yeah. The loch's burst its banks a couple of times, but not for about twenty years. Still, weather's getting worse now. I do worry about the village here sometimes.' Sally trailed a hand along a row of barrels next to them. 'There was talk about the Laird fortifying the loch's defences, but I don't know if it ever happened.'

'Who is the Laird here?' Liz knew that many communities in Scotland still had a titular Laird; a lord who owned the land and sometimes the properties across several villages or towns. Many of the old Scottish noble families had sold their land over the years, and many couldn't afford the upkeep on their castles, so had sold them to national organisations who opened them up to the public.

But even before she'd come to Loch Cameron, Liz knew that it had a privately-owned castle that sat on the other side of the loch to the village, towering over it like something out of a gothic romance novel. Now that she'd seen its pointed turrets and elaborately manicured gardens, she could see its appeal; she'd read online that it also boasted a private beach at the edge of the loch. Some of it was hidden behind woodland, and Liz suspected that the whole estate probably stretched for miles.

'Hal Cameron. Nice guy, actually. Not one of these old duffers you sometimes get, out of touch with the local community. He's probably our age, and he's done a lot for the village.

He's the local landowner, but he's helped quite a few local busi-nesses thrive with business grants and almost non-existent rents for their commercial properties. He sponsors a farmers' market every month, and he rents the castle out for weddings. You'll meet him at some point, I'm sure.' Sally stopped walking at the end of a long passageway stacked with barrels. 'Well, I think that's pretty much it for the archive,' she added. 'Shall we go back up? I can start taking you through the financial records in detail, if you like. Seeing as you've already looked at the accounts.'

'Sure.' Liz followed the other woman as she made her way carefully along the rows of barrels and old bottles, stacked care-fully in racks. At least she was learning a lot about the distillery, though the person she wanted to speak to most – its owner, Ben Douglas – was mysteriously absent.

THREE

It was a novelty for Liz to have a five-minute commute in her car back to the whitewashed cottage she was now calling home. Previously, her journey into the office in central Glasgow had often taken her an hour from her flat if she'd driven it, or forty-five minutes on a packed train. She had to admit that losing a long commute at either end of her long work day wasn't exactly breaking her heart: in fact, she was loving the fact that she could finish her cup of tea and slice of toast in the cosy cottage kitchen, looking out at the cottage's quaint and slightly overgrown flower garden, and be in her office ten minutes later.

In all honesty, she thought as she drove along the twisting rural road from the distillery up to the cottage, she could even walk to work and back every day. That would do wonders for her fitness, which had taken a hit during the past few years of IVF.

Once, she had been really into running, but she just hadn't had the energy for it whilst she and Paul were trying for a baby. The treatments put such a stress on Liz's body that, some days, it had been all she could do to get out of bed and hold it together at work. Her moods had been up and down; she'd gained weight and found it impossible to lose it.

Since she wasn't having the hormone injections now, she did feel better, and was slowly starting to establish a better relationship with her body again. But it was slow going. Walking to work and back every day would help bring her back to something near what she used to be, at least. She wasn't so bothered about how she looked or how thin or fat she was; it was more about appreciating how her body felt and what it could do, rather than endlessly focusing on what it couldn't.

The cottage sat on a rocky point that reached into the loch, giving it a natural vantage point over the water and great views to the castle opposite, and to the imposing green and purple hills to the left. Liz had found it for rent when she had looked online after being offered her new job: there were few properties available for rent or for sale in Loch Cameron, but this one suited her perfectly.

It had just been redecorated, and though it retained a sweet cottage sensibility, Liz was delighted with its more contemporary touches.

The cottage itself, like the whole row of old stone cottages that lined the loch, had a bright whitewashed exterior which made it stand out on the horizon. This one, owned by Gretchen Ross, an elderly woman that Liz had only so far spoken to on the phone, had blue painted window frames and a blue front door under a porch. The porch was solid at the top, but open in a kind of trellis-work at the sides, where white and pink roses threaded their way up and hung prettily over the door.

Inside, floral wallpaper covered the cosy sitting room, featuring wildflowers just like the ones in the garden at the back of the cottage. An authentic-looking fireplace with light green tiles patterned with pink roses acted as a centrepiece, with a comfy upholstered chair with a hydrangea pattern, a vintage pink chaise longue and a plain cream sofa.

Liz had rented the cottage unseen, apart from the photos on the website. So, when she had first walked in, she had been slightly dreading a cottage reeking of mildew and full of dusty trinkets. However, she couldn't have been more delighted with Gretchen's cottage – and when she laid out on the pink chaise longue, she felt like a decadent socialite. *If only there were someone to feed me chocolate-dipped strawberries,* she'd thought jokingly to herself.

Liz let herself in with the key she'd found under a plant pot when she'd arrived a week before. Gretchen had asked a local friend to leave it there for Liz, as she couldn't get out so easily nowadays. *Scones and bridge tournaments, that's how they get you,* she'd exclaimed brightly on the phone when Liz had rung the care home number and been put through to Gretchen's room. *You think you're moving into a care home, and then you realise it's a geriatric cult. Honestly, Liz, if it's not whist, it's canasta and I just can't spare the time to get over to the cottage much now, not being able to drive any more.*

Liz had liked Gretchen straight away and promised to come over and visit her soon.

Well, that would be lovely. But I will come and visit when you're settled, dear. Till then, the cottage'll look after you. It's a little bit magic like that, Gretchen had assured her.

Liz walked into the sunny kitchen and dropped her handbag on a blue leather Chesterfield-style chair which faced a blackened fireplace. The Chesterfield was very comfortable, despite the fact that it was losing some of its stuffing. A large wooden dresser stood at one end, showcasing a beautiful array of vintage crockery, and the large window overlooked a cottage garden full of bright wildflowers.

Liz filled a copper kettle with water and placed it on the old range cooker, flicking a switch as she did so. Then, she reached for a mug and a floral porcelain teapot. She'd got quite into making tea in the teapot, the slow, old-fashioned way.

She sat down in a floral easy chair next to the kitchen table and breathed out a long sigh. A lot of things in Loch Cameron seemed to move in the slow, old-fashioned way, and some of it – like Gretchen's cottage – was charming. But some things were rather frustrating.

For instance, she'd had a bit of an opportunity to look at the sales reports for the company that afternoon, after she and Sally had gone through some of the main financial records, and it wasn't encouraging reading. Her predecessor, Brian, who had apparently been in the job for twenty years, seemed to think that taking the owners of a few independent off-licenses out for a boozy dinner every month was the key to successful sales. Seeing as Brian had retired with liver disease, Liz thought it was likely that approach hadn't worked out particularly well for him.

There was no evidence that Brian had approached many of the major retailers for years; he seemed to believe that, if people wanted Loch Cameron Single Malt, then they'd buy it from one of the few independent sellers that stocked it. There seemed to be no awareness in the company at all that people would buy Loch Cameron whisky if they saw it in the supermarket, whether they knew the name or not: if people tried it and liked it, as they would, because it was good, then they'd buy it again. It wasn't complicated.

Liz had come up against this kind of view before in the drinks industry. It was probably the same in any field: there were always small, specialist makers that wanted to be exclusive, desirable and collectible. And there were the big boys who sold a popular product everywhere, from petrol stations to airports and supermarkets. Both were good business models in very different ways. But the difference between Loch Cameron Distillery and a successful boutique drinks company was that Loch Cameron Distillery wasn't making any money, and she wasn't convinced that anyone had ever really intended the business to be so exclusive and hard to find in the first place.

Loch Cameron Distillery wasn't exclusive and boutique-y. It was just poorly managed.

The challenge – her challenge now, as Sales Director – was to be able to present the big retailers with a compelling enough story to persuade them to stock Loch Cameron Distillery whisky in the first place, and that was what was missing. She'd learned plenty today about the distillery, and she knew it had an amazing history. But no one else did, and that was the problem.

For another thing, the distillery seemed to have little social media presence, and its marketing – now that she'd managed to have a quick look at what was out there – was only the old, traditional trade media, like the various whisky magazines that she knew only a certain sort of person subscribed to, and old-fashioned leaflet inserts in magazines aimed at the older generation: classic motoring, gardening and fishing titles that no one under the age of fifty read.

It wasn't that it was bad, being over fifty, of course. It was just that Liz knew that only catering to one age group would bring the distillery limited success. Whisky was now considered a cool drink by young people, middle-aged hipsters, parents of young families and all kinds of other groups. It seemed that Loch Cameron Distillery was, however, not aware of this fact.

Liz poured her tea into the floral mug and gazed out at the wildflowers in the back garden, blowing gently in the breeze.

Well, here I am, she thought, sipping her drink. *For better or worse*. It was a world away from her old life, but, after all, that was what she had wanted. She was looking forward to throwing herself into something new.

The cottage'll look after you. It's a little bit magic like that, Gretchen had told her. She hoped that was true. Liz felt like she could do with some magic in her life right about now.

FOUR

The next morning, Liz arrived early at the distillery, keen to have time to reorganise her office before everyone arrived. The car park was empty, apart from a muddy pickup truck. *Perhaps a gardener was doing an early shift*, she thought, or, more likely, they had left it here overnight.

She had walked into work, leaving her car parked in the lane next to the cottage. Apart from a passing tractor and a couple of early dog walkers, the roads had been deserted. Liz had cut into a field for part of the way, following a flattened grass footpath past some cows who regarded her with equanimity.

As she'd walked along, Liz had marvelled at the deep green blanket of verdant luxury that surrounded her. The hedgerows at the edges of the fields were thick with red hawthorn berries and glossy holly, and little thrushes and great tits twittered in the occasional oaks that grew in between, flying in and out of the hedges. In the long grass at the edge of the flattened path, she came across a long white feather with a light brown stripe and held it up in amazement. She'd never been much of a one for wildlife, but it was so pretty that she decided to take it with her and ask someone at the distillery if they knew what it was. The feather felt like a good luck omen.

Liz took another deep breath of fresh lochside air. She'd been in Loch Cameron a week already, settling in to the cottage, but the clean atmosphere was still a revelation to her. All she could hear was birdsong, and there was a smell of pine in the air from the surrounding trees.

Pulling her laptop bag onto her shoulder as well as her handbag, she picked her way across the car park. She had worn walking boots for her walk into the office, and she had a pair of heels in her bag; she was keen to get into her office and change before anyone saw her in her smart suit and muddy boots. That would be a fine first impression to make on the elusive Ben Douglas, if he chose to appear at the wrong moment.

Walking into the cobbled courtyard, Liz was struck again by the beauty of the scene. Everything was so quaint, from the original cobbles to the whitewashed buildings – so like Gretchen's cottage – and the hanging baskets and window-boxes that boasted an explosion of colourful blooms.

Liz wondered if there were regular tours around the distillery. It was standard practice at other whisky-makers, but if Loch Cameron Distillery wasn't operating them, that felt like another missed opportunity. Surely, tourists would love to visit this charming location.

By now, she was developing a long list of questions for Ben and the other staff. Liz smiled to herself. *Don't make them hate you from sheer efficiency,* she thought. She'd have to make a point of introducing her ideas slowly, not all at once, or she might put someone's nose out of joint. Liz sighed and turned the key that Carol had given her at the end of the previous day in the side door that led to the corridor of offices.

There had been so many times in Liz's career that she'd had to introduce her ideas carefully out of fear of outshining her boss, or hold back on forging ahead with what she knew was a great idea, to avoid hurting someone's feelings. The more senior she'd got in sales, the more of a problem it had become: because she was a woman, other women perceived her as unfriendly or somehow betraying the sisterhood if she didn't listen to their ideas, or want to have eternal meetings about everything rather than actually make a decision.

If I was a man, no one would have a problem with me being decisive, she thought for the hundredth time.

'Early start?'

Liz looked up in surprise to see a tall, black-haired man dressed casually in jeans and a black T-shirt walking towards her. Her first thought was that he might be the gardener whose truck she had seen outside: he had a few days' worth of stubble growth on his chin, and his skin had the kind of tan you only got by being outside a lot.

'It's all right. I work here. I've got a key.' She held it out as proof.

'Oh. So you're not robbing the place?' he asked, amused. Now he was closer, Liz could see that his eyes were dark brown, with long, soft lashes. She could also see that either he worked out, or gardening kept him very fit, because his arms were muscular, and made an educated guess that the rest of him was pretty fit too.

'No! Of course not. I'm Liz. I'm the new Sales Director.' She held out her hand, and he shook it. 'Do you work in the gardens? I was just admiring them. The hanging baskets are lovely.'

'Oh, thank you. I like them too. But, no. I'm Ben Douglas. I'm so sorry I wasn't here yesterday to welcome you. I was unavoidably detained.' For a brief moment, a dark expression crossed his face, and then it was gone.

'Oh, goodness,' Liz blushed, feeling like a complete idiot, 'I'm so sorry. I saw that truck outside, and...'

'We met at the interview. I mean, I know it was online.' He

gave her that amused look again, and her stomach did a little flip. 'Still, maybe I should have had a shave before I came in to the office.'

'Oh, no. Yes, the interview. I'm so sorry, I just didn't recognise you,' Liz floundered, at once mortified that she hadn't recognised him and that he had, against all the odds, caught her in her muddy walking boots. She was also slightly irritated that he was teasing her, and at herself for assessing her new boss' fit body.

'No harm done. Welcome to the distillery.' He gave her a broad grin, and Liz's irritations fell away. There was something very charming about Ben Douglas' smile: his whole face lit up, and his eyes had a twinkly, playful warmth she liked very much. It was as if, when he smiled, someone turned on twinkly fairy lights like you did at a party. 'Do you like your office?'

'I do.' Liz walked into it and put her handbag on the chair. 'Thank you.'

'Let me know if you want anything changed, moved around, or whatever. I don't mind if you want new furniture, or a new chair. Or we can even paint the whole thing lilac if you want. It's your space, so do what you want with it.'

'Well, I'm not much of a lilac girl, but I'll think about it.' Liz smiled back. Was she imagining it, or did Ben hold her gaze for just a little too long as he stood in the doorway, his hand on the doorknob?

'Oh. Red Kite.' Ben nodded at the large white feather Liz carried. 'That's a lucky find.'

'Ah! I was hoping someone would tell me what it was.' Liz turned the long, sloping feather in front of her face. 'I found it on the walk in this morning. It's so pretty! I don't think I've seen a feather like this before. It was just sitting there in the long grass, just where I was walking.'

'You did well to find that. I don't think I've ever found one. May I?' He walked into the office and held out his hand. She passed it to him, and their fingertips brushed each other. For a brief moment, Liz had a strange feeling; it was like electricity, but not. A kind of pleasant tension from his touch.

Well, that's just ridiculous, she thought.

'Wow. That's a tail feather, I think.' He stroked the edge of the feather very gently and smiled, returning it to her. 'Keep it. Put it somewhere in here for good luck, perhaps,' he suggested.

'I will, thanks.' She smiled up at him, and there was a moment where neither of them said anything. Liz found herself lost in Ben's soft brown eyes.

She came to her senses, blinked and cleared her throat.

'Your dog has a bed in here,' she said, a little abruptly. 'Henry? We met yesterday, but I guess he's not here yet.'

'Oh, right. Sorry. I'll take it away.' Ben nodded, looking a little dazed. 'Henry decided this was his office when Brian left. He does have a bed in my office too, but he always seemed to prefer it in here.'

'That's all right, I don't mind him being here at all. I love dogs.'

'Ah, me too. Henry's a good soul, but he does think he's a human,' Ben chuckled. 'When he's in my office I always get the impression he thinks he could do things better than me. Which he probably could, to be honest.'

'I'm sure that's not the case. He's a dachshund.' Liz raised an eyebrow coquettishly, and then immediately wondered why she was being coquettish. That moment just now had thrown her a little. Somehow, there was an... energy between her and Ben that was... something. Flirty? Charged? She didn't know. But it was *something*.

'Yes, but dachshunds are very bright. Well, when you're ready, let's get a coffee and talk. Henry and I are next door. Sound good?'

'Sounds good,' Liz replied, relieved that he had returned to his usual business-like self. She waited for him to leave before she rummaged in her bag for her lipstick, reapplying it quickly and checking her hair in a hand mirror. She laid the Red Kite feather down on her desk, thinking that she'd find a little bottle or vase to put it in when she returned.

She was almost at the door when she remembered to change her muddy boots for her office heels.

Dear lord, Liz. Concentrate! she berated herself.

There would be no more odd flirting and charged moments between them. Liz was here to work.

As she was changing her shoes, Liz realised that Ben hadn't said where he was yesterday on her first day – simply that he was *unavoidably detained*. Liz didn't know him well enough to ask more details, but she remembered the momentary look that had crossed his face as he'd said it. Other than that moment, their first conversation had been lighthearted and pleasant.

But for that one moment, Ben had looked haunted.

FIVE

'So. All settled in? You were going to rent a cottage nearby, I think?' Ben sat across from Liz at his desk, a wide, dark wood thing topped with green leather and held down with bronze studs. 'Did you find one?'

Ben's office was the same size as hers, but laid out so that when he sat at his desk, he had his back to the window. His wallpaper was tartan and a large portrait of a bearded man in a gold frame hung over a blackened fireplace.

'I did. Gretchen Ross' cottage, up on Queens Point,' Liz replied.

'Ah, Gretchen. Lovely woman.' Ben nodded. 'She's at the care home now, I believe?'

'Yes. I've got to go and see her soon. We've only ever spoken on the phone, but she seems great.'

'Indeed. She was great friends with my father, in fact. He was a bibliophile, and Gretchen worked in the book world most of her life.'

'Oh, really? Is that him?' Liz pointed at the oil painting.

'Goodness, no. That's Iain Raymond Douglas, my ancestor. He's the one who established the distillery.' Ben looked up at the portrait. 'Somewhat of a tyrant, so the legend goes. But he had a vision, and we're still here. So, I have him to thank for all this.' Ben waved his hands at their surroundings. 'My father passed away some years ago,' he added, shortly.

'I'm sorry to hear that,' Liz said.

'Thank you. We weren't close, though.' Ben's friendly demeanour had shifted somewhat; his twinkly expression had faded.

'My dad died when I was younger. I don't see my mum much. She lives in Australia,' Liz offered, to break the tension that had lowered suddenly at the mention of Ben's father.

'Australia's a long way away. Why did she move there?'

'Oh, usual story. I grew up in a small village – Auchen-toshan, if you know it?'

'I do, of course. Another small distillery village.' Ben nodded.

'Yeah, I actually worked in the distillery when I was a teenager. I don't know if I told you that at my interview.'

'I don't think we talked about that, but it's good to know.'

'No, I didn't think we got to it. But I loved it – I think it's what gave me the passion for whisky, in the first place. It was like a family there, too, you know. Everyone looked out for everyone else, and I was the youngest. I was like the kid of the family.' Liz smiled at the memory. 'It was a place I could go to get some peace and quiet, away from my mum and dad arguing all the time. I used to do my homework in the office.'

'Sorry to hear that. About your parents.' Ben picked up Henry, the dog, who had been sniffing around under the desk, and put him in his lap.

'Thanks. Just standard family stuff, I guess,' Liz said, brushing over the truth somewhat. When she talked about her parents, she always made it sound like their arguments were just normal family bickering, but the truth was that it had been much more serious than that. Her dad had been ill and unable to work for many years, and that had made money very scarce at home. Her mum, a nurse, had worked all the hours she could to make ends meet, but that had meant she was always tired, and her temper was short.

When Liz's dad had died, her mum had tried to hide the fact that it was a relief, but Liz understood. It was terribly sad. Liz had loved her dad so much. But, after years of debilitating pain, it was the kindest thing for him when he had passed away, quietly, one day on the sofa. Liz had come home from the distillery where she'd been revising for her Highers and found him.

'Anyway, Mum fell in love with an Australian guy. He's kind, and she has a good life. It was tough for her for years, so I'm glad she has someone looking after her now. It's just been hard to find the time to get over there. I will, this year, probably.'

Liz didn't explain that the reason she hadn't been able to see her mum in Australia was that all her time and money had been swallowed up by the IVF for the past few years.

Again, it had been something that she and Paul had argued about before they finally split. Liz had been ready to sacrifice seeing her mother for a few years if that was what it took to get pregnant, but Paul had been of the opinion that they should still go. Liz had been so hyper-focused on the fertility treatment that she hadn't had the head space for anything else.

Paul had said that family was important. He was right, of course, although Liz and her mum hadn't ever been that close: she was always closer to her dad, and when he'd died, she'd thought that she and her mum would grow closer, but they never had.

If I ever had a child, she would think to herself, *I'd always make sure we had enough money, and we never argued about it. And I'd love that child so much. I'd tell her every day.*

There had been many days where Liz hadn't even seen her mother, let alone be told that her mother loved her. It wasn't because her mum didn't love her, but for those years, all of her energy went into her work, and Liz had felt like an inconvenience rather than a daughter. Her mum's patients had got all of her love.

'Good. So, we should talk business.'

'Yes. Let's.'

'Right. Well, first, I wanted to say how happy we are to have you start in this role. You're well known in the drinks business as a top Sales Director. You're a person with business acumen, insight and great instincts. So, I'm really happy that we managed to tempt you over to Loch Cameron.' Ben's smile returned.

'Thank you, that's very kind.' Liz nodded.

'So, I don't know if you've managed to look at the financials, and the sales reports from the past few years, but—'

'I have,' Liz interrupted. 'You're not in great shape. I guess that's why I'm here.'

'It is, yes.' Ben sighed and sat back in his chair. 'Loch Cameron Distillery is a family-owned business, as you know. It's an old, established brand, but we don't make enough money. And, if I'm honest, I need some inspiration from someone who knows the market. I know whisky, and I'm passionate about how we make it. But, honestly, I don't have the expertise to take us from traditional niche brand to... I don't know what. Better than where we are, anyway.'

'That's your first problem. You don't know what you want the brand to be. What are your aims for the company?' Liz sat forward. 'Do you want to be a boutique specialist? Mainstream family favourite? Supermarket discount brand? Hipster cocktail bar brand?'

'I don't know. Not a supermarket discount brand, I can say that at least.' Ben shuddered.

'Well, what then?' Liz was pushing him, but clearly, nobody had asked any difficult questions at the company for some time.

'I don't know. I think we're more of a boutique product, maybe?' Ben shrugged. 'We're just a whisky firm. We make two whiskies: a Ten Year Old and a Twenty Year Old. We do it well, but that's all we do. I don't know that we're different in any way to any other distillery.'

'Believe me, you are. It's just a case of defining what's special about Loch Cameron whisky, and that's what I'm great at. Tell me what's special about your Single Malt,' Liz suggested.

'Well, we use all local ingredients. We don't buy the mash in from somewhere else. Everything that goes into the whisky comes from within five miles of Loch Cameron: the peat and the grain. And we use the loch water.'

'That's good. What else?' Liz made a note on her pad.

'Umm. It's a family business. It's been run by a Douglas since 1785. We've got the biggest storage vault in Scotland,' he added, stroking Henry's silky black ears.

'Sally showed me yesterday. You have some desirable vintages down there, I think.'

'Oh, gosh, yeah. I think we've got some that date back to the 1850s. Lots of others. My dad used to look after them like they were his babies.' Ben rolled his eyes.

'Well, that's another feather in your cap. You can sell some of those vintages to collectors. Depending on what you've got down there, you could even do auction events, or make a museum out of the vault. Showcase the really old stuff.'

'Do you think so? I doubt people would be that interested.' Ben frowned.

Give me strength, Liz thought, covering her frustration with a smile.

'Again, please believe me when I say that they would be interested,' Liz assured Ben. 'Whisky collectors are a growing specialist market. If you let people know about what you have in your vault, and make a name for yourselves as a distillery of ancestry and tradition, then you can build a reputation for your Ten Year Old and your Twenty Year Old as having some of that quality pedigree,' she explained, patiently.

'I see.' Ben smiled. 'I can see why you had such glowing recommendations.'

'Thank you. So, my next question is, do you do tours here? Because you should. The building itself is interesting, and really attractive. I've noticed you don't have a gift shop or a café,' Liz added. 'Most distilleries are tourist attractions now as well as businesses. There's the tour, the tasting – at some places you can even do a day course and make your own whisky.'

'No. We don't do any of that. My dad resisted it, and I always have, too,' Ben sighed. 'Just the thought of all the health and safety stuff I'd have to put in place to have the general public here. And, it is a working distillery. I'd just think people would... get in the way.'

'Most whisky distilleries are active, and most hold tours and have gift shops,' Liz repeated, patiently. 'You have to do it to compete. I would strongly suggest you do both of those things. A café would also be nice. You could have people onsite selling food connected with the whisky in some way, like whisky fudge cake or whisky in the coffee, that kind of thing. Or, find some local artisanal caterers who would like to operate here and they can run the café.'

'You're right, I know,' Ben sighed. 'Look. These are all great ideas, but before we get onto looking at the sales reports, I want to let you know that I've received an offer for the business.' He set Henry back down on the floor and folded his hands on the desk, a serious expression on his face.

'What? From whom?' Liz was taken aback. Ben named a large, international beverage company.

'How much?' she asked, and Ben supplied a generous sum. 'Wow. So, why employ me at all, then?' She was annoyed, and perhaps it showed, because Ben got up and walked around to her side of the desk, perching on the edge of it.

'Because I don't want to take the money. I don't want to sell the business,' he said, quietly. 'But I fear I may be forced to if the brand can't make a better name for itself – which is where you come in.'

'Oh.' Liz frowned. 'You know, that's a good offer. I've seen your accounts, remember,' she added, a little archly. It was one thing, coming into a new company where there was so much work to be done. It was quite another to be told that the whole thing could be swept from under your feet at any minute. 'You're sure you won't take it? Because if I need to look for another job, I need to start looking now.'

'Liz. I don't want you to look for another job. I want you to help me rebuild Loch Cameron Distillery so that I don't have to take the offer. That's what I'm telling you.' Ben clasped her shoulder, his warm touch enveloping her.

'How long do we have? Before you make a final decision?' Liz tried to ignore the electric feeling his touch enflamed in her; she moved away, but not because she didn't like the sensation. Rather, because she did, and she didn't know what to make of it.

'I don't know, exactly. I mean, the offer won't stay on the table forever. Three months, maybe. Then, if things haven't at least improved, I'm going to have to plan a phased close. There will come a point, based on our current income, when we can't afford to keep the lights on anymore. And I don't want it to come to that.'

'I doubt your employees do, either,' Liz remarked. 'Do they know the distillery's in trouble?' She thought of Simon, the Master Distiller, who had so proudly showed Liz his father's portrait on the wall.

'No, of course not.' Ben looked haunted. 'And I'd prefer that they didn't have to.'

'Right, but if you're considering closing, you owe it to them to give them as much notice as possible to find something else,' Liz counselled. 'Loch Cameron is a small village, and if your employees are mostly local...?'

'All local.' Ben looked glum.

'Right. Well, even more reason, then. It won't be easy to find something else,' she continued. 'And, might I say, I would have appreciated knowing that I had three months to turn the business around before I said yes to the job.'

'I'm sorry. I know I should have said something, but if I did, I didn't think you'd take the job. And I knew we really needed you,' he sighed.

'That doesn't really make me feel any better about it.'

'It's not strictly three months. It might be six,' Ben said. 'I just need... help. I need business to improve at least, by then. Otherwise, yes, I will take the offer.'

You need a bloody miracle, Liz thought, but she didn't say it. She thought for a minute.

On one hand, she could turn around now and go back to her old job. She knew that Sharon would have her back in a heartbeat, and she'd only just left. She didn't think they'd finished recruiting for her replacement yet.

But did she really want to go back? No. She didn't.

Liz didn't want to go back to long commutes on busy trains, where people sneezed in her face and pushed her around. She didn't want to go back to sitting in traffic, or being expected to be the first in the office and the last out. And she couldn't go back to her old flat. It had too many memories of her and Paul.

Most of all, she didn't – couldn't – go back to passing the hospital every day, where she'd had to go twice, both times when she'd miscarried.

As much as the nurses told her that miscarriage was something normal that could happen as part of fertility treatment – and it could also happen if you weren't doing IVF, of course – it didn't make it any easier to bear the grief of losing her babies.

Yes, they were early, they were just weeks along, but Liz had still felt a horribly deep loss. They had pulled at her heart, her almost-babies. Her would-have-been children.

There were many reasons for Liz to leave Glasgow. But not having to see the hospital where she'd had to go, both times, for the nurses to kindly make sure that everything was over, was right at the top of the list.

Liz loved her little cosy cottage and was grateful for it. She loved the fact she could walk to work across the fields, with views of the loch, and come to work in her little office with its exposed brick walls and leather seat, where Carol might make her a really great cappuccino, and where Henry could pad around her office as she worked. But she was also grateful that this was a place with no memory for her; Loch Cameron was a blank slate.

Because those memories still haunted her, and she couldn't think about them.

This was somewhere she could recover from everything that had happened to her, but it was also somewhere she could make a real difference. And, that, too, had been missing for a while in her old life. Once upon a time, she had been known for taking ailing companies and turning them into successful ones. Then, she'd been recruited by the biggest firm in the industry because of her reputation, and that had been fun in a different way.

Yes, she'd been great at her job and won various awards. But the last company she'd worked for hadn't really needed her to make them successful. They were already successful. Liz's efforts were just icing on the cake, and she had started to feel a little... unnecessary.

In Loch Cameron, Liz *was* the cake. And, she realised that she had missed being *needed*.

'Right. Well, I'll do what I can.' She let out a long sigh. 'But you have to do *exactly* what I say, sales-wise. And that means we have to relaunch the brand, ideally develop at least one new

product, and we have to present to all the big retailers. Three
months isn't enough time to get a deal with them. They can take
a lot longer to even come back to agree to a meeting. Fortunately, I have good contacts there, so I can get us in the door.
But even six months is a challenge to get them to sign on the
dotted line. I'm just warning you.'

'Okay,' Ben sighed. 'Whatever you say. I just... well, to coin
a phrase, I want to make Loch Cameron Whisky great again.
You know, we had a Royal Warrant, back in the day. It would be
great to get that back, too.'

'You had a Royal Warrant?' Liz looked up from her pad and
pen. 'You mean, the whisky was approved by the Queen?'

'Yeah. We lost it in the 90s, though. Too much competition,
and I think Dad slipped up somewhere. I'm not sure of the
details.'

Liz wondered what else had been missed over the years;
how many other *slip ups* had there been that had cost the
company money?

'Right. Well, that's something we need to get back, then.'
She wrote ROYAL WARRANT on her pad and circled it.

You do like a challenge, she thought to herself. *Or, at least,
you used to.*

It was time to see if the old Liz was still there: the one who
had turned around three ailing drinks companies and turned
them into multi-million-pound enterprises. Did she still have it
in her? She didn't know. But she was going to try.

SIX

Liz was walking along the cobbled high street in Loch Cameron, spending a pleasant lunch break browsing the local shops. The sun glinted on the loch which bobbed with a faint tide: unlike some inland lochs, Loch Cameron was connected to the sea, via a long estuary, which was why there were still fishing boats moored up on its sides. Liz had seen the fishing boats coming back from their catch when she'd been walking to work; she imagined how cold it must get in the winter, leaving your warm bed and going down to the loch at two or three in the morning, only to be greeted by freezing wind, rain and the bite of the cold water.

Not for me, she thought, happy that her sweet little cottage had thick stone walls and a log burner that kept her very cosy – not to mention the piles of blankets and quilts on her vintage, white painted cast iron framed bed.

Even though Liz had always been a city girl, she could definitely appreciate Loch Cameron's old-fashioned charm.

Loch Cameron village stretched alongside the opposite side of the loch to the castle, which stood on the hill across a small, arched iron bridge which was painted blue. Liz knew that you had to cross the little bridge to get to the castle grounds, but she hadn't walked over it yet.

The photographs on the castle website had showed a stylish interior, full of antique features such as four-poster beds bedecked in velvets and tassels, a library full of leather-bound books, a music room with a grand piano and a stunning Great Hall covered in wood carvings and ancestral weapons, with a magnificent wooden double staircase, carpeted in deep red. That wasn't even counting the manicured gardens which boasted topiary animals and sloping lawns down to the loch, and pictures of the private beach she'd heard about, which featured a stone circle where people could have their wedding ceremonies, if they wanted to.

Liz had thought that the castle looked like an amazing place to have a wedding – not that she could foresee it for herself.

She had a purpose, now, and that was good: she had to try as hard as she could and help keep Loch Cameron Distillery open for business, since so many local people depended on their jobs there.

Ben needed her help. He'd been very open about that. And that was what she was going to focus on. Not weddings, and castles, and dreams. Work had always been her refuge, not the idea of a white dress and a band and a ceilidh.

The small high street consisted of perhaps ten or twelve shops: a small fashion boutique, a whisky shop, a book shop, a butcher, bakery and a small local grocery; there was also a post office that also seemed to sell all manner of essentials from bars of soap to newspapers. As well as that, there was a lovely old stone inn bedecked with hanging baskets, a hairdresser's that looked closed, a tiny primary school and a community centre. Liz had heard that there was a small café, too, but she hadn't seen it yet.

Behind the high street, a number of white cottages stood in an elevated position overlooking the high street and the loch;

Liz knew that path, as it was the one that led to Queen's Point and Gretchen Ross' cottage. Behind the cottages there was a newer development of red brick houses.

Liz had lingered outside the bookshop which was called *Pageturner's,* thinking about going in to browse, until she'd seen that there was a hand-lettered sign in the window that said OUT TO LUNCH – BACK SOON. Above her head, a shop sign featuring a flaking gold italic script hung above large lead-lined windows. There was a wooden trolley of books on sale outside, covered in a plastic cover, and a black wooden sign with gold lettering that said:

NEW & SECONDHAND BOOKS
WE BUY BOOKS

Clearly, the owner trusted the people of Loch Cameron enough to leave the trolley out while he or she was at lunch, which Liz thought was charming.

As she passed the community centre, she noticed a bustle of women carrying bags heading inside. There was a sign outside that said COFFEE 'N' CROCHET MORNING – CAKES AND SANDWICHES, and Liz's stomach grumbled as she read it. It was her lunchtime, but she hadn't thought to bring anything to eat, thinking that she'd buy something in the village. But, so far, she hadn't got as far as the bakery which was where she planned to find a sandwich or something similar.

Might as well see what's on offer in here, she thought, and followed the women inside.

Inside, two women were pulling out chairs and arranging them in a circle, while another two were unpacking Tupperware containers of cakes and sandwiches onto a trestle table. Another woman was stacking china cups and saucers at the end of the table next to a catering-sized box of tea bags and a hot water urn.

'Hello! Come in, don't be shy,' the woman stacking the cups called out. 'Tea? Cake? It's all fer charity.'

'Yes! I'd love some, and a sandwich, if there's one available.' Liz approached the table and surveyed the generous spread.

'Ach, yes of course! Egg and cress, tuna, ham, avocado and tomato.' The woman peered at the neat labels on the plates that were still covered over with cling film. 'Bess made them. She's a legend at sandwiches, so yer in good hands.'

The woman was older than Liz, perhaps fifty or so, with her curly hair in a grey-blonde bob. She wore a grey jersey dress patterned with a design of green apples with black leggings underneath, with flat-soled lace up boots. Her voice was confident, and her smile was warm and friendly.

'I'll take the egg and cress, please. And a slice of cake, I think,' Liz laughed, looking at the resplendent Victoria sponge that was dotted with strawberries and cream on one plate, and a huge chocolate layer cake that stood next to it, gleaming with glossy icing. As well as that, there was a tray full of chocolate brownies, one of oatmeal cookies dotted with raisins, and a plate full of millionaire's shortbread. 'May I have... hmm. It's so difficult to decide! I think the Victoria sponge. And a cup of tea.'

'Certainly, dear. That'll be two pounds fifty.' The woman cut a generous slice of cake and put it on a paper plate for Liz, and filled another plate with a round of thick sandwiches, oozing with filling.

'Is that all?' Liz did a double take. She'd expect to pay that for a slice of cake, never mind a whole lunch.

'Aye. We're volunteers, an' as I say, it's all fer charity. We give tae the mother 'n' baby group so that they can keep goin', givin' formula tae the mums that need it, an' fundin' the health visitor tae get over here from a few villages away. Loch Cameron's pretty, but it can be lonely fer new mums,' the woman explained. 'I'm Sheila, by the way. Haven't seen you before?' She ended with a question in her voice as she handed Liz a cup of tea in a grey-green china cup and saucer.

'Liz Parsons. I just moved here. I'm working up at the distillery,' Liz explained, struggling to hold the cup as well as two plates, groaning with food. 'I'm just on my lunch break, exploring a bit,' she added.

'Aha! Workin' wi' Ben Douglas, then?' Sheila asked.

'Yes. Still finding my feet a bit,' Liz confessed. 'Still, everyone seems really nice.'

'Aye, they're a nice bunch. Sally's a good soul. Take a seat. We're goin' tae start crochetin' in a minute, when we're settled,' Sheila added, gesturing to the circle of chairs that one of the other women had arranged in a circle in the middle of the room. 'D'you crochet?'

'No. Well, I've never tried,' Liz confessed.

'Ah, well, we can teach ye, if ye like. Plenty o' spare hooks an' wool.' Sheila smiled. 'Bess! This is Liz, she's just moved to the village. Workin' up at the distillery.' Sheila introduced the woman next to her who was now fiddling with the water urn.

'Oh, hi, Liz.' Bess grinned at her, after she made a face at the urn. 'Damn thing. It gets hot quickly but then it turns itself off and won't turn back on again.' She took a screwdriver out of the top pocket of her flannel shirt and lifted up a control panel on the back of the urn. 'Nice to meet you, anyway. Sorry, it just annoys the hell out of me when it does this,' she explained.

'Bess's our resident handyman. Handywoman, I should say,' Sheila explained, grinning. 'She runs a wee business round the village. Repairs, plumbin', that kind o' thing.'

'Wow. That's impressive. I can't even change the washer on a tap,' Liz confessed. 'I bet you're busy.'

'Can't complain.' Bess ran a hand through her black curly hair and smiled bashfully. 'I like my job. Gets me out and about. No day's the same as the one before, and I get to help people out.'

'Sounds great.' Liz sipped her tea. 'I know what you mean. I've always been in sales, and part of the reason I love that is meeting new people, and not being stuck in the office all day.'

'Yup.' Bess frowned at the urn, twisting her screwdriver in the back of it. 'Hmph. Let's see if that did anything,' she muttered, and flicked the heating switch on. A light came on. 'Yes! Fixed it.'

'See? A legend.' Sheila raised her eyebrow at Liz, smiling. 'Bess, can ye find a hook and some wool for Liz? She's goin' tae join us in the circle today.'

'No problemo.' Bess nodded, and gestured to Liz to follow her. 'Nice to have a new member of the group.'

'Well, I didn't say I was going to join. I'm sort of just here for the food,' Liz protested, smiling, but Bess laughed.

'Look, Sheila's the boss. She'd going to get you to try, at the very least. My advice? Don't resist. It's way easier that way.'

'Okay.' Liz grinned back. She liked Bess and Sheila immediately, and she had a great lunch to eat for a bargain price. She could definitely try knitting – or crochet, if that was different – for once. In her new life, maybe she would be the kind of person to start crocheting. Anyway, she definitely didn't hate the idea of coming here once a week and hanging out with Bess and Sheila, and eating huge slices of cake.

That was definitely something she could get used to.

SEVEN

'So, first, ye need tae learn how tae make a chain stitch.' Sheila handed Liz a plastic crochet hook and a small ball of black wool. 'You havenae done this before? Have ye knitted?'

'Neither. Total newbie, I'm afraid.' Liz finished eating her immense slice of Victoria sponge, which was delicious but left her feeling quite sleepy. She wiped her hands on a napkin before taking the hook and wool.

'Not to worry. Here, watch me. Make a loop, then stick the hook through it. Then, wrap round once an' pull through; wrap around again an' pull through. See? Like a chain.' Sheila's quick fingers demonstrated with her own bright yellow hook and a length of red wool.

'Umm. Okay.' Liz followed suit, as well as she could, but her chain looked far less neat than Sheila's.

'Good!' Sheila grinned. 'You're a natural. Okay. Now we're goin' tae start wi' a basic square. We make a circle of six chain stitches, like this.' She linked her stitches together with one deft movement. 'And then we go up two chain stitches like so, then we go back intae the main hole. Watch, this is a different move now.' Sheila's quick hands went over and under the wool she held in her hands and, magically, a small crocheted panel appeared between her fingers.

'Wait. I didn't see how you did that.' Liz peered at Sheila's hands. 'Can you do it again?'

'Sure.' Sheila demonstrated the movements again. 'So now, what yer doin' is goin' in and out of this central hole. In, wrap around, pull through third loop, pull through second loop. See?'

Liz tried to copy the movements, but her wool slipped off the hook.

'Agh!' she cried, good-naturedly.

'That's okay, Liz. It takes a bit of practice.' Bess sat down on Liz's other side. 'Let me introduce you to the rest of the crochet coven. This is June, Kathy and Mina. Ladies, this is Liz. Just moved to the village.'

'Welcome! Nice to have some new blood.' June, probably the oldest member of the group, looked up from a very complex-looking green and blue garment she was working on. Liz thought it might have been a jumper. June had short grey hair and lined black skin; her brown eyes were piercing yet kind, and Liz felt that she was being assessed thoroughly in that sharp gaze.

'Nice to meet you, Liz.' Kathy nodded. 'I heard you say you're up at the distillery? My brother works up there. Simon?'

'Oh, yes, I've met Simon.' Liz smiled at Kathy, who looked a little younger than her, and had vivid, bright pink hair on one side of her head, with the other side dyed a deep black. Tattoos covered her arms, and she was dressed in stripy tights, heavy black boots and a black minidress with a crocheted pink cardigan over the top. 'What do you do, Kathy?'

'I'm studying. Doing my PhD in archaeology,' Kathy explained, her hands moving effortlessly on a small crochet square as she talked. 'My thesis is on the Ring of Brodgar.'

'Wow. That sounds amazing.' Liz frowned at her wool,

attempting the new stitches again. 'So you weren't tempted to work at the distillery as well?'

'Not for me, no. Simon took after Dad. I didn't,' Kathy answered, one eyebrow raised.

'Fair enough.' Liz sensed that there might be some tension between Simon and Kathy, but it wasn't her place to comment. 'So what d'you plan to do when you've finished your PhD?'

'There are some good research projects going on. I'd like to get a Fellowship.' She shrugged. 'We'll see.'

'Ah, she's desperate to get away from Loch Cameron, this one,' the woman sitting next to Kathy said. 'Can't understand it, myself. Hi, Liz. I'm Mina.'

'Hi, Mina,' Liz said with a grin. 'Nice to meet you.'

'Same here. I've seen you around,' Mina replied, detangling a clump of blue wool. 'How are you finding the village so far? I moved here a year ago with my family and we love it.'

'Yeah. I am actually really enjoying it,' Liz said, aware that she sounded like she was surprised by the fact that she was enjoying Loch Cameron. 'Sorry. I didn't mean to sound like I didn't expect to. It's just that it's really different to what I was used to. But I like the slow pace, and the cottage I'm staying in is really nice.'

'Oh, right. You're at Gretchen Ross' place?' Mina asked, then laughed. 'Ah, you must think I'm so nosy.'

'You are,' Bess muttered, not looking up.

'Thank you, Bess.' Mina grinned. 'Well, I am a little curious, yes. But I don't think curiosity is a bad thing, is it?'

'Depends on your point of view,' Bess murmured, catching Liz's eye with a smile.

'Not at all, Mina,' Liz replied, straight-faced. 'Yes, I'm at Gretchen's cottage. It's lovely.'

'It is, isn't it? I actually looked at renting it when we moved here, but it was too small for us. I've got three kids. We needed more bedrooms, and my husband Sanjay said, *No, Mina! I can't swing a cat in here!* So we got one of the new builds in the new estate,' Mina explained. 'At that point, Gretchen had just moved out and it had been renovated to what it is now. Very nicely done, I thought. Apparently, the Laird's girlfriend did the redecoration. She's American, you know,' Mina added in a conspiratorial tone, as if being American was gossip-worthy in some way. *Perhaps it was, in Loch Cameron,* Liz thought.

'Is she?' Liz asked instead, politely. 'Well, she did a great job. It's homely without being too old-fashioned.'

'Exactly,' Mina said, unrolling a new colour of wool and starting it on her hook. 'So, why Loch Cameron?' She gave Liz a shrewd look. 'Not many people's choice for a new life, even though it is pretty sometimes, eh? We came because we started using a new factory out this way. We make jams and chutneys, and the factory space where we were was too expensive. We got such a good deal up here that we moved up from Birmingham, if you can believe it,' Mina chattered on. 'Business has never been better.'

'It sounds like you're doing really well,' Liz said, politely. 'I know something about that market, and it's not an easy one.'

'Ah, well, you know. We try.' Mina smiled. 'But you were saying. Why you moved here.'

'Oh. For the job, really,' Liz said, vaguely, feeling colour bloom in her cheeks. She didn't want to discuss her real reasons for coming, or why she'd snapped up a job at the distillery when she'd seen it. 'Fancied a change.'

'A change from what?' Mina watched her with that shrewd gaze.

'Mina. None of our business,' Bess interrupted. 'Sorry, Liz. She doesn't mean anything by it.'

'Oh, no. It's fine.' Liz shook her head.

'I can be nosy, Liz. You just have to ignore me.' Mina waved her hand in Bess' direction. 'This one always keeps her cards close to her chest too. I still don't even know when her birthday is, so I can bake her a cake.'

'I'm just not that into birthdays, Mina,' Bess muttered. 'I told you that.'

'Ah, who isn't into birthdays?' Mina tutted. 'If I was your mother, I'd make sure you had a big party.'

'Well, you're not. Though I appreciate the sentiment.' Bess rolled her eyes. 'Shall we all just get back to doing some crochet now and leave Liz alone? She's never going to come back if you hound her for her life story on day one.'

'Fair enough,' Sheila interjected. 'Liz, I hope we havenae scared you off. You're welcome back at the group anytime. We're harmless, really.'

'Oh, don't apologise,' Liz chuckled, and she meant it. 'Actually, it's been really nice. But I do have to head back to work now.' She stood up and handed her hook and wool back to Sheila. 'Thanks for the amazing lunch, too.'

'Ach, you're welcome, hen. We're here every Tuesday, if ye want tae drop in.'

'I will. Thanks, everyone.' Liz picked up her bag and gave them a little wave.

It had been nice, chatting with a group of women. Liz hadn't lied about that. It had been a long time since she'd done it: yes, she had girlfriends, but in the past couple of years they'd mostly fallen away. She'd been so busy with work, and with the IVF, that she hadn't had much time to keep up with friends, and most of the friends she had at work were definitely work colleagues first and friends second, if at all. There had been Sharon, who she still exchanged texts with here and there. But, since Liz had left Glasgow, she knew that her friendship with Sharon was likely to go a little quiet. Not because they didn't like each other, but because Sharon was busy with work and her family. That was just what happened.

Liz had liked the crochet coven a lot. It felt good to have

somewhere to go in Loch Cameron that wasn't work or the cottage – which, though she loved it, could be a little lonely.

Even for a confirmed workaholic like Liz, the crochet group felt like a welcome space where she could switch off her work brain and have a little fun – and the cake was a definite bonus. It was exactly what she needed.

EIGHT

'Drinks trolley!' There was a knock on Liz's office door.

'Come in.' Liz looked up from her contacts database with a frown. Ben stuck his head around the door frame.

'Hi, Liz. Hope I'm not interrupting? Just thought you might be interested in a little tasting session. We've just opened a cask of the Twenty Year Old.' He opened the door and Liz saw that he was holding a small wooden tray holding glasses, a small decanter and a jug of water.

'Oh! All right, come in!' Liz got up and helped him with the door, which he had pushed open with his elbow. 'Don't spill anything,' she cautioned him.

'Not my first time opening a door while carrying whisky.' Ben's eyes twinkled at her. 'How are you, Liz? Getting on all right? You've been shut up in your office for a while so I thought, if Mohammed won't come to the mountain, the mountain'll...' He trailed off. 'Well, you know.'

'The mountain will bring me single malt whisky, straight from the cask?' Liz chuckled. 'That's not a terrible situation to be in. Though I'm not sure you make a really good mountain.'

Liz had been hiding in her office a bit, it was true. She felt slightly ill at ease talking to any of the staff, knowing that they might lose their jobs within months if she and Ben couldn't save the distillery. She felt hopeful that the business could be salvaged, but the strain of not saying anything to Carol or Simon or to any of the rest of the staff was difficult. Liz had wondered if she seemed cold or unfriendly to them: she didn't want to, but she also didn't want to go out there and make friends with everyone, only for them to all get laid off in six months' time. Plus, it would be so much easier not to accidentally talk about the trouble the distillery was in if Liz didn't talk to anyone much.

Still, as a naturally sociable person, the enforced silence was driving Liz a little bit mad, so she was grateful for Ben's intrusion.

'Are you telling me I'm not a mountain of a man?' He set the little tray down on her desk and met her eyes with a flirtatious look. 'Come on, now. Quaker Oats based all their adverts on me.' He adopted a dramatic pose, flexing his arms heroically. Liz couldn't help but giggle.

'Oh, that was you?'

'Yes. I don't talk about it much, so don't mention it to the others. They'd just get jealous of my pecs. And my massive...' He broke off, pausing.

'Your massive *what?*' She laughed out loud at his cheekiness.

'Fortune,' he finished, with a grin.

'Right. My lips are sealed.' Liz feigned seriousness.

Ben poured some of the amber liquid into each glass. 'Water?'

'The same amount as whisky, please.' She watched him pour the drinks. Even though they'd been joking around, Ben was very good-looking, and Liz wondered if he knew that she thought so. He was dressed casually, like he always seemed to be, in blue jeans and a faded rugby sweatshirt. He was perhaps not a mountain of a man, but Liz was aware that he was attractive, and had an air of pleasant masculinity about him.

'I see I've got a connoisseur on my hands,' he murmured, handing her a glass. 'Slainte Mhath.'

Liz returned the traditional Gaelic toast, and took a sip of the whisky.

'Mmm. That's really good.' She let the taste develop on her tongue, allowing the oxygen in her mouth to change the balance of aromas, sweetness and smokiness. 'Peaty, but still sweet. Not too heavy.'

'Yes. She's a good one,' Ben noted. 'We should probably have a talk about how to market it.'

Liz frowned. Ben hadn't specifically mentioned that she would be required to be responsible for marketing in her interview, but since she'd begun working at the distillery, she'd realised that he expected her to do both sales and marketing.

'What?' he asked, looking at her expression. 'You're frowning.'

'No, it's just that... I'm the Sales Director. I have done marketing before, just not for a while. In big companies, Marketing and Sales are different departments. I know that in small firms like this, sometimes they get lumped together,' Liz explained. 'It's fine. It's just not exactly what I expected. It wasn't clear in my interview or the job description.'

'Ah. That's my fault. I'm sorry, I just assumed...' He trailed off. 'It's just because you're so competent at everything you do, that I just thought you'd do it. You don't have to. I guess I could look at hiring someone else.'

'No, that's not necessary. I just... there have been some unclear expectations, since I joined,' Liz said, patiently. 'I just think we should probably talk more to make sure we're on the same page.'

Liz laid her hand on Ben's arm. It was a reflexive gesture,

not one that she had thought out beforehand. He looked down in surprise at her hand.

Ben's skin was pleasant to the touch; black hair covered his muscular forearm, and she felt that same jolt of electricity that she had felt before. She missed being able to touch a man. Not even in a sexual way, but just the everyday, affectionate touch that couples took for granted. She had always loved the way that Paul's body felt next to her in bed; she had always held his hand when they were out together, walking along.

As soon as she touched Ben, she realised that her train of thought was inappropriate, and she pulled her hand back. Ben wasn't her boyfriend – he was her boss, and he wasn't there for her to touch because she missed basic human intimacy.

'Sorry,' she mumbled, looking away.

'Um. No problem,' he said, giving her an unreadable look. 'Anyway. I better... yep. Head off. Back to the old grindstone.' He picked up the tray. 'And, you'll get no argument from me about improved communication. Okay? I'm very happy to communicate with you as much as you need.'

'Okay. Thanks for the dram,' she said, feeling awkward. Probably, Ben hadn't thought anything of what had happened. It was such a small thing; Liz was blowing it up out of all proportion.

'My pleasure.' Ben avoided her gaze. Was it going to be awkward now, between them? Because she'd touched his forearm, ever so briefly?

You're just imagining it, Liz told herself. *It's fine.*

'See you later, then,' he added, as he got to the door. He gave her a lingering look, and Liz felt herself blushing.

Oh lord, Liz, she thought, remembering the moment in her office when her fingertips had grazed Ben's as he'd given the Red Kite feather back to her – the feather that still lay on her desk, waiting for her to find it a little bottle to display it in. *Get a hold on yourself. Why are you even blushing right now?*

It was mortifying, having that very obvious physical reaction to Ben and not being able to control it. Why was she having it at all? All she could say for sure was that Ben held some kind of fascination for her, and the way he was looking at her right now wasn't helping.

'Yes. Okay. Later. Whatever.' She tried to sound breezy, but it came out as if she was being dismissive.

'Right.' Ben nodded and closed the door behind him.

Oh, great. Now he thinks I'm rude as well as weird, Liz thought, making a screamy face but in silence so that Ben didn't hear anything next door. *Arghhhhhhh.*

If she was being totally honest, Liz did find Ben attractive. She had from the moment she'd met him. But there was no way she was interested in getting involved with a work colleague: it was thoroughly unprofessional, especially in her position as a director. If you were a man, people were more likely to overlook you having affairs at work. But, if you were a woman in a senior position, you were expected to be perfect and unassailable, and definitely not having any kind of romantic attachment to a colleague, not least your boss. It was the ultimate cliché.

University studies showed definitively that women lost over fifty per cent of their authority in the workplace as soon as anyone knew who they were sleeping with.

Touching someone on the arm isn't quite the same as sleeping with them, Liz, she reminded herself. *Let's not get carried away here.*

Anyway, aside from all that, Liz just wasn't ready for any romance. She'd come to Loch Cameron to get away from everything, and she had absolutely no intention of getting involved with anyone now that she was here.

Ben could flirt with her if he wanted; that was fine. But she wasn't going to engage with it any further. Her heart was just too raw.

NINE

'It's not much further,' Ben called over his shoulder, flashing Liz an endearing smile that she couldn't help but return.

'Okay,' she shouted back, over the wind, concentrating on not appearing too out of breath as she climbed the lush green hill speckled with purple heather.

It wasn't quite what Liz had expected for a typical work day at the distillery but, in fact, she and Ben were nowhere near the distillery today. Instead, Ben had proposed a research day out to give Liz an insight into the location surrounding the distillery, so she could see for herself how the whisky got its particular flavour.

'Since you were talking about finding a story for the distillery, I thought this might help,' he called back to her, his voice being taken by the wind. 'Might give you some ideas.'

Liz was glad that Ben had advised her to wear hiking boots and a waterproof jacket. It was freezing cold, and the further up the hill they went, the colder and windier it became. When she'd seen these hills from afar, driving up from Glasgow, she'd thought how beautiful and tranquil they looked. They were beautiful, but Liz had realised about half an hour ago that when you were walking up them, they were very far from tranquil. Plus, she'd had to pay attention to where she was putting her feet, as there were frequent holes and dips where you could easily turn your ankle.

In fact, Liz had never owned a pair of hiking boots, and she had once had one of those waterproof jackets that came packed in a small travel bag, but that had been years ago and she must have lost it. Luckily, when she visited the only clothes shop in the village, Fiona's Fashions, Fiona had recommended some extremely comfortable boots and a blue rainproof jacket that didn't actually look too bad on.

Liz was grateful for both items now, as she followed Ben up the tussocky hill. The wind had been tangling her hair, so she'd tied it in a makeshift ponytail – luckily, she'd thought to bring a hair band on her wrist.

'Here we are.' Ben stopped ahead of her, pushing his dark hair out of his eyes and grinning. 'The entrance to the fairy world.' He tapped a large, egg-shaped stone that lay incongruously against the side of the hill.

'This is it?' Liz panted, coming to stand next to him. 'How on earth did something like this get up here?'

The stone was as tall as Liz's waist and wider than her arms could reach. It was curiously smooth, and she couldn't see anything else like it around them.

They were alone on the hill, accompanied only by the sound of birds cawing in the morning air. Liz thought they might be crows, but she wasn't really an expert.

'No one knows. That's part of the mystery.' Ben raised one eyebrow. 'Legend says that the Fairy Queen would invite the women from the village up to the Fairy Stone once a year and take them into the fairy world to teach them the secret of distillation.'

'Only the women?' Liz smiled, pushing her fringe out of her eyes. 'I like this Fairy Queen. Very progressive.'

'Yeah. Back in the day, after the monks brought the knowledge to Scotland, distillation was considered a woman's art because it was a bit like witchcraft.'

'Get on with you,' Liz laughed. 'You're pulling my leg.'

'I most certainly am not. The making of *uisge-beath*,' he pronounced the Gaelic word *usk-a-bar*, 'involved knowledge of distilling alcohol, but the locals used herbs in it too which meant you had to know their properties. Likely, the early makers of *uisge-beath* – the English called it Aqua Vitae, Water of Life – were also herbalists. Back then, that early whisky drink was considered medicinal. It was only later that it became a drink as we know it.'

'So, distillers were herbalists, and therefore witches?'

'Yeah. Kind of.' Ben trod a few steps over to the right and plucked what looked like a weed to Liz from the grass and brought it back.

'What's that?' She took it from his outstretched hand, and was taken aback at the slight buzz of something that came from their fingertips touching. It wasn't an electric shock – anyway, what around them could have given them one? They were standing on a hill in the middle of nowhere. No, this was something else. Something just between them. That same electricity she'd felt before.

Liz felt the blush blooming on her cheeks again, like it had done before in her office, where she'd totally mortified herself by blushing after touching Ben's arm and then trying to play it too cool afterwards. Doubtless, Ben thought she was probably suffering some kind of cheek pigment malaise, or a middle-aged breakdown of some kind.

'Oh!' she said, making an involuntary exclamation. 'Hmm. Sorry, something stuck in my throat.' She coughed on purpose a few times.

'You all right?' Ben watched her, amusement lighting up his eyes.

'Fine. What was this again?'

'Wild thyme. Smell it.' He kept a little and rubbed it between his fingers. Liz gazed at him vacantly for a second. 'It smells good. You just crush the leaves a little,' he prompted her, clearly thinking she didn't understand.

'Oh. Right.' Liz cleared her throat, masking the fact that she had temporarily disappeared somewhere for a moment. Maybe this was the door to the fairy world, after all; that would explain the sudden strangeness she felt between her and Ben. Not an unpleasant strangeness at all: it was... magical, somehow.

But it was probably the stunning location doing the hard work when it came to magical vibes, she told herself. The view was utterly breathtaking: they had gone far enough up the green and purple hill – purple, because it was covered in heather – to see for miles across the loch, the village and further into the fields and across to other, distant hills, ringed by clouds. It made her feel like she had stepped out of the ordinary world altogether.

Come on, Liz, she thought to herself. *It's just a crazily romantic environment. There's nothing happening between you and Ben. Pull yourself together.*

She crushed the small leaves between her fingers and sniffed them.

'Wow. That's aromatic. Pungent.'

'I'll take that as "good".' Ben smiled again, meeting her eyes with his soft-lashed brown gaze.

'Yes. Good,' she breathed. There was a brief silence, where she gazed back into his eyes and couldn't think of anything else to say. The silence stretched out between them.

'Umm. Do you want to try something else?' he asked, awkwardly breaking the moment.

'What do you mean?'

'Other herbs. Meadowsweet, Creeping Thistle, Angelica.

They're all here.' He looked away, jamming his hands in his pockets.

'Oh, I see. You know a lot about the local plants, then,' Liz said, relieved that she could steer their conversation away from the strange energy that was between them.

'Yeah. When I was a boy, I'd range around on these hills all day, finding herbs and taking them home to look them up in my father's books. Bit of a nerd, really, but when I got older, I realised that's what the early whisky makers did too.'

'Are you a witch, then?' she joked.

'No. I don't think so. But if I'd have been born a few hundred years ago, maybe I would have been, yes.'

'Ha. I think whatever time I was born in, I'd be an entrepreneur of some kind. I spent a lot of my childhood making up schemes to make money from my friends.' Liz sniffed the wild thyme again.

'Junior capitalist. My father would have loved you. Like what?' Ben leaned against the egg stone.

'Oh, I made things and sold them. Jewellery, cakes, that kind of thing. When I got older, I had a T-shirt business. I'd make them to order.' Liz smiled, thinking about it.

'You drew them?'

'Yup. I'd draw what people wanted. But then I realised hand-drawing every single one wasn't cost effective, so I started making a range of standard designs and posting them online. People could just buy them from my online shop. I did that all through university as a sideline, in fact.'

'I'm very impressed at your commercial acuity at such a young age.' Ben met her eyes, and Liz felt that same shiver of electricity pass through her.

What was it? There was some kind of connection between them, and it was a new sensation for Liz. In every romantic relationship she'd had, she had felt love and affection for her partners, but not this kind of magnetism that made her want to be close to Ben. There was something in his mere physical presence that made her feel a little dizzy, but also felt warm and real and *right,* somehow. She wanted to be near him.

She made an effort not to gaze into Ben's eyes again. That kind of ridiculous romantic moment had no place in a work relationship, and Ben was her boss.

'Thank you,' she said, shortly. 'I ended up in the right career, I suppose.'

'You surely did,' Ben agreed. 'Not sure I did, though. Come on, let's head down. I was going to walk you over to the peat fields. They're not far.'

They started to walk down the hill again, which was much easier than going up, Liz was relieved to find.

'Why d'you say you're in the wrong career?' Liz raised her voice over the wind.

'You've seen the accounts. I know everyone thinks I'm doing a bad job of things at the distillery.' He shrugged. 'My dad was a real boss. He managed the place with an iron fist. Not a grain of barley came in that he didn't know about. I... I never wanted to be in charge, you know? I'm passionate about the whisky. But not the business,' he admitted with a sigh.

'Well, it's not everyone that gets handed the keys to a family business,' Liz replied. 'I don't want to sound disapproving, because I'm not. I understand what you're saying, about the job being thrust upon you. But the distillery is such a privilege to own. You must know that.'

'Oh, I do. I do. And I realise I must sound very privileged, like you say. I really do get that.' Ben reached up to a tree as they passed it and touched a leaf; Liz was starting to see how he was out in this wild environment, and how much it meant to him.

'But you never wanted to take over the business,' Liz finished for him. 'You never wanted to be CEO.'

'No. If I'm honest, I didn't,' he replied. 'Is that awful? I think you're the first person I've ever admitted that to. I'd prefer to be the Master Distiller, like Simon and his dad. I love the craft of the thing, and I love the land. The plants. The wind. The rain. The soil. I just don't love spreadsheets and reports and...' He waved his hand vaguely. 'You know. All that.'

'Well, I'm not sure anyone really loves spreadsheets,' Liz said. 'But they're useful. I love what they can tell me, and how they can make me better at my job.'

'You should be CEO.' Ben tapped her gently on the arm as they walked; another twinge of electricity shot through her. *Oh, for heaven's sake*, she thought, shaking her arm imperceptibly as if to shake off whatever energy Ben had somehow transmitted to her. *I can't work in the office next door to this guy if this keeps happening. How am I going to concentrate?*

'Well, that job seems to be taken for now.' Liz sounded more sardonic than intended. 'Maybe one day.'

'Maybe,' Ben replied, giving her an unreadable look. Liz looked away, feeling a flush spread over her cheeks. *Seriously, you're going to need to calm down*, she berated herself. *Or this new job really isn't going to work at all.*

'So, you didn't get on with your dad?' Liz asked, more than anything to steer the conversation back towards something that would mean she wasn't going to blush every five seconds, like some kind of weather beacon. Honestly, it was mortifying.

'Umm. It's complicated.' Ben picked a leaf from a bush and handed it to her. 'Bay. One of my favourite smells.'

'Mmm. It's lovely.' Liz sniffed the green, pungent leaf and held it out to him, but he shook his head.

'Keep it. Put it in a casserole or something.'

'All right.' Liz put the leaf in her pocket. 'You were saying? About your dad?'

'Agh. I'd rather not talk about him. He was a difficult character,' Ben sighed. 'Let's just say he made life difficult for me in some ways. You might think the money made things easier, and it did, in a way. But we were never close. That was partly because I went away to boarding school. But we never saw eye to eye. We were just too different, and... other things happened which were difficult.'

'Other things?' Liz caught his gaze, but he looked away.

'I'll tell you another time,' he said. 'It's not that I don't want to talk to you. I do. I... I enjoy talking to you, Liz. But I guess some things take time. Maybe in the future, okay?'

'Okay.' Liz found that she liked the idea of a future where she and Ben shared the deeper, more personal things about themselves. *Just as friends,* she thought, doggedly. 'I understand. I... I have some things that I guess I don't really want to talk about, either. Not yet, anyway.'

He gave her a long, thoughtful look.

'Yeah. I can see that,' he said, nodding. 'You've got pain written in you. I can see it.'

'You can see my pain?' she asked, looking at him askance.

'Yeah. Like, in your aura, or whatever.' His fingers traced the air around her head and her body. 'I'm not saying I'm one of those woo-woo hippies, or anything. I can't actually see it. More that I just see it in you... in a more abstract sense.'

'Oh.' Liz didn't quite know what to make of what Ben had said, but she didn't dislike the idea that he saw something in her that wasn't obvious to everyone else. 'Well, I guess we all have some pain, here and there. If we're grown-ups. By now, enough life has happened to scar us all in some way.'

'That's true.' Ben put his hands in his pockets as they walked along. 'Heartbreaking, but true.'

'Well, life is heartbreaking, isn't it?' Liz sighed. 'No point pretending otherwise.'

'I guess so,' Ben said, as they approached a field dug into long black furrows. 'And, on that bombshell, this is the peat field. Rather like life, peat is the accumulation of thousands of years of events. All pressed down into itself, rotted and mulched into something beautiful. I feel like there's a metaphor in there somewhere.'

'Are you saying that peat is like life because all the terrible things ultimately make for transformation into something great, like whisky?' Liz felt a smile turn up the edge of her lips. 'Because, if you are, that's probably the most dour, Scottish sentiment I've ever heard.'

'I am, and it's not dour at all,' he said with a laugh. 'Yes, life breaks our hearts. But we can at least pour our heartbreak into something good, right? And enjoy the most delicious of things?'

'We might as well,' Liz sighed.

'Yes. We might as well.' Ben reached for her hand and gave it a quick squeeze. 'Life's too short to be sad all the time, Liz Parsons.'

And, before Liz could react, he strode away into the field, calling for her to follow him.

TEN

It was a sunny Saturday, and Liz was looking forward to putting her feet up. It had been a demanding few weeks, and she felt like despite all the research and reading she'd done, she still only knew a tiny sliver of what she should know about the company.

However, to Liz, *putting her feet up* meant that she had decided to read the company ten-year business plan in bed with a cup of tea. It was very rare that she didn't work on a weekend; that was one of the secrets of her success, in her own mind. If you wanted to be the best, then you had to put in the hours, and that meant more than the standard nine to five. Even more so if you were a woman, trying to succeed in a male-dominated environment like the drinks industry.

Paul had not appreciated the working at the weekends and into the evenings. He'd said *all you do is work, eat and sleep. You have to make some time for me.*

At the time, all Liz could think about was the IVF and doing everything she needed to stay on top of her job. She'd argued with Paul. Didn't he realise that everything she was doing was for them both? For their future?

When she looked back, she could see that she had been obsessed by her work. And, if she was really honest with herself, she knew why.

It wasn't just the fact that she was ambitious. And it wasn't just that she knew she had to work harder and smarter than all of her male colleagues to get ahead. There was something else driving her, and there always had been.

As a child, Liz had witnessed her mother and father fight endlessly about money. Her dad had suffered long periods of unemployment because of illness, and her mum had worked around the clock as a nurse. An honourable job, but a badly paid one – and, as the years wore on, an occupation that took more and more from her mother until she could hardly stand anymore.

The long shifts, often doubled because of emergencies and staff shortages. The sheer, bone-numbing tiredness of being on your feet all day and having to care for strangers. It got to Liz's mum, after a while. And, though she loved nursing – *who'd do it if they didn't care about people?* she'd say to Liz after a long shift, as she lowered herself into a chair with a deep groan – it changed her.

It wasn't just that Liz felt like she hardly saw her mum, growing up. She also distinctly remembered thinking, aged ten, as she watched her mother fall asleep on the sofa, how noble her mum's job was, but also how tough it was to survive on one income when it wasn't very generous to start with.

By contrast, sales was a good job for someone who was motivated to make a good salary, and unlike nursing, it wasn't a set wage. Liz was gifted when it came to sales, and her commissions reflected that.

But she was like her mother more than she'd thought, perhaps, because she had overworked herself for years. She was addicted to work. She loved it, but it had exhausted her and Paul had hated it. However, she supposed that it didn't matter now, if she overworked herself – well, it only affected her, now. It didn't matter if she read business plans in bed, because there was no one around to object any more.

A pang of homesickness clutched at Liz's heart. She missed Paul – or, perhaps more accurately, she missed having *someone*. She had loved Paul, but he hadn't ever really understood the depth of who she was. She had never felt truly *seen* with him.

Paul had listened to her explanation of her childhood carefully, and told her that she didn't even have to work. He would look after her, and she'd never be poor again.

It was kind, and it was thoughtful. Paul was a good man. Liz had thought of all the people that probably dreamed of someone saying those words to them, and felt bad. But the truth was that Paul had listened, but hadn't heard her. Because what she had told him was the reason why it was important for her to work.

No, she never wanted to struggle for money again. But she also never wanted to have to rely on anyone else, because that person might get ill and not be able to support her, just like her dad had had to rely on her mum to pay all the bills. Then, that person might die and leave her alone, having to look after herself, like her dad had. And – though Liz didn't blame her for wanting something good for herself – when her mum had finally retired from nursing, within a year she'd gone to live in Australia with the man she'd just met, but described as *the love of her life*.

Part of Liz thought that it would have been nice if her mum had tried thinking of Liz as the love of her life for once, but she wasn't that invested in judging a woman who had kept a roof over her head for her whole childhood. It was what it was, and Liz knew that the only person she could rely on was herself.

That was what Paul had never understood. But perhaps it was something in Liz that had also pushed him away. She was accustomed to men – before Paul, too – telling her she was too much. Too much of what, Liz was never clear about. Too successful? Too hardworking? Too confident? She'd never thought that these were bad things. How could someone be too successful or confident or even too nice? But she was, apparently. She had been judged many times by many men – lovers, boyfriends, colleagues, bosses.

Her friends had assured her that men who thought she was *too much* weren't worth her time. But it was a theory that would mean she was lonely a lot of the time, she thought. Even Paul had ended up thinking she was *too much*. Her work was too demanding; the IVF took *too much* from them both. She was *too much*, in the end.

She was sipping her mug of tea and looking at her laptop screen when there was a knock at the door.

Who is knocking at this hour? she thought crossly, looking at the bedside clock, which read 10.34 a.m. She sighed and put the tea on the rattan bedside table. She'd been reading the accounts for about an hour and making notes. She thought it was earlier, but she must have slept late and not started work until after nine.

Usually, Liz was up at dawn. However, she did feel refreshed for an extra couple of hours in bed. *Maybe it's the lochside air*, she thought as she wrapped a fluffy pink robe around her and tied the belt around her middle.

She opened the front door, expecting the postman.

Ben Douglas stood on the doorstep, holding a carton of eggs and a bag of courgettes.

'Good morning.' He smiled brightly.

'Oh. Hi.' She was immediately aware that her hair was straggling around her shoulders and needed a wash; she took the hair band from her wrist and twisted her hair up into a quick bun. She cleared her throat. 'I mean, good morning.'

'Not a morning person, eh. Not to worry. Me neither.' His eyes twinkled as he looked at her.

Who knocks on their employees' doors without warning at ten thirty on a Saturday morning? I might have had a man here.

Yeah, right, she thought. Liz wasn't looking for any romantic entanglements in her life right now: she wanted to throw herself into her new job and find the old Liz. Find that old spark she used to have, before everything had gone wrong.

'Um... well, I am, but I was just doing some reading,' she replied, thinking *at least this is a thick robe. Nothing revealing.*

'Ah. Well, I wanted to drop you round these.' He held out the groceries. 'From the house. Housewarming present.'

'From your house?' Liz took the eggs and the bag of courgettes. 'Thank you. That's kind of you.'

'Yes. I've got a smallholding. Nothing fancy, just some chickens and a veggie patch. Oh, and a goat.'

'A goat? Really?'

'Aye. Mae. I'd have brought you some goat milk but she's been wilful lately.'

'I see,' she said, pushing her fringe out of her eyes. 'I've heard that about goats.'

'Mae thinks she's queen of the village.' Ben held out his hands in an apologetic gesture. 'Who am I to argue?'

'Just to be clear: your goat's called Mae?' Liz couldn't help but laugh.

'Yeah. Like Mae West. Wilful, but beautiful.'

Liz snorted, imagining a goat wearing a revealing evening gown. *Revealing what, though? Hooves?*

Despite being in her dressing gown, and the unexpected segue into talking about stubborn goats, Liz found that she was starting to enjoy her conversation with Ben. She hadn't realised how lighthearted and fun he could be.

'Hey. Don't make fun of Mae. She could have had it all, but she chose to live with me and eat all my grass,' he added, a smile at the edge of his lips.

'Well, it's important that Mae lives as authentically as she can, I guess.' Liz made a serious face. 'Did you want to come in? I can make you a cup of tea. And maybe a courgette omelette, now.' She stood aside as if to welcome him in.

'Ah, that's a nice idea. But I was wondering if I could tempt you to a little tour of the village, and then maybe lunch at Myrtle's Café? It's the best Loch Cameron has to offer. As an official welcome. And, to apologise for the fact I wasn't here on your first day,' Ben explained, a hopeful and optimistic look on his face.

'Oh. Err... well, I have some reading to do, so...' Liz demurred.

'Oh. What're you reading? I love a good book. Crime, mostly, but I'll read anything.' Ben seemed a little nervous; Liz could swear that he was talking to fill the time.

'Nothing like that. The company business plan, if you must know. I had a brief look when I started, but I really wanted to get into the detail,' she explained.

'You're... reading the business plan? On a Saturday?' Ben actually took a step back from the doorstep.

'Yeah. Why not? It pays to be prepared,' she said, a little defensively.

'No, no... it's just...' He blinked a few times. 'I don't think I've ever done that – not on a weekend. And it's my company.'

Liz fought the impulse to say anything as churlish as *and it shows*, and just smiled instead.

'Well, I like to be thorough,' she replied, crisply.

'I'm very pleased to hear it, don't get me wrong.' Ben smiled. 'But it's a lovely day. Why don't you leave the business plan at home and come out? I was thinking I could take you to a couple of local stockists and introduce you.'

Well, if it's a work thing, I really should go, she thought.

'In that case, then okay.' She stood aside. 'But give me a minute to get dressed. Okay?'

'Just so you know, the fluffy pink robe look is in around

Loch Cameron this season. But, sure. If you want to get all formal about it.' Ben shrugged.

'Such a comedian. Come in and wait. I won't be long,' Liz instructed him, ushering him into the cosy sitting room. 'Read a book while you wait,' she called over her shoulder as she went to the bathroom, waving her hand at the cute white rattan book-shelf that Gretchen had left stacked with paperback romances. 'Or, the business plan's on my laptop, on the bed.'

'A book is just fine, thanks,' Ben replied, standing with his hands clasped behind his back and his head on one side, reading the spines of the books. Liz noticed that he was whistling quietly under his breath, and that he was wearing a brown corduroy jacket with leather patches on the sleeves.

If the elderly professor look was acceptable in Loch Cameron, then the fluffy robe probably wasn't as much of a fashion faux pas as it might have been elsewhere, Liz thought playfully. Still, she thought for a good few minutes in the shower about what she was going to wear.

She wanted to look nice. It wasn't a date. But she had to make a good impression nonetheless. What outfit said "laid back Saturday smart" as well as made her look good?

What does it matter what you look like, Liz? she asked herself, and had no good answer.

It just does, okay? she answered herself, mulishly.

She absolutely wasn't dressing for a date.

Was she?

ELEVEN

'So, this is Myrtle's. I'd say it was famous, but that would be overstating the truth a little.' Ben gestured to the small café in front of them both. 'But only a little. Myrtle does some amazing scones, if you like that kind of thing.'

'I do.' Liz took in the unusual exterior of the café, which was made up of remarkable stained-glass windows.

She didn't think she'd seen anything like it before. The wooden café door was painted red, but boasted a glass panel featuring a rising sun over water, and a rainbow beyond it. The café windows were a patchwork of coloured squares of glass, joined by black lead piping: cornflower blue, rose pink and bottle green glass reflected the loch.

A chalk board next to where they stood advertised:

COFFEE – TEA – SANDWICHES – CAKE OF THE DAY

'What a remarkable place,' Liz commented.

'Yeah. A real one-off. Myrtle took the place over years ago, from when it was a barber shop. Hence the windows.' Ben looked up at the façade, shielding his eyes from the sun.

'It's gorgeous.' Liz loved the look of the place, and when Ben ushered her inside, she loved it even more. Inside was a cosy café with four sets of mismatched tables and chairs – the tables were a scrubbed pine, but the chairs were a mix of wooden dining chairs painted white or red. A couple of upholstered stools sat at one table, and three 80s-style metal dining chairs surrounded another.

An aged leather recliner sat in the corner of the café next to a small side table: *that was the best place to sit*, Liz thought, as it was next to the window. She imagined sitting there with a cup of coffee, watching life in Loch Cameron go by, albeit at a snail's pace, and tinted blue through the glass.

The walls were filled with shelves carrying knick-knacks, plants and books, and there was a welcoming smell of coffee and baking. Liz felt instantly at home.

'Mornin', Ben.' The woman behind the counter looked up from cutting some sandwiches. 'And who's this? Come in, dearie!'

'Liz Parsons. I've just moved to the village,' Liz replied, returning the woman's friendly smile.

'I'm Myrtle McGarry. A pleasure tae meet ye, Liz.'

Liz's gaze travelled over the walls, which were thoroughly covered in a variety of keepsakes and odd items. One wall was completely covered in postcards. One wall held bookshelves, with a hand lettered sign: BOOK SWAP: TAKE ONE, LEAVE ONE. Liz thought that she might bring down some of the romance novels stuffed onto the shelves at the cottage and swap them for something else. It wasn't that she disliked romance, but she wasn't exactly in that headspace right now.

The third wall showcased a shelf of male and female mannequin heads wearing a variety of hats. Bonnets, military-looking caps and a formal trilby sat on their respective heads, alongside a mannequin head with a beard wearing a straw boater, and a large teddy bear at the end of the row who wore a French beret.

Welcome to rural Scotland. Liz smiled to herself. *Adorable, but also a little eccentric.*

'Liz has just joined us as Sales Director at the distillery,' Ben explained. 'She's going to turn the company around.'

'Er... well, I don't know about that, but...' Liz demurred.

'Oh, that's great. An' I'm sure ye'll be fantastic.' Myrtle looked delighted. 'Always nice tae see a young woman makin' her mark.'

'Thanks, Myrtle.' Liz was touched by Myrtle's kindness.

'Not a bit of it! Us workin' women got tae stick together, aye. Anyway. Listen to me, bletherin! What'll ye have?' Myrtle placed both hands on the top of the glass counter and looked at them both expectantly. 'I've just made some nice, thick ham an' salad sandwiches. Good thick granary bread, just come in from the bakery. Or there's cheese, or smoked salmon...' Myrtle reeled off a list of delicious-sounding sandwich fillings.

'Ham salad sounds great for me, Myrtle. Thanks. And a cup of tea?' Liz asked.

'Same for me. And can we get some scones and jam, too?' Ben pointed to a plate of huge, yellow scones in the glass display. 'Honestly. They're the best I've ever had,' he added to Liz.

'Great. Who doesn't love a scone?' Liz agreed.

'Right ye are, both o' ye. I'll bring it over in a minute.' Muriel busied herself pouring hot water into a pretty blue teapot and reaching for a couple of matching cups and saucers.

'So, what d'you think of Loch Cameron so far?' Ben asked as they settled themselves at the table with the white and red painted chairs, passing her a cushion from the empty chair on his side of the table.

'I like it. I'm getting used to the slower pace. Slowly.' Liz laughed at herself. 'I'm not too good at it, though. Being slow,

that is. I'm kind of used to a frantic environment. Frantic life,'
she sighed. 'Still, it's not good for you, after you've done it for a
long time.'

'No, it isn't,' Ben agreed. 'I know what you mean about the
pace here. When I was younger, and I'd come back from university in the holidays, it all seemed so archaic and deadly boring.
But, then, you get older, and somewhere that things don't
change becomes... reassuring.' A cloud passed over his expression for a minute, then it was gone. 'Anyway, I'm glad that
you've brought your busy energy with you. We could do with
an injection of energy at the distillery.'

'Thanks. I'll try not to be too full on.' Liz smiled as Myrtle
approached the table, carrying a tray with the tea and sandwiches. 'Wow. This looks great! Thanks, Myrtle.'

'You're most welcome, dear. Be back wi' the scones in a wee
while.'

Liz watched Myrtle as she tucked the now-empty tray
under her arm and wiped the other tables down with a cloth
before sashaying back to the counter. Myrtle had a definite
style about her: she was perhaps in her late forties or early
fifties, and wore a long, bohemian pink skirt and a *Phantom of
the Opera* T-shirt under a silver threaded cardigan. A number
of crystal necklaces hung around her neck, and she wore large
gold hooped earrings with a word that Liz couldn't quite make
out emblazoned within them. Her dyed auburn hair was
pulled up in a loose bun. Liz liked her immediately, and
decided that she would definitely come back to the café after
today.

'Full on is good.' Ben poured milk into his cup. 'Milk?'

'Yes, thanks. Well, I guess so,' Liz said, watching as Ben
poured the milk into her cup too and nodding as he picked up
the teapot. 'I did come to Loch Cameron for a new start, and to
slow down a little.'

'You said that in your interview.' Ben filled both cups with strong, amber liquid. 'I was curious about why. You don't have to tell me, by the way. If it's personal.'

Liz sipped her tea, which was strong and hot.

'It is personal. I'd rather not talk about it just now, if that's okay,' she said, quietly. She didn't know Ben Douglas well enough to disclose something so close to her heart. 'I'm just not ready.'

'Oh, of course. But, if you do need someone to talk to, I like to think I'm not a traditional boss. My door is always open, and I mean that as a friend as well as a colleague. My dad was the one you could never talk to. I prefer to be a friend that happens to be in charge.'

'There's a fine balance with that kind of thing, in my experience,' Liz replied, neutrally. What she actually meant was that she had come across the "I'm not your boss, I'm your friend" type before and it usually didn't work very well, mostly because employees felt that they could take liberties.

However, she had to admit that it had been a while since she had felt this comfortable talking to anyone. There was just something about Ben that soothed her nerves.

'Why don't you tell me about you? Are you married? Do you have children?'

Ben looked very uncomfortable. 'No,' he said, shortly. There was an awkward silence.

'I'm sorry, I... that was rude of me,' Liz blurted out, wondering if she could get this conversation any more wrong.

'No, it's all right. It's a normal question.' Ben smiled at Myrtle as she set a plate of enormous scones down in front of them. 'Thanks, Myrtle. They're huge!'

Myrtle nodded, pleased, and looked up as the phone rang in the back of the café.

'Enjoy! Sorry, I should get that.' She excused herself and trotted back towards the kitchen.

'I don't have kids. And I'm not married. Not anymore,' he

said, awkwardly. 'I was married, but it didn't work out. I wanted kids. It wasn't to be,' he admitted with a sigh.

'I'm sorry.' Liz felt awful. 'What happened? She didn't want children?'

'Kind of. It's a long story. I'll tell you another time.' He gave her an evasive look.

'Of course. I feel like I ruined a nice lunch, now.' Liz felt as though she'd been too nosy – but, after all, as Ben said, they were normal questions to ask. How was she to know that there was clearly some drama hidden there?

'What, with these scones?' Ben raised an imperious eyebrow. 'Don't be daft. Seems like we've probably both been through some bad times. But, remember, this is a new start for you. You're going to get there, okay? And, I think you're going to be great for the business too.'

'Thanks, Ben. I appreciate that,' Liz said, taking a bite of her sandwich, which was delicious.

'Leave room for scones,' he said, picking one up and slathering it in butter and jam. 'You'll regret it if you don't.'

'Okay, okay!' Liz laughed, feeling the mood lighten again. The thing was, though, that she wouldn't mind opening up to Ben. She felt safe, talking to him – here, up on the windy hill, in the office. There was just something reassuring about being in his presence, and she knew, instinctively, that he would never judge her. She didn't know how she knew, she just did. It was a feeling; an instinct. And Liz had learnt to trust her instincts over the years.

She hoped that she could trust Ben when it came to work, and being her boss. And, perhaps she had found a friend, too. Even though she had, secretly, pooh-poohed the idea of Ben's "friendly boss" self-image, she found that she was open to being Ben's friend as well as his colleague. It wasn't so bad, eating scones in a cute café on a Saturday. It was, arguably, quite a lot more fun than reading work documents on your own at home.

TWELVE

The bell on the door jangled as Ben and Liz entered the dim interior of the small shop. Outside, a sign that looked like it had been there for years proclaimed the name of the shop as The Wee Dram. In the window, faded posters for Cinzano and Martini Rosso competed with a classic globe-style cocktail cabinet with the legs removed. The top of the globe had been rolled back to reveal a tarnished cocktail shaker and two crystal highball glasses next to a bottle of whisky and a selection of other liqueurs.

It's cocktail o'clock somewhere in the world, Liz thought, as they went in.

'Ah, Ben! Good to see you, dear boy. I had no idea you were coming in.' An older man, sitting in a black leather armchair behind an impressive green baize-topped table, set a glass of what looked like whisky back on it and rubbed his hand over his white beard. The shop smelt strongly of cigars and was lit by gold-hued lamps; it was bright and sunny outside, but – judging from the contents of the man's glass – Liz thought that inside The Wee Dram, it was clearly cocktail o'clock all day long.

'Hello, Grenville. I just thought I'd pop in with our new Sales Director and introduce her to one of our most treasured stockists.' Ben gave the man a vigorous handshake, and held out his other hand to introduce Liz.

'Liz Parsons, this is Grenville McNulty. Owner of The Wee Dram, and tireless promotor of Loch Cameron Distillery. Grenville, this is Liz, who's taken over from Brian.'

'Oh! A woman!' Grenville looked surprised, as if Liz had come into the shop in a false beard and moustache and had only now revealed her disguise. 'Well, now. Hello, young lady.'

'Lovely to meet you, Grenville,' Liz said, pointedly using his name when he hadn't used hers, and shaking his hand firmly. Being called *young lady* when you were an internationally renowned businesswoman and well into your thirties was irritating, but it also wasn't anything she hadn't experienced before. Liz knew for a fact that if she'd been a man, Grenville wouldn't have called her *young man* on meeting her. 'So, how many units do you sell for us every week?'

'Ah, well. Straight to business, is it?' Grenville looked momentarily surprised.

'Us young ladies are known for it.' Liz gave him her hundred-watt sales smile that she knew told him she was good fun and could take a joke, but also that she wouldn't stand for any of his sexist remarks.

'Hahaha! Touché.' Grenville laughed delightedly, and took her arm. 'You and I are going to get along famously, I can see that, Miss Parsons.' He guided her to a glass cabinet at the back of the shop. 'Now, then. Numbers, shmumbers. This is the most important place in the shop. D'you know why?' He peered at Liz over the top of his silver-rimmed, half-moon glasses.

'Please tell me.' Liz looked back over her shoulder at Ben, who raised his eyebrows as if to say *yes, he's a character. Just go with it.*

'Because here I have some of the oldest bottles of Loch Cameron Distillery single malts in existence. Ben's father, Jim Douglas, God rest him, gave these to me in 1965, and they've been here ever since. Of course, you have older in the archive, Ben. But none elsewhere, I don't think.' He tapped the glass case proudly and fixed Liz with a friendly stare.

'Look how beautiful these are!' Liz leaned forward to look at the bottles, which were wrapped and stored so carefully. 'And does anyone buy these?'

'Now and again. There are some loyal customers.' Grenville adjusted his glasses. 'But, as you can imagine, it's a luxury for most. I do move about twenty bottles a week of the Ten Year Old, since you asked.'

'Well, that's something,' Liz said, keeping her tone positive, though eighty bottles a month was nothing in her experience, especially if this was one of the distillery's main stockists. 'It would be nice to sell those vintages, though, wouldn't it? If we could widen the interest. Tell more people about you and the shop. Do you get much online business?' she asked.

'The internet? Goodness, no.' Grenville made a face. 'Sometimes people order over the phone. But, mostly, they just come in.'

'I see.' Liz wasn't overly surprised that Grenville didn't have an online presence. *One of these days, it'd be amazing if one of these old duffers turned around and showed me a hundred thousand Instagram followers,* she thought, drily. 'Well, maybe that's something I could help you with.'

'Hmm. I don't know about that.' Grenville looked like Liz had just suggested he stick a rhino horn up his bottom. 'However, I've been on at Ben for years to start doing tours of the archive. People would come from miles around, don't you think, Miss Parsons?' His eyes twinkled at her over his glasses, and Liz found herself softening towards the old man.

'I do, actually.' Liz turned around to look at Ben. 'I've told him that already. It's a no-brainer.'

'A what? A *no-brainer*. What a remarkable expression!' Grenville laughed delightedly. 'Yes, Ben. That's exactly right. My goodness, your father would have loved this firecracker.' He patted Liz on the arm in a fatherly way that Liz found she didn't mind too much. 'Start running tours of the distillery and the cellars. I'm sure it would be a big hit.'

'You know,' Liz mused, 'Grenville would be a perfect tour guide. If you were willing, Grenville? And if you can manage time away from the shop? You seem to be very knowledgeable and passionate about the distillery.'

'Oh, my goodness! What a thought.' Grenville picked up a spiral bound notepad and fanned himself with it theatrically. 'I mean, yes, I'd love to. I do know a lot about the distillery and the whisky. And I was great friends with Ben's father. If you think I could do it, Ben, it would be an honour.'

'I'm not sure I have any choice in the matter.' Ben smiled widely. 'But, it's a great idea. I can really see Grenville in the role. If he's up for it.'

'Well, I can't say I wouldn't like some time away from the shop,' Grenville mused. 'I have been thinking of starting to run more reduced hours. The custom isn't what it was. I could do a couple of tours a week at the distillery, certainly. And close for two afternoons a week.'

'I think you'd find that there would be ways to increase custom at the shop from the contact with new customers at the tours, too,' Liz suggested. 'If people enjoyed their tour with you – and why wouldn't they? A charming, local character such as yourself – then it would be easy for them to come and find the shop in the village and continue their whisky experience. That benefits you, but it also benefits the village as a whole if we make it somewhere known to be full of whisky expertise. A place whisky enthusiasts can visit and really immerse themselves in the history and the culture.'

'That's true. My, my, I would never have thought of that!' Grenville glowed at the compliment. 'They could come here and I could teach them all about the different malts and distilleries. All the old stories.'

Liz thought that, if she could persuade Grenville, then he would be amazing at making some short, sharable videos for social media. He had that kind of old school, classic camp way about him that people would love, whatever he was talking about. She'd have to shoot the films herself, but it would be worth doing. She smiled to herself, feeling some of that old spark coming back. This was just the kind of thing she had done before – a fun part of the job where she could use her creativity, and she loved it.

'Yes. In fact, Ben,' Liz turned to him, '*you* could also do a walking tour of the local area, like you did with me. Tell people all about *uisge-beath*. You could even make it, out there in the hills, if you had some equipment in a little campervan or something,' she suggested. 'You could show them the local flowers and plants, just like you showed me.'

'Oh, no. I don't know about that.' Ben blanched at the idea. 'I didn't mind taking you. But I don't know about a group of strangers.'

'Why not? It's unlikely you'd get anyone difficult. And if you did, just push them off the top of the hill.' Liz shrugged, smiling sweetly.

'No, it's not that. I dunno. I'm shy in front of people I don't know.' He jammed his hands in his pockets and looked down at his feet. 'But Grenville doing the distillery tour's a great idea.'

'Well, Grenville, let me have a little time to get everything set up, and I'll be in touch.' Liz made a note on her phone. 'And, Ben, don't think I'm going to forget about the *uisge-beath* walk thing. I think that's got legs, too.'

'Hmmph. Maybe.' Ben gave her a half-smile.

'Certainly. I shall look forward to it. Ben, don't you let this one go. She's a marvel.' Grenville leaned over unexpectedly, took Liz by the shoulders and kissed her firmly, once on each cheek.

Despite the fact that Grenville's kiss was a little inappropriate by modern standards, Liz didn't really mind. Yes, Grenville was one of those old-fashioned men, who probably needed to be told not to call grown women *young lady*. But he also seemed like a sweet man with a good heart. Liz found that she liked him more than she expected to.

Ben and Liz said goodbye, and walked back out onto the high street.

'I knew it'd be a good idea to show you around the village.' Ben looked like he wanted to hug her, but he settled for giving her a huge grin instead. 'If I didn't know it before, then I definitely know now, you're a hundred per cent the right person for this job, Liz.'

'Thank you. He's quite a character.' Liz looked up at the exterior of The Wee Dram. 'Thanks for bringing me here. I have to say, I had a preconceived notion of what it'd be like in there. I mean, I was right,' she laughed, and Ben laughed too.

'Yeah. It's kind of... traditional, let's say,' he chuckled as they walked along.

'Right. The window really doesn't do it any favours,' Liz agreed. 'But Grenville is a real treasure. I hope you don't mind me kind of taking over in there. I just thought, he'd be so great as part of the team. He's got that kind of old school gentleman charm people would love.' Liz realised they were walking past the book shop she had noticed earlier, and she stopped to look in the window.

'Liz, if it wasn't clear already, then I don't mind you doing your job.' Ben stopped next to her, but instead of looking in at the shop window, she felt his gaze on her. Liz glanced up at him, and a long look passed between them. Ben reached over and, without warning, he brushed a stray hair from her cheek.

'Oh... thank you,' she said, feeling a blush come up in her cheeks as it often did around Ben.

'You're welcome.' He smiled, and his fingertips stayed on her cheek for one second longer than they should have.

'I know that I can be a little direct in my work life. It's just how I am.' She cleared her throat, returning to their conversation and pretending that the moment hadn't happened. Though it had, and it was probably the most erotic thing that had happened to Liz in a long time.

'Are you apologising for being great at what you do?' Ben raised an eyebrow. 'Because it sounded like you were, just then.'

'No, I wasn't apologising. But, sometimes, people have found me a little... too much.'

'Liz. I don't know what happened in your previous work-places. Or, in life in general.' Ben touched her shoulder, gently. 'But please know that I do not, or will ever, think you are *too much*. And whoever told you that you were *too much* was a complete idiot.'

He was staring intensely into her eyes, and she returned his gaze steadily. For a long moment, neither one of them spoke.

'Okay,' she said, quietly.

'I just meant...' Ben trailed off, still holding her gaze. 'Never mind. I meant what I said.'

'Thank you,' she breathed.

'You're welcome,' he replied, quietly.

There was something happening between them, and Liz was unprepared for it. Yet, caught in the moment, she found that she wanted to pursue this unexpected new feeling of... what? Attraction? She wasn't blind. Ben was an attractive man, for sure. Tall, dark and handsome, as if someone had animated one of those old-fashioned romance novel covers and brought one of the dashing heroes to life in front of her.

But it wasn't really that, even.

She was aware of Ben as a man. Not just as a boss, or a friend, showing her around the village. She didn't know him that well, yet, but there was a chemistry between them that she could feel, like a kind of cloud of sweetness that she wanted to wrap around her. When he'd touched her cheek just then, she'd wanted to melt into the ground.

He was an unusual man: seemingly not afraid of letting her take the lead, or her being a strong woman with definite opinions. In fact, between the two of them, Ben was the gentler one, being the one who enjoyed roaming the Scottish hills as a boy, collecting herbs. He was shy; he didn't like the idea of taking people on a tour of the hills, even if it was to talk about his favourite subject. Liz was the one who didn't think twice about standing up in front of hundreds of people to make presentations, like she'd done so many times in her career. Liz was the one that had always been driven to success.

There was something deeply attractive to Liz about a man who told her that she was never *too much*. And that knowledge, that she didn't have to dim her light or try to be less than she was around Ben, was somehow intoxicating.

She had the compelling urge to reach up and wrap her arms around Ben's neck, and kiss him. *Come on,* she thought. *You were just semi-appalled that Grenville kissed you on both cheeks, and that was more or less acceptable as a greeting.*

Snogging your boss in the street without warning would definitely be inappropriate.

'Do you want to go in?' Ben murmured, inclining his head at the shop door they had stopped in front of. 'I'm at your disposal for as long as you want me. As a tour guide,' he added, his voice still low. There was something delicious in being the one chosen for Ben's quiet, intimate tone of voice that made Liz shiver a little.

Liz didn't know how to answer that. *Yes. I want you at my disposal,* she thought. *Whatever that means, or could mean.* Instead, she cleared her throat.

'Let's continue the tour,' she said, and pushed the door open.

THIRTEEN

'Liz Parsons, I presume?' The sprightly, elderly woman stood up to welcome Liz as she walked into the day room at the care home. In fact, as Liz walked in, she realised that the room was a large conservatory, with a glass roof and plenty of hanging plants. Tasteful rattan furniture was arranged in groups here and there, with easy chairs dotted around. In the corner, a coffee machine sat next to a tray of muffins and other pastries.

'Gretchen?' Liz walked over to the woman's table.

'The very same.' Gretchen Ross held out her hand and shook Liz's firmly. 'Lovely to meet you at last. Thanks for making the trip out here to see an old lady.'

Gretchen was dressed in an elegant plain green kaftan-like dress and matching long wrap, with her silver hair up in a loose bun. She wore glasses halfway down her nose and had been reading a novel, which she turned face-downward on the table when Liz arrived. Despite her age, she had good skin and bright, intelligent eyes.

'A pleasure. It was a lovely drive.' Liz sat down at the table, putting her handbag on the chair next to her.

'Yes, it's not a bad spot.' Gretchen waved at the coffee machine. 'Do help yourself, dear. It's all free.'

'Oh. Can I get you something while I'm up?' Liz did feel a little peckish: she'd only had a cup of tea before leaving the cottage that morning.

'I'll have a flat white and a muffin, dear. Thank you,' Gretchen requested, yawning. Liz, walking to the snack station, glanced back at Gretchen and saw that she was holding court at her table with two elderly men, one a shorter fellow with a bow tie and a checked jumper, and one taller with glasses and a more cautious expression. She smiled to herself. Clearly, even if you were in a care home, the old boy-meets-girl magic could still happen.

Liz came back to the table with the drinks and cakes, and Gretchen said goodbye to the two gentlemen like a benevolent monarch.

'Sorry about that. Bridge tournament coming up, you see.' Gretchen sighed. 'It all gets very involved. Still, it keeps us off the streets.' She chuckled drily at her own joke. 'So, Liz. How're you finding the cottage? All okay? I hope you're warm enough. Zelda, the girl before you, did persuade the Laird to come and install central heating, not before time. The controls are a bit twiddly, but an intelligent woman like you shouldn't have a problem working it all out.'

'Oh, it's lovely, thank you. And I haven't used the heating much yet. It's a bit chilly in the evenings, but not much. I've just put a cardigan on, or got into bed early.'

'Wonderful. Well, mind you use it, if you need it.' Gretchen nodded. 'So, tell me about yourself. I know you're working up at the distillery. How's that been?'

'Good, I think. It's early days, and there's a lot of work to be done. But I think I can make a difference.' Liz started talking about her job and what she'd done before, explaining what she did as a Sales Director. Gretchen listened carefully, asking insightful questions. When Liz mentioned the fact she had often worked in male-dominated environments, Gretchen nodded sympathetically.

'Ah, yes. Publishing was much the same, once upon a time. Of course, now, it's largely female dominated, but it's still very male up at the top. Glass ceiling, as they say,' she sighed. 'I made some inroads, as did some other women I worked with. But even in the 80s and 90s, when feminism was all the rage, you were expected to be the Publisher's secretary rather than the Publisher. Of course, I ignored that,' she chuckled. 'In fact, I insisted on having a young, gay male secretary when I finally became a Publisher. Andrew, his name was. Lovely looking boy, too.'

'Wow. I'm impressed.' Liz thought that she wouldn't mind turning into someone like Gretchen, one day.

'Ha. Thank you, dear. It was all above board, of course. We were great friends and still are. I just loved seeing the look on those stuffy old dinosaur's faces when they had to make an appointment with Andrew to see me. I used to peer through the crack in the door from my office into Andrew's office, outside.' She giggled conspiratorially.

'Gretchen, I feel like you have a lot of stories to tell. And I want to hear all of them,' Liz told her with a laugh.

'Well, make sure you come and see me again, and I'll tell you whatever you want to know. But we were talking about you, dear. You must have struggled with sexism, over the years. Successful women always have to.'

'Yeah. I mean, things have definitely improved. But the drinks industry is still a bit of a boys' club. That's why it's nice to be at Loch Cameron, if I'm honest. It's still all men. But at least there's less of them,' she laughed. 'And, Ben seems like a good guy. He's not threatened by me, which is refreshing.'

'Ah, Ben Douglas. Yes. Interesting young man.' Gretchen nibbled her muffin. 'His father was a tyrant. He kept the distillery afloat in some difficult years, but he was never a loving father. Everyone knew that.'

'That's sad. I kind of get the sense from Ben that they had a troubled relationship,' Liz said.

'Mmm. I shouldn't wonder. So many young men grow up in the shadows of their fathers, and Jim Douglas was one of those men who was obsessed with perfection. He lost his wife, Gillian, when Ben was young. Packed the poor boy off to boarding school. That was just what was done in some families, of course. I expect the same thing was done to Jim when he was young. Just six when they get sent away, many of them. Breaks your heart, doesn't it?'

'It's very young to be away from your parents so permanently.' Liz felt a pang of sadness for Ben, and his father. 'Neither of them ever stood a chance.'

'Well. It can make you resilient, I suppose.' Gretchen raised an eyebrow. 'Some sink, some swim. I don't wonder that boarding school helped make Jim Douglas as hard a man as he was. But Ben... well. He's a very different character.'

'He told me he doesn't really want to be CEO. I think he'd rather be a farmer, or a painter or something.' Liz smiled, thinking of Ben. 'He's good with people, but he doesn't have the killer instinct. And he doesn't want to put the hours in, in the way that you have to, to make a company a success. Especially in an industry as competitive as the one we work in.'

'You'd make a good CEO. I can tell that already.' Gretchen sipped her coffee, giving Liz a shrewd look.

'I'd like to. And, yes, I think I could do it.' Liz wasn't embarrassed to admit that. It had always been her ambition.

'Good. Then you will, I'm sure.' Gretchen nodded. 'Now. Tell me about why you really came here. I know it wasn't just for a job, because someone like you would never come to Loch Cameron unless you were escaping something.' She sat back in her chair. 'You might as well tell me. And, if you think I'm going to tell anyone, look around. Half of these old duffers are deaf, anyway.'

'You don't miss much, Gretchen.' Liz ate some of the pastry she'd chosen for herself, thinking about what to say. She found that she did want to tell Gretchen about the IVF, and about Paul. There was something about the woman that inspired trust.

FOURTEEN

'I always had a picture in my mind. You know, of the family I wanted,' Liz began. She looked nervously at Gretchen, her rational mind wondering whether it was okay to open up, but Gretchen patted her hand reassuringly.

'Yes. We all grow up with that, I think,' the older woman said. 'Either society makes us think we want it, or we really do.'

'Well, I really did. Do,' Liz corrected herself. 'Unfortunately, my body had other ideas. I couldn't get pregnant. I had a long-term partner, Paul. When we met, we knew that was what we both wanted: two kids, a house in the suburbs, security. You know? All the things you're supposed to want.'

'Indeed.' Gretchen looked wistful.

'Yeah. Well, it turned out that I couldn't get pregnant without help, so we started IVF,' Liz went on. 'The first round didn't work, but we were hopeful. And Paul was so lovely. He really looked after me. I'd get home from work, and he'd run me a bath, he'd have dinner ready. He'd rub my feet, give me back massages, everything. Hug me when I felt tired and overwhelmed.'

'He sounds like a real find,' Gretchen observed.

'He was. Is, I suppose,' Liz sighed. 'But we did three rounds of fertility treatment and it still hadn't happened. And in that time, I had two pretty distressing miscarriages. I'm sorry. Do you really want to hear about this?' She stopped herself, feeling anxiety bloom in her chest. Yet, it was a relief to talk about all of it.

She'd talked to Sharon, especially over the past year, about the IVF and her worries about Paul who had grown more and more distant. But, though she and Sharon had agreed to stay in touch, Liz felt they'd lost touch a little recently. It was understandable, seeing as she'd moved more than two hours away, and they no longer worked with each other, so it wasn't as easy to grab a quick coffee and catch up between meetings. Life was busy; she knew Sharon was always juggling her own family and a frantic work life.

'I'm happy to listen.' Gretchen bit off one side of a biscuit and regarded Liz with a kind expression. 'Honestly, dear, you have to remember that, at this point in my life, there's not much I haven't heard before. And I can tell you that there's absolutely nothing that can shock me anymore, either. So, you're in safe hands.'

'Okay.' Liz gave Gretchen a grateful smile. 'It's good to have someone to talk to that isn't a work colleague, too. It would be really inappropriate to tell them this. But still...'

'Of course. I was the same, when I was working.' Gretchen nodded. 'I worked mostly with men, then, and as far as they were concerned, I didn't have a personal life. I couldn't be a woman, to them. In many ways, I sympathised with Margaret Thatcher at the time. She was a woman working with a lot of chauvinist pigs, of course. So, she had to be stronger than all of them. The Iron Lady.'

'Were you the Iron Lady of the book world?' Liz wiped her

eyes, where a tear was threatening to leak out. 'I can't imagine that.'

'Oh, yes, I was.' Gretchen chuckled. 'I had a couple of women friends I worked with, as time went on. By the time I retired, things were a lot better in terms of women having decision-making roles in the industry. But, when I started as an editor, I had a choice: be a woman, and have all the men I worked with continually asking me out and never listening to anything I said, or beat them at their own game. So, I worked twice as hard as them, and I got results. I found new authors, worked on their manuscripts, made them bestsellers. I got promoted above most of those young men, in the end. Hired Andrew as a secretary, and I ruled over them all with a rod of iron. Just the men, of course. I hired as many female editorial staff as I could, and treated them very nicely.'

'I love that.' Liz had to smile. 'I wish I'd had a mentor like you at work.'

'I would have been very happy to mentor a bright young thing like you.' Gretchen patted her hand. 'Anyway. You were telling me about Paul. And the miscarriages. I'm sorry to hear about that. It's a very distressing experience. Even though it's so common, so they say, but that doesn't make it any easier when it happens, does it?'

'No.' Liz took a deep breath. 'I lost the first baby at two months. But there were complications, so I had to go into hospital to have a D&C. The nurses were so lovely. But it was still awful. And I felt like such a failure.'

'I had one in my thirties. I was seeing a man, but we weren't that serious.' Gretchen frowned. 'Lovely man, really. He wanted us to get married when he found out I was pregnant, but I didn't want to. Then, I lost the baby. So, I understand the feeling of being a failure. But you know that you're not, don't you?' Gretchen gripped both of Liz's hands. 'It's important that you know that.'

'I know. I mean, I guess so.' Liz let out a long breath. 'It's hard not to feel like I failed as a woman, you know? My body didn't do the one thing it was designed to do. And I... I lost Paul because of it.' She started to cry. 'Oh, goodness, I'm so sorry,' she sobbed, trying to stop, but failing. Liz was aware that she was in a public place, with many of the tables and seating areas around her occupied with the other residents of Gretchen's care home.

'Here you are, dear,' someone handed her a large cotton hanky, 'keep it. I've got plenty.'

Liz looked up blearily and saw an elderly man wearing a bow tie, shirt and obligatory old-man knitted jumper over his cord trousers standing by the table. His face was lined, but his eyes twinkled softly. Gretchen smiled up at him affectionately.

'Thank you, Alun. That's kind of you,' she said. 'Liz and I were just having a bit of a heart-to-heart.'

'Oh, I won't interrupt. Girl talk, and all that.' Alun nodded. 'I just thought you might need something to dry your eyes. I know you ladies don't like to spoil your makeup.'

'Thank you.' Liz took the hanky and wiped her eyes. 'That's so sweet.'

'Not a bit of it. I rather miss being there to supply hankies, mints, that kind of thing, since my Elsie passed,' Alun replied. 'And may I say, whatever it is, dear, you'll rise above it. I can see you're a strong one, just like our Gretchen.'

'Thank you, Alun,' Gretchen said, firmly. 'I'll see you later, at bridge.'

'Looking forward to it.' Alun straightened his bow tie, and nodded politely to them both before going over to the coffee machine.

'Sorry about that,' Gretchen muttered. 'Some of these men can't stand to see a lady in distress, that's all it is. It's rather sweet, really, but they don't always know when to keep their distance.'

'Oh, no, I didn't mind at all,' Liz protested. 'What a lovely man.'

'Well, look. I was just going to say, before Alun decided you needed saving,' Gretchen rolled her eyes, 'you must remember that you didn't lose Paul because you couldn't have a baby. It sounds like he was very supportive in the whole process. It was more that the whole thing was so overwhelming that it was just a huge pressure on your relationship. And, if he got distant with you, then he just got to the place where it was too much for him. You didn't fail him. Things just didn't work out, that's all.'

'He thought I was *too much*.' Liz picked up on the phrase that haunted her life. 'Other men did, too. I was too successful. Too confident. I don't know. I never understood it. It's like saying you're too nice or too kind. Madness.'

'Ah. That old chestnut.' Gretchen raised an eyebrow. 'I heard that plenty from men in my life too. What you have to realise is they're not saying we're *too much*. They're worried that they *aren't enough*. No real man would ever worry he wasn't enough for a woman like you. He'd just be delighted to be around you, you mark my words.'

'Did you find someone who didn't think you were too much?' Liz asked her.

'Of course I did. More than one. Legions.' Gretchen chuckled. 'You just have to stop trying to be someone you're not and they'll flock to you, I promise. For as many men in the world who want a little woman, there are just as many that adore a powerful one.'

'Hmmm. I want to believe that.'

'You should. I lived it. I know,' Gretchen sniffed. 'It's never the ones you expect, either. Often the younger ones went for me. They liked that I had money, confidence, my own life. That I didn't need anything from them. That was...' Gretchen lowered her voice '*Super sexy* to them. Believe me.' She winked.

'Oh, goodness.' Liz let out a loud giggle. 'Gretchen!'

'What? Just being truthful.' Gretchen gave her a 'cat that got the cream' look.

'Did you want kids? Do you have any?' Liz asked.

'Yes. I had a daughter. I adopted her when I was in my mid-thirties. People thought I was mad, as a single working mother.' Gretchen looked sad. 'But I got to the stage where I knew I wasn't going to settle down with anyone and have a family. And I wanted to work. So, I adopted.'

'That's really nice to hear. Obviously, Paul and I considered it. I just... I had the very strong instinct that I wanted my own child. My own flesh and blood,' Liz admitted.

'Of course! Adoption isn't easy, but it suited me at the time. It wouldn't suit everyone.'

'Do you have any other family?' Liz asked.

'I have a grandson, who I see now and again, but not much. He's too busy, off living his life,' she chuckled, dryly. 'Still, he's a good boy. My daughter – Stella – died a couple of years ago. Car accident.' Gretchen stared out of the large bay window in the day room onto the gardens beyond. 'He hasn't wanted to see me much, since then. I don't know why. He's just coping with it in his own way, so I'm not going to push him.'

'Oh, no. I'm so sorry to hear that.' Liz held Gretchen's hand. Her heart ached for the other woman.

'It's been very hard.' Gretchen looked back at Liz, and Liz could see the difficult emotions she was struggling to keep under control. 'She was fifty. She had an extreme nut allergy, and the doctors said that she must have accidentally eaten something containing nuts when she was driving. I mean, she would never have knowingly eaten anything nutty. But anyway, she went into sudden anaphylactic shock while driving, and there was an impact. She died almost immediately, they told me.' Gretchen took in a shaky breath. 'There was a sandwich in the car with her. It must have been in that.'

'Oh, God, Gretchen! That's terrible! Did you ... I mean, you could sue the company, if it said there weren't nuts in it.' Liz was appalled. You heard about these freak accidents, but you never thought they'd happen to you, or anyone you knew.

'I was eighty at the time, dear. I didn't have it in me to sue anyone.' Gretchen gave her a brave smile. 'And I was grieving. I still am. I miss her so much.'

'I can only imagine. What was she like?' Liz asked, gently.

'Beautiful. She was always beautiful. I adopted her when she was two. Never any trouble. She went to full time daycare when she was little, because I was working. We lived in Edinburgh then, and then we moved back to the cottage when she started school. I had a nanny come and pick her up from school, make her dinner and all that, and I'd always be back by six-thirty. I made sure I put her to bed every night.' Gretchen smiled at the memory. 'We read so many books. I was definite that I was going to instil a love of books in her, and I did. She grew up to be a librarian.'

'She sounds great.' Liz held Gretchen's hand tightly. 'I'm so sorry you lost her. It's unthinkable.'

'I had her for forty-eight years.' Gretchen let out a long sigh. 'And that's so much more than some people get. My heart breaks for you, trying so hard to have a child and not having that time at all. Not yet, anyway. It could still be in the cards for you.'

'Oh, I don't know, Gretchen.' Liz exhaled. 'I'm thirty-seven now. Every year that goes past, it gets less likely. And I'd have to start all over again with someone, and that's assuming that they would want kids. They might not. You know what they say about the likelihood of women over forty finding love. You're more likely to get struck by lightning. Or something like that.'

'Pfft. Those so-called "statistics" are probably made up by men,' Gretchen tutted. 'Anyway, in this day and age, that's all changed. Maybe in the 80s, yes. But fifty per cent of marriages end in divorce these days, which means there's a lot of people in their forties and fifties becoming single again. Even younger too, I suspect. So, there are plenty of fish in the sea, Liz. Should you want to go fishing.'

'I guess you're right,' Liz agreed, reluctantly. 'I suppose it's more the fact that going fishing's the last thing I feel like doing right now.'

'Fair enough, dear. It's just as nice having a picnic on the riverbank with your friends. To continue the metaphor,' Gretchen explained. 'Just remember that you've got a friend here, should you need one.'

'Thanks, Gretchen. And, same here.' Liz enveloped Gretchen in a hug. 'I'm sorry I cried all over you. But it did help, to talk about things a bit.'

'Any time.' Gretchen patted Liz's arm affectionately. 'I'm always here. The only distractions I've got are bridge and canasta.'

'Well, I wouldn't say that was strictly true, Gretchen. You seem to have plenty of male admirers,' Liz cautioned her friend with a wry smile.

'Agh. Yes, I suppose so,' Gretchen sighed. 'But they do grate on one, after a while. There's only so many boiled sweets and mugs of cocoa one has a tolerance for.'

'No, but you've got moxie. And they seem to like it,' Liz giggled, watching Alun across the room as he tried, unsuccessfully, to seem like he wasn't staring at Gretchen. 'You should be kinder to them.'

'Oh, dear lord. Save me from having to be kind to old men. I miss the younger ones.' Gretchen rolled her eyes, but she shot Alun a sweet smile anyway. 'You've got to give them something,' she said, out of the corner of her mouth, to Liz, who suppressed another laugh.

'Gretchen, I want to grow up to be just like you,' she said, feeling much better than she had before.

'Be careful what you wish for, dear.' Gretchen stood up carefully, leaning on the glass-topped wicker table to steady herself. 'But I wish you all the very best. And come and see me again soon, all right?'

'I will,' Liz promised.

FIFTEEN

'She's escaped!' Ben said when Liz opened the door to the cottage. She was still in her pyjamas.

'What?' Liz rubbed her eyes sleepily. 'Ben? It's a Sunday.'

'I know. Sorry. But I followed her this way and I think she's gone into your garden.' Ben dashed to the side of the cottage and peered over the small blue-painted wooden gate that led to the garden. 'Sorry, I'm out of breath. I've just run from the house up here.'

'Who's escaped?' Liz blinked, wishing she had her robe on. The cold morning air coming up from the loch was freezing her bare toes.

'Mae,' Ben hissed, tiptoeing back to the front door. 'My goat, remember?'

'Your goat's in my garden?' Liz was well aware of the ridiculousness of that statement. 'What is this, like, some kind of prank? Am I on camera?'

'No. I'm serious. Mae escapes pretty frequently; I don't tie her up or anything, that would be cruel. Mostly, I keep the gate to the garden shut and she has plenty of room to run around, and the hedges are tall. But she does tend to squeeze through the trees and get out. I've put wire netting up, but she just ate through it.' Ben had lowered his voice.

'Why are we whispering? Does she speak English?' Liz replied, copying his tone.

'You think that's funny, but she's clever. I wouldn't put it past her to have learnt what we're saying.' A smile pulled at the side of Ben's mouth. 'Goats are smart.'

'Dear lord. Okay, come in for a minute.' Liz beckoned Ben inside the cottage and led him to the kitchen window. 'We should be able to see her from here, if she's invaded Gretchen's flower garden.'

'She might be hiding. She does that,' Ben suggested. Liz took in the fact that he was wearing only a thin T-shirt, shorts and trainers.

'I can't see her.' Liz looked out of the window. 'Aren't you cold, also? You look cold.'

'Yeah, kinda,' Ben admitted, shivering. 'I had to run out in what I was wearing, and I'd just come in from a run. I should've grabbed a hoodie at least, but Mae runs fast.'

Liz had to admit that her gaze had been drawn to Ben's muscular forearms, thighs and the suggestion of a toned stomach under his T-shirt. She blinked, looking away on purpose. But, *damn,* Ben certainly kept fit.

'I've got an oversized hoodie here. Wait, I'll get it.' Liz went to the bedroom and rummaged in the corner cupboard for a moment until she found her favourite, men's size sweatshirt. She'd got it on holiday with Paul one year when they'd gone to a basketball game in the US and Liz had surprised herself by having a great time. She'd never really thought of herself as a sports fan, but she'd really enjoyed the speed and athleticism of the game – hence the sweatshirt. Nowadays, she didn't really keep up with watching basketball on TV, but she wore the sweatshirt sometimes as a reminder of a happy time.

As Liz pulled the sweatshirt out, she realised that she hadn't actually worn it since she'd split up with Paul. Touching its soft-ness brought back a raft of sudden memories: the day she'd bought it at the American stadium; wearing it after her first miscarriage as she'd lain in bed and cried. She'd washed and washed it, but it still reminded her of Paul. Bad days and good days.

She walked back to the kitchen and handed it to Ben.

'Here. Probably your size,' she said, not wanting to get into a discussion about where the sweatshirt had come from. Ben didn't ask, but took it gratefully.

'Thanks. Look. There!' He pointed to a corner of the garden, where there was a sudden flash of grey fur. Ben ran out to the front door, the sweatshirt half over his head. 'Come on!' he yelled.

Liz swore under her breath. Did she really want to go on a wild goat chase in the Scottish landscape?

Here we go, she thought, as she pulled on her walking boots and a fleece top and ran out of the cottage. She thought leaving the cottage door open was probably okay, but she grabbed her keys too and pulled the door closed after her, just to be on the safe side.

Old habits die hard, she thought as she ran after Ben. She hadn't quite got into the rural mindset of leaving your door open all day just yet.

Ahead of her, Ben was running along the mud track that led past her cottage and up to Queen's Point, the outcropping of rock that reached out over the loch. Legend had it that Mary, Queen of Scots had met a lover here, secretly; Liz had read that on Gretchen's ad for the cottage when she'd found it online. She didn't know how true it was, but it was a nice thought and added to the general romantic appeal of the cottage.

Unfortunately, that's all wasted on me, Liz thought as she broke into a jog to catch up with Ben. *I'm not here for romance.*

However, she also hadn't planned on chasing a goat through the highlands in her pyjamas, and here she was. *So, I suppose that's proof that you shouldn't rule anything out*, she thought, wryly.

Ben stopped and waved for her to catch up.

'She went that way. Little minx. She'll eat all the plants if we're not careful.' Ben pointed into another garden which belonged to the next cottage along the Point from Gretchen's, a good few hundred yards and around a corner. Liz hadn't said hello to the owners yet.

'Come on. We'll do a pincer movement and trap her.' Liz started tiptoeing towards the side of the cottage.

'Right.' Ben approached the cottage, and then broke off to go to the other side of it where another gate led into a wraparound garden much bigger than Gretchen's.

A man that Liz estimated was in his sixties opened the front door, holding a saucepan in one hand and a tea towel in the other.

'Guid mornin'. Can I help ye?' he asked, frowning.

'Oh. Yes. Good morning.' Liz broke out her best sales smile, guaranteed to charm even the most hostile of customers. 'I'm so sorry to bother you. I'm Liz Parsons. I'm renting the next cottage down.'

'Oh, the Ross cottage. Aye.' The man nodded with equanimity, but his frown remained. 'And yer sneakin' round ma cottage because...?'

'Look, I know it sounds mad, but my friend over there,' she waved at Ben, who smiled uncomfortably, 'well, the thing is, he's lost his goat. And we just saw her go into your garden.'

'A goat?'

'Yes. In your garden,' Liz repeated, wishing she was wearing real clothes and not pyjamas covered in a fleece. It was even worse that the pyjamas had cartoon cats on them.

'I see. And ye need tae get it, I suppose.'

'Before she eats everything. Yes.' Liz nodded.

'Hmm.' The man frowned at her again, his craggy face half-covered with a thick greyish-ginger beard. Liz thought he could have stepped straight out of *Lord of the Rings* or some other Norse-inspired fantasy tale – apart from the tea towel, which was slightly incongruous.

'Hi. Look, I'm so sorry we've disturbed you,' Ben joined Liz at the door, 'it's just that time is of the essence. Before she runs off again,' he explained.

'Ben Douglas. Is that ye?' The man peered at Ben and broke into a smile. 'Havenae seen ye up here for a while. It's Angus McKinnon.' He tapped his own barrel-like chest. 'Used tae work for yer dad.'

'Oh, hi, Angus!' Ben nodded vigorously, and shook the man's outstretched hand. As if by magic, the Viking's gruff exterior changed into friendliness. 'Yes, I remember. You were a handyman for us, weren't you? I was away at university a lot when you were working at the distillery, I think.'

'Aye. But I remember ye when ye came home. Always oot in the fields, up the mountains. Yer dad could never find ye tae do any work,' the man chuckled. 'I heard yer runnin' things now.'

'As best I can, yes.' Ben smiled, but Liz could sense he was a little uncomfortable, as he always was when his father was mentioned.

'The goat, Ben,' Liz reminded him, under her breath.

'Right. Yes. Angus, would you mind? It's just that Mae'll eat anything she can find, and I wouldn't want you to lose your vegetables or whatever.' Ben bounced on the balls of his feet, a little impatiently.

'Ah, right! Yes, go round. I'll come with ye.' Angus went to one side of the house, and Ben followed Liz to the other.

'There she is!' Ben whispered from behind Liz.

Sure enough, a large goat stood in the middle of a well-kept lawn at the back of the cottage. She was chewing something that definitely wasn't a plant and staring back at Liz and Ben with a contemptuous look on her narrow face.

'Look, she's got a sock from the clothes line!' she whispered. Angus – or someone else at the cottage – had obviously hung out laundry at some point, and Mae seemed to have chosen one of a number of white socks from the line to eat.

'Oh, goodness,' Ben muttered. 'Well, I guess it could be worse.'

'Angus' pants, you mean,' Liz murmured back, stifling a sudden giggle.

'Liz! It's not funny,' Ben shushed her. 'Did you see that guy? He could eat me for breakfast. Now I have to explain to him that my goat's eating his underwear.'

'Come on. It is a *bit* funny.' Liz started laughing out loud as Angus appeared at the other side of the garden and took in Mae with the sock in her mouth.

Ben edged past Liz and started to move towards Mae, making a clicking sound.

'Mae, be a good girl. Come on,' he crooned. The goat eyed him and continued chewing. 'Mae-Mae. Who's a good girl?' he continued, reaching out his hand. Liz watched as Angus crept up on the goat from the other side of the garden. She was laughing so hard now that she couldn't have helped if she'd tried.

Mae skipped a few steps away from Ben, as if she knew what he was up to. *She probably does,* Liz thought.

'Mae. Don't be silly. We both know what's going to happen here.' Ben reprimanded the goat sternly, which set Liz off even more. 'Liz. It's not funny,' he called out, casting an amused glance at her. 'You could help, you know.'

Liz held onto the gate and wiped her eyes, still giggling. It was the goat's face that really did it: there was something in her flat eyes with their odd, striped pupils that spoke of mayhem.

'I can't,' she managed to stutter. Ben grinned at her and started to laugh.

However, as if Mae knew that Ben was temporarily distracted, she made a break for it and ran straight at Angus, the white sock still in her mouth.

'Aghhh!' Angus flailed for a moment and then stood stock still, staring Mae straight in the eye as she ran at him. Ben flung himself after Mae, and as the goat collided with the mountainous Angus, Ben landed on top of them both in one confused man-goat tangle.

'Ben!' Liz ran over to them, temporarily concerned that someone had hurt themselves, but Ben looked up at her, smiling. 'Are you okay?'

'I'm fine. Angus bore the brunt of it.' Ben got to his knees, carefully holding Mae's collar. The fall seemed to have surprised her, and though she got to her feet readily, she seemed unharmed. 'Damn goat! Angus, I'm so sorry for all this,' he added.

'Ah, no harm done.' Angus dusted himself off and stood up. 'Not every day I get tae wrestle a goat in ma own back garden,' he chuckled. 'Would ye like some tea? Ye might need it after that.'

'That's kind, Angus, but I better get this one home.' Ben tapped Mae on the head. 'So sorry, again. I'll replace the sock.'

'Nae bother. I've got more.' Angus shrugged. 'Good tae meet ye, Miss... sorry, I forgot yer name.'

'Liz Parsons. I'll come and say a proper hello another time. When I don't have a mad goat in tow.' Liz opened the cottage's side door, standing back so that Ben could hustle Mae through it. 'Come on. Let's get her back home.'

As Liz followed Ben and the goat onto the pathway that ran

alongside all the cottages, she reflected that, sometimes, it was nice to embrace the unexpected. There was no way that she could have predicted her morning so far, and she liked that. She liked the fact that in Loch Cameron, her life was different. Anything might happen, and that made her hopeful.

SIXTEEN

'We need some kind of local angle. I'm thinking a new range that can revive the Loch Cameron brand.' Liz stood at the head of the board room table and pointed to the screen behind her, which showed the traditional logo and bottle labels Loch Cameron Distillery was known for. 'People respect the Loch Cameron brand, and they recognise that it's historic and family-run. But our market share is – frankly – abysmal. Almost every other single malt distiller sells three times or more than we do per year, and most of them have updated their messaging, their sales outlets, the way they reach people. Look at all these other traditional, family-run distilleries' Instagram accounts. See how they're interacting with customers here?' Liz flicked through a few slides showing the Instagram accounts of some of their competitor distilleries.

Ben opened the door to the board room and gestured to Liz to continue.

'Sorry I'm late,' he said, his face curiously blank. 'Had a last-minute thing I had to attend to.'

'No problem.' Liz continued with her presentation, but she was slightly annoyed at Ben's lateness to the meeting. It wasn't like she didn't know meetings overran, and schedules got busy at the last minute – especially for CEOs. But Liz had seen Ben in his office five minutes before the meeting started, sipping coffee with Henry curled up by his feet.

It didn't seem like that was too much of an emergency.

'And, when it comes to stockists, we go out to specialists only. No representation in the supermarkets. No representation in the other big market sellers. It's no wonder that sales are so low. We're not giving people an opportunity to find Loch Cameron Distillery whisky,' she continued.

'I've been saying this for years, Ben.' Sally leaned forward. 'Brian never pushed for those big contracts, and you just let him slack off.'

'That's not fair, Sally. You know Brian was Dad's best friend. I had to keep him in the job: I promised.' Ben looked down at the polished wood table. 'I know I made bad decisions. We've talked about this before.'

'Hey. This isn't about blame,' Liz interjected. 'Whatever happened in the past, happened. Ben hired me to address your – our – sales problems, and that's what I'm doing.'

'Fine.' Sally sat back in her chair. 'Liz, this isn't about you. I know you're doing a great job. I just feel like I've said a lot of this before, and nothing ever got done. It's frustrating, that's all.'

'I can imagine that it must be.' Liz met Sally's eyes with an open, friendly gaze. In fact, she knew exactly how frustrated Sally must be, as she'd been in the same position herself in the past. It was so annoying when you, as the person who worked in the company and could see all the problems, pointed them out but were ignored. Then, a new consultant or new member of staff would come in and say all the same things, and be listened to – and, usually, paid handsomely for doing so. It was just how workplaces were, sometimes.

'I'm not even in Sales. I know that's your expertise, Liz, and believe me, I know you're great at your job. And I'm so glad to have you here. But I could have told you all – and I did, repeat-edly – that you can't sell whisky if it's not in the shops,' Sally repeated. 'Anyway. That's all I'll say.'

'And you're a hundred per cent correct, Sally,' Liz agreed. 'So, that's why I've got meetings set up with three major super-market chains. They know me, so they know I'm going to come to them with what they want to hear. But what they're going to want to hear from me is that we can appeal to the modern whisky market, and can also provide them with the volume they need. Now, I can solve the first problem, but I can't solve the volume issue. How many units can we supply to a stockist, going on normal production rates?' Liz looked along the board room table. As well as her, Ben and Sally, who was the Finan-cial Director, Simon had joined them for the meeting, as had the rest of the Board: Andrea, the HR Director, and Eva, Head of Operations.

'Presently, we turn out twenty-five barrels per quarter. That's around 260 standard bottles per barrel,' Simon clarified. 'So, we're looking at around 6,500 bottles per quarter, full capacity.'

'That's better than I expected.' Liz tapped on her phone, using the calculator. 'I'd anticipate they'd want more, though. And we have to bear in mind that we have to fulfil all of our other orders, as well as whatever other sales routes I open up. I've got to know that we can fulfil big orders if they come in – when they come in – so, can we make more than 26,000 bottles per year?'

'It's possible. We have the storage space, but it means that we have to put more into production. So, we'd need to hire a few more staff. And, obviously, it's ten years after it goes to cask for anything new to be available,' Simon interrupted.

'Yes. But I think I'm right in saying that we have a backlog of existing product in the archive?' Liz looked at her notes. 'Sally provided me with these numbers.' She flicked to a new slide on screen. 'So, yes, if we commit to larger production numbers going forward, that will be reflected in future yield. But in the meantime, we can supply new sellers with our existing stock.'

'That's true,' Simon assented.

'All right, then. So, as I said, it's a two-pronged attack. We get the big stores selling Loch Cameron Ten Year Old, and we also launch a new, more exclusive range that can reinvent us in the market as a desirable, cool brand, without losing any of our historic, high quality appeal. So, my question to you is, what should the focus of our new range be?' Liz cast her eyes around the table.

There was a silence.

'Well, it should be something that is relevant to Loch Cameron. Some local feature,' Ben suggested. 'The landscape – the loch, the water, and the local plants are so important to the taste of the whisky.'

'Okay. I would say that a lot of newer distilleries are emphasising their organic ingredients, or new and more experimental brewing processes,' Liz replied. 'But we're very traditional in that way. And we don't use unusual ingredients, though they are locally sourced. I'm just not sure that's enough to make us stand out.'

'Okay, what then?' Simon asked, pushing his cap back on his head.

'I think it should be something based on local stories. Legends. People, even,' Liz explained. 'Customers love it when companies like ours invest in the legacy of our histories. We know that we're perceived as a trusted, high-quality brand with a family legacy. So I think we should go with that angle, but make it modern and relevant in some way.'

'Are you saying Loch Cameron is old-fashioned and irrelevant?' Simon raised an eyebrow, looking amused. He glanced over at Ben. 'Sounds like you've been judged, Douglas.'

'That's not what I meant at all,' Liz insisted, firmly. She wasn't going to let Simon railroad her presentation and bring it back to him and Ben's rivalry.

'I know you didn't, Liz,' Ben interjected, ignoring Simon. 'I get what you're saying. But it shouldn't be about the Douglases. It should be about someone else, in the past. People who have been important in the development of the whisky, maybe. Or in the village.'

'Yes. Exactly.' Liz nodded, relieved that she hadn't offended Ben, and that he seemed to be on her wavelength. 'I don't know who, but we can have more of a think about that. Everyone – that's an invitation open to you, too,' she added. 'We need to bring Loch Cameron Distillery into the twenty-first century. And, ironically, we're going to do it by bringing out something about its past.'

'Okay. Thanks, Liz.' Ben shot her a warm smile. 'Let's move on, but let's all consider it a task for next week's meeting to come with some ideas for the focus of our new range. I'm excited about that.'

Ben's eyes stayed on Liz's just a second longer than she expected, and a warm glow spread from her stomach into her whole body. There was a strange electricity that he seemed to elicit in her, and it didn't seem to care whether they were in a board room with other people or alone on a windy hill, looking for herbs and wild flowers. Liz cleared her throat and sat down, breaking his gaze and looking down at her laptop.

Whatever it was that happened when Ben looked at her, it was confusing, and she didn't need to be confused in the middle of the weekly meeting. She was here to do her job.

I'm not the kind of woman who gets flustered in meetings, she scolded herself. *Stop it. You're acting like a schoolgirl.*

Whatever it was that she was feeling, Liz didn't welcome it. Her work was the one place that she could focus away from her emotions, and that had been the one thing that had kept her

that the sun was out. Firs, oak and ash trees were dotted along
the edge of the loch, sometimes in deep clusters, and sometimes
just a lone tree here and there, like the king or queen of its own
small glade.

The village was full of gentle activity. Liz would have struggled to describe it as busy, but there was a rhythm to it, in its
own way. Older ladies carrying baskets and tartan tote bags
either walked briskly from shop to shop, or stopped to gossip at
the edge of the street. A small van stopped outside the butcher's
shop, and a young man got out, opening up the back and taking
out some large boxes.

Parents of young children passed her here and there, with
little ones in pushchairs and prams or holding toddlers' chubby
little hands. Liz smiled at them all, though her heart wrenched a
little every time. She didn't begrudge those parents, of course.
Today, seeing happy families with small children filled her with
a sense of hope. That could still be her.

She'd taken a footpath that led uphill at the end of the little
cobbled high street, following her instincts and wondering
where it led. First, it had taken her through a dappled forest,
where a gurgling stream wound through pine and spruce trees,
following the hill down to the loch.

Then, at the top of the hill, as Liz paused to catch her
breath, the path widened to a plateau, and she saw the chapel.

It's probably big enough to hold twenty people at the most,
Liz thought, as she walked up to it and held out her hand to
touch its aged grey stone wall. Above the arched oak door, old
carvings had partly crumbled away, but she thought she could
make out grinning gargoyles and the flick of a scaly tail. Liz
wasn't much of one for old churches, not being very religious,
but she seemed to remember reading somewhere once that
many of the older ones had quite mythical carvings relating
back to old beliefs or local legends. The gargoyles were meant to
scare bad spirits away, that she knew – and perhaps the scaly

tail had once belonged to some kind of Loch Ness-type mythical beast that people believed lived in the loch here.

People believed some pretty strange stuff in the past, after all, she thought. And Loch Cameron was one of those ancient, rural communities where there were probably a lot of old legends.

However, the door to the chapel was closed, so Liz sat with her back against its outer wall, facing the loch, and drank some water from the bottle she'd brought with her. As she sat there, she looked at the closest tombstones: none of them seemed more recent than about a hundred years old, and many of them were older than that.

I guess it's full, she thought, shading her eyes from the sun. Prime location. The place to be when you're dead in Loch Cameron. Or, at least, it was.

Finishing her drink, Liz stood up and inspected the stones.

MURIEL PEABODY, the first one read. 1776–1834. OLD MAID.

Nice, Liz thought. *Poor Muriel. No one had anything to say about her other than her marital status.*

She walked on to another stone.

RICHARD MCCULLOCH
1887–1950
FOR GOD AND SCOTLAND
AT REST

Liz noted that Richard's stone had no mention of his marital status. Plus, he got a rousing epithet: For God and Scotland. *Muriel probably would have liked that too,* she thought as she walked on between the stones. *I wonder if anyone asked her.*

Liz doubted it.

ANNIE CONSTANTINE
'AUNT ANNIE'

1791–1875

Liz stopped at Annie's stone, which was also engraved with a rose. *I wonder why she was 'Aunt Annie'*, she thought. The rose was a nice touch. And, she had lived for a long time, given the period in history and the likelihood of disease.

Liz walked past some family burials, not wanting to linger at the stones that listed children in their graves at a young age, of which there were surprisingly many. She realised she was looking for other women's stones: women who had been buried alone.

Dark, she thought. *Is this because this is how you see your future? Buried alone, perhaps after being found because your ten cats are making a racket?* Liz smiled to herself. *Maybe,* she thought. *Maybe these are my people, now.*

But it was more than that, she realised. There was something sad about the lone women in this graveyard who were afforded such little acknowledgement. Aunt Annie was a little different: Liz got the feeling that Annie had been much loved.

She looked at some more: there were four OLD MAIDS that Liz could find in the graveyard: Muriel Peabody, Elspeth Anderson, Felicity Black and Evelyn McCallister.

Of course, Liz reflected, being an "old maid" meant you hadn't married, but it also meant you hadn't had children. She thought about how she would feel if, in death, she was defined only by her childlessness, and a wave of sadness passed over her. How awful that was! How awful to look ahead and see herself alone, as Muriel had been, in old age.

Liz had no way of knowing whether any of these women were spinsters by choice or not. Of course, if they had chosen not to tie themselves to a family, she understood.

She had made herself stop thinking about the baby game show; she had stopped thinking about herself as a competitor for some unlikely chance at that sepia-tinted, nostalgic future photo of herself and a child. When the thought threatened to make a reappearance, sometimes when she was at home, alone, at night, she locked it away in a box in her mind.

We're not thinking about that anymore, she told herself, firmly.

Instead of being sucked back into that old train of thought, Liz got out her phone and took some photos of the women's gravestones. She didn't quite know what she was going to do, but she knew that she didn't want Muriel Peabody, Elspeth Anderson, Felicity Black and Evelyn McCallister to be forgotten. At the very least, she could find out more about them for her own satisfaction.

If they hadn't had children, Liz wanted to know why. She wanted to know these women's stories: who were they? Who had they loved? Where had they lived, and what secrets and sorrows did they each hold? No one could be adequately summed up by their epitaph, it was true, but simply printing OLD MAID on each of their graves wasn't enough. They were human beings: each had lived a full and interesting life, of that Liz was sure.

It felt important to Liz that she know more about these women, if only to prove to herself that her own life was still important in the light of her own infertility. She had to believe that, if her lifelong goal wasn't going to come true, that it wouldn't become the thing she was judged on by the rest of the world, or, worse, that she measured herself against and was found wanting.

The gravestones were a sign, Liz decided. If this was her new life, and if children weren't part of the picture, then she owed it to herself to come to terms with her new truth, no matter how difficult it was. In which case, she also owed it to these four women to be known as more than OLD MAIDS.

Muriel, Elspeth, Felicity and Evelyn wouldn't be forgotten; at least, not to Liz. She felt hopeful about her new life in Loch

Cameron, and part of that hope was connected to those women. If Liz could make a new life, then so could they, even so long after they'd lived. Their legacy was in Liz's hands, and she felt good about telling a different story for them. She was starting to feel good about her new life, overall. Day by day, a brighter sliver of light lit up Liz's darkened life, and every day she felt just a little happier.

EIGHTEEN

Liz held the letter in her hand and stared at it uncomprehendingly.

It had arrived the day before, but she'd been busy at work and hadn't even looked at her mail until this morning, when she was eating breakfast in the sunny kitchen of the cottage. She'd eaten half a piece of toast and was sipping a cup of tea as she opened the envelope. Life felt good, today. It had been feeling a little better every day since she'd been in Loch Cameron.

The letter was from the IVF clinic. She blinked as she recognised the logo on the top of the letterhead, remembering that she had had a frantic day of notifying all her contacts and accounts of her new address in Gretchen's cottage before she'd moved.

Dread roiled in her stomach. She didn't quite know why; the IVF clinic contacting her wasn't a bad thing. Perhaps it was because she'd been enjoying not thinking about her fertility for the first time in what felt like forever.

She focused on the letter, reading it with a sinking feeling.

The clinic was writing to remind her that she was able to take one more round of IVF, if she wanted to. The doctor had advised that much more beyond one more might not be worth it, and then, of course, she and Paul had broken up. She had discounted the idea of any more rounds.

Liz stared at the letter. She had known another round was an option, of course, but getting the letter and seeing the information in black and white – a reminder of everything she was trying to forget – was still a shock. But it was the last paragraph that had really made her tense.

She had spent weeks slowly unwinding in Loch Cameron; enjoying her new job, discovering the women's graves in the village cemetery and thinking how she might rewrite their histories a little. It was nice to have something else to focus on rather than the possibility of a baby. She had been slowly healing, trying to forget Paul; trying to reconnect with herself.

Now, somehow, all of that fragile peace had been swept away.

It wasn't the clinic's fault. They were doing what she'd asked them to do. It was Liz. Had she changed, somehow? She didn't know. But since she'd had some time out of the fertility game show she had competed in so fiercely, she'd started to... heal.

In the final paragraph of the letter, the clinic added that it also provided sperm donation services and was available for consultation.

Sperm donation?

Liz continued to stare at the piece of paper in her hand until she realised that her tea was dripping from the cup; she was holding it at an odd angle. She swore, got up and poured the rest of the cup in the sink, wiping her robe with a tea towel.

She had never even considered donation from a stranger before.

The letter said that it would be possible for her to do another round of IVF on her own, if she had a sperm donor. She had always thought that the father of her child would be Paul, but that hadn't worked. Could she try again, with a stranger's DNA making up half of her baby? Did she want to put herself through another round of IVF when the likelihood of getting pregnant was so low?

Liz had relocated to Loch Cameron and plunged herself into her new job with the aim of deliberately not thinking about fertility or having a baby. And, yet, the sudden possibility was there. She felt blindsided, realising the possibility that perhaps she'd been too deep in grief to see before. She could still have a baby. Maybe.

Do I want that? she asked herself. She really didn't know. Somehow, it had been easier when she thought that the IVF was over. That it was a clean break, destined never to be.

Now that she knew there was a possibility to hope again, half of her wanted to jump at the opportunity and call the clinic right away. But the other half felt a kind of grief for the future her who would be disappointed yet again. She'd just started to regain an equilibrium in her new life. Did she really want to upset that?

It would be different, doing fertility treatments on her own. There would be no Paul to hold her at night when she ached with exhaustion. There would be nobody to talk to, to share her fears with. And if the treatment was successful, she would be a single parent from the start. Was she really ready for that?

Carefully, Liz folded the letter and placed it under the vase of flowers that she had picked from the garden the day before. Her heart felt heavy. Her previous lightness had disappeared.

You don't have to decide anything now, she told herself. *Be gentle with yourself.*

Yet, as much as she tried not to think too hard about the possibility, the idea of a child – her child, the one she had longed for – filled her head and her heart, and wouldn't go away.

NINETEEN

'So, what's on the agenda this week?' Liz sat down on one of the slightly rickety wooden chairs that were free in the circle, dropping her handbag on the floor next to her chair and carefully settling her plate on her knee. The Tuesday before, she hadn't managed to make the crochet club, but she'd put a note in her diary to remember to come today.

'Hi, Liz. Not much. Same old.' Kathy flashed her a grin. Today, her two-tone hair was divided into two plaits: one black, one shocking pink. 'How are you?'

'Not bad. Settling in.' Liz took a bite of the thick chocolate brownie she'd chosen for lunch this week, feeling like a naughty child for not eating her sandwich first. 'Mmm! That's so good. I swear, you guys should have some kind of full-time cake business,' she said with her mouth full. She was trying not to think about the letter from the clinic. It felt like too much to think about: every time she started to consider the possibility of a sperm donor – and the possibility, once more, of being a mother again, however slight – she became overwhelmed by a wave of hope, and an equally large wave of fear.

'Ha. It's a thought!' Sheila chuckled. 'I think we're all tae busy for that, though. Tuesday lunchtime's one o' the only times we can ever get together. Mina's got the business tae run, Bess's always oot and aboot, fixin' pipes an' puttin' up wallpaper, Kathy's got her studies – an' I dinnae think June's got a cake business in her nowadays. No disrespect, June, aye.'

The older woman gave Sheila a regal stare.

'How dare you, Sheila Briggs. I could run a cake empire if I wanted to,' she scolded, poker-faced.

'Of course. How silly of me.' Sheila grinned. 'I know ye could, June. Ye could probably run the country too while ye were crocheting that doily.'

'This is it. I just choose not to, in my dotage,' June said, crisply, with a twinkle in her eye. 'Liz. How's things at the distillery?'

'Good, thanks.' Liz reached for a crochet hook and a ball of wool from a pile of materials on a side table and frowned at them, trying in vain to remember how to start. 'I've forgotten everything you showed me last time, Sheila,' she confessed.

'I'll show you. Chain stitch first – make a loop, then wrap the wool around the hook and pull through.' Mina, sitting next to her, held out her hook and demonstrated the stitch slowly, before pulling the thread so that all the stitches disappeared.

'Right. Okay.' Liz started the stitch again, getting something that roughly resembled Mina's neat loops.

'Right. Then, remember, go in through the middle hole.' Mina demonstrated the next steps slowly, letting Liz follow along. 'Right. That's it. Now carry on,' she said, watching patiently as Liz fumbled with the wool. 'You're getting it. Well done!'

'So, how's the jams and chutneys business, Mina?' she asked as she frowned at her wayward stitches.

'Ah, mustn't grumble. We're doing very well. And, Ashoka – that's my eldest – got a special merit in school this week for her spelling. So, we're very happy.' Mina glowed with pride. 'Sanjay reads to the kids every night before bed. We think books are so important,' she added. 'Do you have a family, Liz? We didn't even ask you last time.'

'Umm... no.' Liz felt sudden anxiety twist in her stomach. She looked down at her crochet, avoiding eye contact.

'No? Not met the right guy, eh? Ah well, there's still time. But the biological clock goes tick-tock, tick-tock,' Mina tapped Liz on the knee. 'Perhaps you'll meet someone here.'

'I don't think so. And children aren't likely,' Liz said. She didn't want to talk about it, not least with people that she didn't know. Even if they were friendly and welcoming.

'Oh? Why not?' Mina pressed on, crocheting away.

'Mina,' Bess was sitting on the other side of Liz today, 'that's personal.'

'What? It was a normal question,' Mina protested. 'Liz, I'm sorry if it's too personal. You can of course ignore me, I will not be offended.'

'No, that's all right,' Liz looked up, clearing her throat. 'I actually... can't. Have children. At least, I haven't been able to so far. I've been doing IVF for a couple of years but didn't have any luck.' She tried to keep her voice steady, but she couldn't help it when it wobbled.

'Oh, no.' Mina dropped her crochet and turned to Liz, clasping both of her hands around Liz's. 'I am so sorry. What a shame for you.'

'Thanks.' Liz took a few deep breaths, wanting to keep her emotions under control. 'Sorry, I really didn't want to end up talking about this.'

'And you don't have to,' Bess said, calmly. 'We totally understand if you don't.'

'But yer also welcome to talk about anythin',' Sheila added. 'Many's the time this lot've listened to ma woes aboot ma kids. An' the menopause.'

'Oh, the *menopause*,' Bess and Mina chorused, laughing. 'Just you wait, Kathy.'

Kathy frowned, and continued on with her crochet.

'Hey. I've got the kid thing to do first, maybe, if I ever find anyone worth doing it with,' she muttered.

'Anyway, Liz, what I'm saying is that there's nothing new you can say we haven't heard,' June said, leaning forward in her chair. 'I know you don't know us, really. But, over the years, we've ended up talking about goodness knows what on our Tuesdays. The girls were here to help me when I lost my husband, two years ago. Bess never wants to talk about her feelings, but I think she likes to be here anyway. She knows she has somewhere to go if she wants to.'

'That's fair.' Bess smiled over at June, who nodded. 'We're here for you, Liz. It sounds like you've had a pretty hard time recently.'

'I guess I have.' Liz heard her voice catch. She thought about the letter from the clinic again, and the overwhelming feelings overtook her again. She started crying. 'Oh, no. I'm so sorry.'

Tears rolled down her cheeks, and she started sobbing, feeling the weight of her emotions in her heart and her lungs. It felt as if she was drowning as she fought for breath.

She felt a warm hand on her back, solid and present.

'Ach, pet. Ye poor wee lassie.' Sheila had come to stand next to her, and her hand made wide, reassuring circles on Liz's back. 'Aye, let it oot. Best thing.'

Liz sobbed her heart out, then, finally letting something go inside her. She had been resisting it for so long: she had been fighting to stay in control. But all she'd been doing was damming up her emotions until they were too powerful, and the barrier she'd hidden them behind was breached.

She had lost Paul. She had lost two babies. And she had lost her whole future.

That was how it felt, anyway. And, in a way, the letter from the clinic just made it worse, because it had given a tiny shard of hope again. And hope felt like the absolute worst thing that could have been offered to her right now.

All that loss reverberated and crashed through her body like a storm. She felt as though it was never going to end; it hurt, coming out of her. Her body ached and her heart felt used up and exhausted. *I can't put myself there again,* she thought. *I just can't.* The thought of building herself up only to lose again was too much.

Yet, as she cried, Liz realised that her heart would never hurt as badly now as it had when Paul had actually left, and on the days when she had lost her two babies. The hurt she had been damming up inside her heart in response to those events needed to be purged – and, now that she was letting it go, she was starting to feel a little lighter.

Of all the places and times that Liz would have liked to express her emotions – not that she was usually a fan of doing it at all – a community centre in rural Scotland with a group of virtual strangers doing crochet, on a Tuesday lunchtime, was pretty far down the list of ideal situations. Yet, here she was, crying in front of five other women she'd only met two weeks ago.

'I'm so sorry, Liz.' Kathy handed her a tissue. 'My friend's doing IVF now. It's so tough. You're a warrior for doing it in the first place.'

'Ugh. I don't feel much like a warrior right now,' Liz mumbled, trying to get herself under some degree of control.

'Well, you are,' Bess said, staunchly. 'I've got nothing but respect for you. I couldn't do it.'

'*Men* wouldn't do it,' June added. 'Think of all the things we do that they wouldn't. Don't ever think you're not strong,' she scolded. 'It takes strength to do what you're doing now, too.

Experiencing your emotions. Letting them out in front of other people.'

'June's right,' Mina agreed. 'My husband Sanjay couldn't run the business and be a mummy at the same time. He's got no idea of what I do to hold the family together.'

'Ach, love him, but my Phil's the same. He cannae put his trousers on without me tellin' him which leg's which,' Sheila added.

Liz laughed, despite herself.

'Ah, there now. That's better.' Sheila patted Liz on the shoulder. 'I'm goin' tae get ye another cuppa, hen. An' then you can tell us whatever you want to get out there. Or nothin'. Whatever ye want, okay?'

'Okay,' Liz said, wiping her eyes. Mina pulled up her chair closer to Liz's and put her arm around Liz's shoulders.

'I'm sorry I upset you,' she said. 'But I think it was strangely for the best, mmm?' she asked. 'Now. My mummy used to say to me, miracles happen often. We just have to look for them, and recognise them when they occur. Your miracle might be a baby, one day. But it might not, and Parvati – that's the Hindu goddess of fertility – might bless you in another way. I think you will be blessed, one way or another.' Mina nodded, seriously.

'That's kind, thank you, Mina.' Liz squeezed the woman's hand. 'Don't apologise. This has been going on for months. I guess I just couldn't hold it in anymore.'

'Hmm. Holding in emotions never works.' Mina shook her head. 'I tell the kids this all the time. If you're sad, cry. If you're happy, laugh. If you have worries, tell Mummy. Very simple.'

'It is. You're right,' Liz sighed. 'I'm going to try and feel my feelings a little more from now on. Ideally, not in the middle of crochet circle every week, though,' she chuckled, ruefully.

'Ah, we don't mind. What else have we got to do?' Mina grinned. 'You can come here and cry every week for a year if you like, Liz. I won't mind.'

'You might regret saying that,' Liz warned. 'And my crochet so far is atrocious. Look at that!' She held out her mangled wool on the hook.

'Never.' Mina tutted. 'Anyway, here's Bess with your tea. Drink up.' She took Liz's crochet from her and started to unravel it. 'Here. We'll start again, and it will be much better.'

'Crochet's a bit like life,' Kathy said, taking a bite of a large, fruit-laden flapjack. 'Sometimes it all goes to crap and looks a mess. But you can usually unravel it and start again.'

Liz smiled.

'I can see that.' She took a drink of tea, and felt it fortify her. She didn't know if she'd ever end up crocheting anything worth looking at, but she'd give it a try. Making a new start in Loch Cameron was also worth sticking at – especially now that she'd found the crochet coven. For a long time, IVF had controlled Liz's life, but now she felt like she was taking her life back, little by little. And if that meant taking some time out for a little crochet, cake and gossip now and again, then so be it. It had been a long time since she'd been a part of a group like this, and she realised, now, that she'd missed it.

TWENTY

Liz was in her office, reviewing her predecessor's sales reports again, when her phone rang. She tended to use the voice command when she was working, and had her phone set up to go straight to loudspeaker.

'Liz? It's Paul.'

For some moments, Liz couldn't reply. It felt as though all the air had been pushed out of her lungs. She stared mutely at the phone screen, where his name showed alongside the photo she'd taken, two years ago. It was – had been – one of her favourites. Paul had taken her on a surprise trip to Lapland at Christmas: the photo showed him in a red knitted hat, smiling softly into the camera. She'd forgotten to take the picture off his contact on her phone.

'Paul?' she stammered. 'What... why are you calling me?' His voice was so familiar, and yet so alien, because Liz had never expected to hear it again.

'I wanted to see if you were okay,' Paul replied. There was a silence, as Liz's heart hammered in her chest. 'I... I miss you.'

He had always had a voice that pulled her in. It had a certain timbre, a quality about it that she couldn't describe, but had always made her feel both protected and happy, like all was right with the world whenever Paul spoke to her.

'If I'm okay?' Liz stammered.

'Yeah. I'm sorry if it's not a good time. I was just thinking of you, and—'

'Why are you calling me?' Liz interrupted him. Her initial dismay had been taken over by a rising anger. This was the man who had walked out on her as she sat on the sofa, crying. For as much as he knew, she might have been pregnant in that moment. She hadn't been, but who did that? Paul had broken her heart and now, here he was, calling her out of the blue because he'd been "thinking of her"?

'I wondered if I could come and see you. And talk.'

'You want to talk to me. About what?' Liz snapped. She was glad she was angry. Anger was better than bewildered and weeping.

'About us. I should never have walked out on you,' he said. His voice was as effective as it had always been; Liz could feel herself responding to it. Despite her anger, despite the hurt he had caused her, Liz yearned to be in his arms. That was where she had always felt most at home.

'No. You shouldn't,' she snapped, again.

'I know.' He sounded so sad that, even though she was angry, it made her heart ache. You didn't spend years of your life loving someone and then just turn off your feelings like a switch. Or, at least, Liz didn't. She couldn't. 'I'm sorry.'

'Well, thanks for the apology, I suppose.' She made herself sound frosty. It was easier that way: Liz would be mortified if Paul knew how she was really feeling.

'I shouldn't have left, that day,' he added, hastily, as if he thought she was going to hang up. 'But I didn't know what else to do. I meant what I said, about the IVF. But I handled it all wrong.'

'Paul. You left. I haven't heard from you. I've moved. I've...'

She broke off, feeling tears rise up in her throat. 'I've... changed my life. You can't just call me, and—'

'I know. Look, Liz. I'm sorry. I'm sorry, but I just couldn't do it anymore. It was too hard,' he sighed. 'But I still have feelings for you. I just want to see you, and talk. Is that possible?'

Was it possible? Liz didn't know. Part of her was desperate to see him again. But she shook her head.

'I don't think so.'

'Are you sure? I miss you, Liz. Don't you miss me?'

Of course I miss you, she thought, a tear rolling down her cheek. She wiped it away, angrily. She wasn't going to let him know how much his voice was affecting her.

'No,' she lied. 'Paul, you can't just call me up at work and do this.'

'I'm sorry. I didn't think... I didn't know you'd be at work,' he replied, lamely.

'It's the middle of the day. What else would I be doing?' She glared at the phone as if it was Paul's face.

'Huh. Some things don't change,' he replied, mulishly.

'What's that supposed to mean?'

'It means, you never stop working. You're obsessed with your job.'

'Well, I don't know if you realise, but you are *supposed* to work when you're at work. The clue's in the word,' she shot back. She exhaled and shook her head in irritation.

When Liz looked back at her past relationship with Paul, she could see now that she had always tried to ignore all his little comments about work. She'd always known that he resented her job, but she could also see now that she'd purposefully lied to herself about how passive-aggressive he was about it. Now that she was talking to him again after a break, though, she could see it so clearly. It was tedious, always feeling like she had to defend herself.

'Liz. Let's not get sucked back into old arguments.' Paul

sighed. 'I just want to see you. I think we need to talk. Okay? If nothing else, please let me apologise to you properly. In person.'

Liz took in a deep breath and let it out slowly.

'Let me think about it. Okay?' she said, finally. She couldn't deny that she had missed Paul. She didn't know what to think, or feel. Only that something in her still wanted him, despite everything.

'Okay.' He sounded relieved. 'I'm not trying to pressure you or anything, Liz. Really, I'm not. I just... there's things that need to be said, still. That's all.'

'I know,' Liz whispered. She felt another tear roll down her cheek. 'Let me have some time to think. Okay?'

'Of course. Well, I'll wait to hear from you, then,' he said; his voice was soft, and it made her heart ache again. 'Bye, Liz.'

'Bye.'

The phone screen went black and Liz stared at it for a long moment.

Then, she started to cry.

TWENTY-ONE

'Wow. This is quite something.' Liz leaned forward in the driver's seat to take in the view of Loch Cameron Castle as they approached it.

After her trip to the chapel graveyard, Liz had been thinking about the "old maids" that were buried there. The women's names had played on her mind: Muriel Peabody, Elspeth Anderson, Felicity Black and Evelyn McCallister.

She wanted to know more about them for her own curiosity, but, three nights before, she had also had the seed of an idea for something more. She'd been washing up in the little cottage kitchen when the idea struck her: what if she could somehow connect those four "old maids" with Loch Cameron Distillery? Ben had told her that women had once been the keepers of the knowledge around the distillery process. What if the distillery could honour the women of Loch Cameron in some way?

On impulse, after drying her hands on a dishtowel, Liz had called Gretchen and asked her where she could find out more about Loch Cameron's past. Gretchen had suggested that they come to Loch Cameron Castle, as the Laird kept an archive of records going back hundreds of years.

'Not a bad old pile, is it?' Gretchen cast a critical eye over the castle's grey stone frontage. 'Still, the Laird needs to do some repairs. You can see the roof's got a few loose tiles.'

'Can you? Your eyesight's better than mine, then.' Liz chuckled as she parked up on the loose gravel outside the castle and got out to open Gretchen's door for her.

'Oh, yes. Well, I'm as blind as a bat without my glasses, of course.' Gretchen pulled a cerise wool cape around her shoulders as she got out of the car.

'Thanks for coming with me. I could have come on my own.' Liz got out and hurried around to Gretchen's side of the car, where she held out an arm for her elderly landlady. However, she was grateful for Gretchen's company today.

Paul's call out of the blue the day before had upset her, and it had been difficult to get through the rest of the day at work. Thankfully, it was a Friday, and everyone seemed to disappear after lunchtime. Liz had noticed Ben leave his office just before twelve, slamming the door so hard that her windowpane shook. She'd heard him stamp down the corridor outside and then heard his four-by-four growl to life in the car park outside before accelerating out of the gravel car park.

Not even midday, she'd thought. But she was happy that Ben wouldn't see her tear-stained face.

'You're welcome, dear. Gets me out of the old folks' home. I'll tell you a secret about the roof tiles, shall I?'

'Please do.' Liz slung her handbag onto her shoulder, wrapping her own coat around her and shivering. The misty morning above the loch was beautiful, but freezing.

'I happen to know that the Laird probably isn't as up to date with the castle's repairs as he would be usually. Due to a certain romance with a certain American.' Gretchen took Liz's arm and raised an eyebrow coquettishly.

'What American?' Liz asked, curiously, as they walked slowly up to the imposing castle door, Liz allowing for

Gretchen's slower pace. 'What's the Laird like? I heard he was youngish. I'd assumed he would be...' She trailed off, not wanting to offend Gretchen. But what she had meant was *I'd assumed that he'd be old*.

'Wizened, like me? Hardly. Hal Cameron's a fine young man; some might say *buff*, but I couldn't possibly comment. He's seeing an American friend of mine, Zelda. That's a whole other story. I'll fill you in later.' She lowered her voice as the castle door opened and a tall, well-built man with light brown curly hair and a beard stood in the doorway.

'Ah, hello, Gretchen. Welcome. And this must be Liz?' He stepped forward and shook Liz's hand. 'Hal Cameron.'

Liz kept a straight face, wanting to giggle at the fact Gretchen had described Hal as *buff*. He absolutely was – Liz could see that straight away. It was more that eighty-three-year-old Gretchen had chosen that word in particular. She was glad she'd come up to the castle; it was cheering her up no end.

'Indeed, yes. Thanks for having us in your lovely castle.' Liz smiled. 'Gretchen's told me so much about your wonderful archive.'

'Ah, well. The Camerons have been here a long time, that's all,' he demurred, leading them inside. 'The least we could do was keep records of what happened in the area. I'm grateful to my ancestors for that, if not their war-mongering.'

They stepped into a cavernous reception hall, and Liz looked around her in awe. A variety of old-fashioned weapons were arranged on the walls in neat lines and circles, while an array of oil paintings hung on the opposite wall, facing the muskets and rifles.

'I see what you mean about the war-mongering,' she said, taking it all in. 'Were these used in battle?'

'Aye. Some have blood on them still.' He nodded, gravely. 'I'm not one for all that, but it was all there when I was born and it'll be there when I die. Ancestry. Tradition. I think if I took it down, my ancestors would start hauntin' me.'

'Are those your ancestors?' Liz pointed to the portraits. 'There's a resemblance, I must say.'

'Aye, yes indeed. Every one a Cameron.' Hal looked up at the portraits. 'Not every one a good man, but I guess every family has a few black sheep, eh.'

'Oh, yes. In fact, Liz, Hal helped me find out about some of my ancestors, not so long ago. I'll have to tell you the story some-time,' Gretchen said, leaning on her stick. 'However, my legs aren't what they used to be, so, Hal – can you take us to the archive, so I can sit down and so Liz can look up what she needs to?'

'Aye, certainly. Come this way.' Hal led Gretchen and Liz down a long, dark wood-panelled corridor which featured many doors leading off it. Liz peeked into some of the rooms as they walked past: drawing rooms with sofas and side-tables, a formal-looking dining room with a highly polished wooden table and a games room with green baize billiard tables made Liz wonder what it must be like to live in such a grand place. She wanted to explore a room filled with rows and rows of antique leather books, but Hal led them on to a door just before the end of the corridor.

Liz helped Gretchen down some stairs and they found themselves in a shorter, below-stairs corridor which was painted an old-looking sage green colour, like an old hospital.

'The old larder and store rooms are down this way,' Hal explained. 'We dinnae really use them anymore, but the area stays cool, so I keep the records down here. Here ye are.'

He opened a heavy oak door onto a medium-sized room in which various glass-fronted cabinets ranged the walls, and a large oil painting of an old-fashioned sailing ship on a choppy blue sea hung over a heavily singed cast iron fireplace. Liz could see that most of the cabinets were piled up with old leather books and large ledgers. One whole wall also held shelves of old-looking books protected by locked glass doors.

Hal brought out a set of keys from his pocket and used one to open the padlock on the glass walled section. Gretchen settled herself into one of three chairs that sat at a wooden table in the middle of the room, sighing.

'Ah, that's better,' she muttered. 'Now, then, Liz. Who was it again you wanted to know about?'

'Muriel Peabody, Elspeth Anderson, Felicity Black and Evelyn McCallister. I have their dates of birth here.' Liz reached into her handbag and took out her notebook. 'They were members of the parish; they're buried up at the little chapel on the hill.'

'Okay. Let's have a look at the dates.' Hal glanced at the notebook. 'Muriel Peabody died in 1834?' Liz nodded. 'Okay. Let's look at the births, marriages and deaths ledger first, an' then I'll pull out the records we have that covered her lifetime. It's varied, what's here, but the Chamberlains used tae keep the records for what happened in Loch Cameron. It might be criminal proceedings, observations on the weather, strange occurrences, weddin's, that kind o' thing. And there're some local census reports sometimes. My ancestors did them intermittently, but they contain some interestin' information.'

'Great. Thanks so much, Hal.' Liz took the leather-bound volumes that the Laird handed her, and laid them on the table next to Gretchen. 'Gretchen? Would you mind looking for any mention of Muriel in those, and I'll take the next person on the list?' she asked.

'Certainly, dear. And help yourself to these, if you like.' Gretchen reached into her handbag for her glasses and a tin of travel sweets, which she placed on the table next to her. 'I'm sure that the Laird'll bring us a cup of tea as well, when he's ready.'

'Oh, he will, will he?' Hal chuckled. 'Okay, Gretchen.

Comin' up, aye. Why d'ye want tae see the records for these women, anyway?' He turned to Liz. 'Bit of a local history enthusiast, or...?' He trailed off.

'Oh, well, kind of, I suppose.' Liz nodded. 'I've just started work at the distillery. I'm the new Sales Director. Thing is, confidentially, the distillery's not doing so well, and I've suggested they launch a new product. But it's up to me to come up with a new concept, and when I was up at the graveyard the other day, I got to thinking about these women. Did you know that the knowledge of distilling was mostly held by women, when the tradition started? There was a time when it was viewed with suspicion, like witchcraft.'

'I didn't know that. Interestin.' Hal took a boiled sweet from Gretchen's tin. 'So, what's that got tae do with these women? Were they distillers?'

'Not that I know of. But, you know, they're buried up in the graveyard with very dismissive headstones. They all just say OLD MAID.'

'Rude,' Gretchen interjected. 'If anyone puts that on my stone, I'll haunt them.'

'Quite.' Liz grinned. For a moment, she thought of Paul, but then banished the thought from her mind. She was aware that she herself could easily become an "old maid" now that Paul had left her and taken her dreams of a family with him. Yes, there was the option of the clinic, but she still didn't feel ready to think about that. Her stomach twisted, thinking of his voice on the phone. She still didn't know what to think about it, but her body told another story. She wanted to see Paul – despite everything.

'Anyway. I thought, why not launch a new range of whiskies named after local women? I thought if I could come and find out more about any of them, that might give some inspiration as to what their special whisky could include. Or, there could be a good story there. Stories sell products,' she explained, pushing the feelings to one side. Now definitely wasn't the time.

'Fascinating,' Gretchen said. 'I love the idea. So, you could have a Muriel Whisky? And a... what were the other names?'

'Elspeth, Felicity and Evelyn.' Liz looked at her notepad. 'Yeah. That's my thinking, at the moment, anyway. Or, alternatively, we could reclaim the whole 'old maid' thing and the whisky could just be one new product called Old Maid, but there could be four collectible bottles, each featuring the details of one of these local women. Something like that. I don't know yet.'

'Oh, I wish I could be one of them!' Gretchen held her hands out in front of her. 'What about: THE GRETCHEN. She's a smoky old bird with an initial bitterness, but warm afterwards,' she chuckled. Liz adored Gretchen's gravelly voice and her quintessentially old school British way of speaking; she thought, if she could choose how she would be as an elderly woman, she would choose to be like Gretchen in a heartbeat. Gretchen was like a bookish, slightly cantankerous, polyester-slacks-wearing version of the Queen, if the Queen had once dated Norman Mailer and was ready to dish.

'Look, THE GRETCHEN's not off the table, by any means,' Liz said with a laugh. 'We might use you if these women didn't have anything happen to them. But I kind of feel like they might have. And I think the historical angle would interest people, you know?'

'Well, I'd definitely buy a bottle of THE GRETCHEN.' Hal patted Gretchen on the shoulder. 'Okay, then. These're in date order, and you can usually see on the spines where they belong – see?' He showed Liz the way that the books were ordered on the shelf. 'I'll go an' make the tea. I'll be back.' He left them to it, and Liz looked at the next dates on her list.

'Okay. Let's see what we can find out,' she mused, and ran her finger along the lines of ledgers and notebooks. 'Come on, ladies. I know you lived amazing lives. Let's prove there was more to life for you than being old maids.'

'Anyway, as an old maid myself, I can very much recommend the lifestyle.' Gretchen sniffed, opening the first book in her pile.

'Good to know, Gretchen.' Liz pulled out some likely-looking books and sat down beside her. 'Let's do this.'

TWENTY-TWO

'So, I was thinking, and Liz was right, last time.' Bess was pouring hot water from the big metal canister into a large teapot as Liz settled herself down next to Mina with some lunch and her crochet hook. She'd actually gone out and bought her own hook and some wool and had been working on a crochet square at home. After a few false starts, it was actually coming along quite well. Liz was strangely proud of it. She'd never crafted anything before.

'What?' Mina looked up as Liz sat down. 'Bess is always thinking. So much going on in that head of hers.' She tutted as her hands turned the wool hat in her hands expertly, her hook going in and out of the wool without her looking at it at all.

'Well, I don't know that thinking a lot's a bad thing.' Liz grinned and sipped her coffee.

'I concur,' Sally chipped in. Liz had tapped on her office door today before she'd headed down to the village at lunchtime, and invited Sally to come with her. She'd remembered Sheila saying that she and Sally were friends, and Sally had accepted Liz's offer of a brisk walk and some amazing cake.

'You should try it some time, Mina,' she said playfully. Mina made a shooing gesture with her hand.

'Sally Burns, you know very well I beat you at the general knowledge quiz last year. Don't make me tell Liz all the questions you missed. I still remember them all,' Mina shot back, grinning. 'Oh, Liz. Ignore us. Sally and I are long-standing rivals. She thinks she has the best general knowledge in the village. She doesn't.'

'Oh. I see.' Liz laughed. 'I had no idea you were into quizzes, Sally.'

'She's a dark horse,' Bess agreed, putting the lid on the teapot and setting out some mugs. Today, some mums with toddlers had joined the space in the community centre, and the toddlers were enjoying a variety of toys and soft play slides, mats and other safe toys. Bess served the mums tea and cake, smiling and chatting to them.

'What were you thinking, anyway, babe?' Sally held out a hand for Bess, who took it and gave it a squeeze. 'Oh, sorry. Liz, you've met Bess. I should have explained, she's my partner.'

'Oh! I didn't know. But that's lovely.' Liz beamed, happy to feel like she was getting to know Sally better. 'I do remember you saying you lived with someone.'

'Yes. We've been together five years. We actually met at the inn, at a general knowledge quiz,' Sally explained, gazing up at Bess with love in her eyes. 'Bess fell instantly in love with me because of my in-depth knowledge of the Suez oil crisis.'

'Yep. That and your amazing legs.' Bess leant down and placed a kiss on the end of Sally's nose. 'The legs might have swung it, though. Anyway. What I was thinking was,' Bess continued, after the mums had gone to play with the kids on the other side of the hall, 'That Liz was right when she said we could make money from our baking. You know that we give all our profits from these coffee mornings to the Mum and Toddler group anyway, right?'

'Yes. It's a lovely thing to do.' Liz nodded.

'Well, it is, but we don't exactly make much. Just enough to keep the mums in free tea and sandwiches, and the occasional new toy for the kids.' Bess smiled as she watched some of the little ones climbing on the padded mats. 'I was thinking that we could do something bigger. A fundraiser. Some of that equipment's getting old, and I was thinking it would be great if we could get one of those big trampolines for the kids. One of those big round standalone ones, with the netting around it? It could go outside in the summer. We could have it in here in the winter. It'd take up some space, but we rarely use this place for anything else anyway.'

'That's a great idea.' Kathy looked up from her crochet. Today, her two-tone hair was in a schoolmarm-ish bun on top of her head, and she wore drainpipe jeans with zips and a long stripy mohair jumper. 'Kids love those things. And a lot of families here can't afford one, or don't have the outside space for one. The kids can really tire themselves out on one of those.'

'Oooh, how fun!' Mina's eyes lit up. 'Ashoka would love that. How much are they?'

'A few hundred pounds I think,' Bess said. 'Sally's niece has one. We bought it for her last summer. They couldn't afford to go away on holiday, so at least it was something she could do outdoors. It worked really well.'

'What about getting the distillery involved?' Liz looked up, thoughtfully. 'We could make it a whisky and cake evening or something. You guys could bake, and I could definitely arrange for some contributions from the drinks side. We could just charge once for the ticket, and then people could have unlimited food and drink once inside. Maybe some entertainment?'

'What aboot havin' it at the inn?' Sheila had been chatting to one of the mums, standing at the edge of the soft play area, and now came over to sit next to Liz. 'Dotty'd let us, I'm sure. She'd do anythin' for the kids.'

'That would be nice.' Liz hadn't been to the inn yet, though she'd seen it from the outside. It was a large, yellowy-brown cobbled stone pub with sash windows and a black slate tiled roof. Every time she'd passed it, Liz had thought how cosy and welcoming it looked, bedecked with hanging baskets of orange, cerise and white begonias and geraniums. 'I don't think we'd have any trouble making a few hundred pounds. Not if the tickets were, say, ten pounds each? What do you think?'

'Sounds good to me.' Mina reached for a chocolate brownie and broke off half of it, eating a corner delicately. 'We can advertise the event around the village. Put up some posters. We could even get an advert into the free paper.'

'When shall we do it, then?' Bess was standing behind Sheila's chair, and now got out her phone. She tapped at the screen. 'What about in two weeks' time? Otherwise it starts to get a bit close to Easter.'

'What about making it a fun Easter event?' Liz countered. 'I can just imagine the inn with bunnies everywhere, an Easter egg hunt for the kids.'

'Oooh. That sounds really nice.' Kathy's eyes lit up. 'Let's do that!'

'And a quiz?' Sally added. 'People do love a quiz. Not just me.'

'We could get some of the school kids involved, to sing. If it could start around tea time and not too late,' June suggested. Today, she wore a floral scarf knotted around her grey hair, a pair of mustard yellow slacks and a nicely fitting navy blue jumper. Liz found herself thinking that June might have been the oldest of them all, but she still had style. 'My granddaughter's at the school, so I'm there a lot to pick her up. I can ask the teachers. I'm sure they'd be up for it.'

'That's a lovely idea.' Liz imagined a choir of apple-cheeked local children singing angelically. The thought of a wholesome night at the Loch Cameron Inn, raising money to buy the little ones of the community some much needed new toys was quite heartwarming.

Liz was starting to feel as though Loch Cameron was her home. And that, too, made her feel warm inside.

'All right. I'm going to call Dotty, then, and see what she thinks. They might already have some kind of Easter do planned.' Bess held the phone to her ear and turned away, starting to pace around the community hall.

'Well, you know what this means,' Mina purred as she resumed her crochet.

'What?' Liz asked.

'Sally better get ready for me to take home the trophy two years running.' Mina flashed them all a devilish look. 'Because I will win. Mark my words.'

'There's even a trophy?' Liz laughed.

'Oh, my dear. Yes. There is a trophy.'

TWENTY-THREE

'Hi, Liz.'

Paul stood up as she walked into the bar at the Loch Cameron Inn, the only pub in the village. Instantly, Liz felt a lump in her throat as she took in Paul's familiar features: his hazel green eyes, his short, dark brown beard, streaked with grey at the front. He had started shaving his head a couple of years ago when he started losing his hair, but she'd always liked that. In the winter, he wore a black knitted hat which she'd always teased him about, which, perhaps instinctively, he took off as she walked in.

Liz wasn't sure how to feel. He had annoyed her when they'd spoken on the phone, and she'd realised some things about him that she hadn't seen before: his little digs about her work, about her being *too much*. But, on the other hand, there were a lot of old feelings there between them that weren't about to go away in a hurry.

'Hi.' She walked up to the bar, where Paul stood next to a row of wooden bar stools. Awkwardly, he leaned forward and placed a kiss on her cheek.

'You look great,' he said, gazing into her eyes briefly before looking away shyly. 'What d'you want to drink?'

'A glass of merlot. Thanks.' Liz unzipped her thick parka and looked around for somewhere to hang her coat. She had, in fact, made an effort with her hair and makeup, and agonised for ages over what to wear to meet Paul. What did you wear to meet the ex that broke your heart? She needed to look good, but also appear like she wasn't making an effort.

After pulling almost all of her clothes out of the white-painted wooden wardrobe in the cottage bedroom and strewing them all over the bed, Liz had ended up with her dark dye skinny jeans – since she'd been at Loch Cameron she'd lost a stone almost overnight, just from the stress of moving and starting a new job, and was therefore amazed when she fit into them again – and a light pink silky blouse that was pretty but not too flashy. She hadn't wanted to wear heels: that seemed too dressy, and anyway, she didn't fancy her chances on Loch Cameron's cobbled streets, especially as it was raining. She'd put on some black leather boots instead with a reasonable heel that still looked smart, but not like she was trying to impress too much. The parka was purely practical.

Liz hadn't been inside the inn yet, and she looked around her for a coat hook in an effort to focus on her surroundings, rather than be overwhelmed by emotion at seeing Paul again.

It was strange, though, seeing him again. So much had changed, including her. She had started to rebuild her life here; she'd started to feel hopeful. But seeing Paul brought back a lot of things she'd tried to forget.

A hand-painted sign just outside the Inn's archaic, huge wooden front door boasted:

BEST WELCOME IN SCOTLAND
COME AND ENJOY OUR HOSPITALITY AND
LOG FIRE

WHISKIES – DRAUGHT ALES – FOOD SERVED

Inside, it was just as welcoming as the sign outside promised. As Liz had entered through the imposing vaulted wooden door – which looked like something straight out of medieval times – she had come into a carpeted hallway with a reception desk at one end. To the right, the bar opened up into a cosy snug, featuring a mix of upholstered and leather armchairs arranged around low tables. A dartboard hung on the wall next to the bar itself, which was made entirely of wood and stretched along the back wall. Six wooden bar stools, topped with red tartan cushioned seats, were arranged neatly alongside. Liz could see that the bar led to another room in which a log fire burned merrily and a TV hung on the wall, showing sports to a couple of older men who leaned against the end of the bar and regarded it over their pints of ale.

She hung her coat on a coat stand near the reception area, noting a huge ceramic vase which held a collection of umbrellas, and a rack of wellington boots with a notice that said:

FOR CUSTOMERS' USE

Paul had taken their drinks to a table, and hung his scarf on the back of his chair. Liz sat down opposite him in a leather wing chair and looked at him, not knowing what to say.

'Well. Here we are,' Paul said, nervously. He'd ordered a soft drink, by the looks of things. 'I'm driving,' he explained, seeing her look at his glass of sparkling water.

'It's a long drive from Glasgow,' Liz said, surprised. In fact, she hadn't thought about how Paul was going to get here. She'd been completely consumed by the thought of what she was going to do and say when she saw him. In fact, she still didn't know.

'Not so bad. Worth it to see you.' He smiled and took a sip

of his drink. Liz's stomach flipped, but it wasn't a comfortable feeling. Part of her was over the moon to see Paul again. But another part of her felt chaotic and unbalanced. 'This is a really sweet little village. I can see why you came here.'

I came here to get away from everything in my old life. And that included you, Liz thought. *I'm happy here. I've started to find myself again.*

'Yes, it's peaceful,' she said, instead. 'I've joined a crochet club.'

'Oh, that sounds nice.' Paul's smile widened. 'I can't imagine you doing something as girly as crocheting. You should do more of that kind of thing.'

'I do enjoy it,' Liz admitted. 'More for the social element than the actual crochet. I just go one lunchtime a week.'

'Ha. Gossip and crochet, is it? I can just imagine,' Paul chuckled. 'We should have toured around these little villages more. Maybe we could have even moved to one of them, and you could spend your life crocheting and baking cakes for me, and I could be a regular at a pub like this. Play darts, watch the football.' He looked around him at the little snug and its cosy, wood-panelled décor hung with prints of men on horseback, and portraits of ladies in ball dresses. 'Sadly, we never seemed to get the time.'

'No, we didn't.' Liz frowned, thinking that she had absolutely no desire to spend the rest of her life baking cakes for Paul while he was propping up the bar somewhere. 'But that wasn't all my fault. You work too. Your job's just as demanding as mine.'

'I wasn't pointing the finger.' He gave her an unreadable look. 'I think, over time, we just morphed into this couple that had one focus. And it ate up all of our quality time together, where we could have enjoyed little weekends in cosy inns. IVF destroyed us, Liz. You have to admit that.'

'Paul. I don't want to talk about that,' Liz protested. 'If you came here just to repeat everything you've already said, I'm not interested. I get it, okay? You didn't want to do that anymore, and you left.' She heard the emotion catch in her voice and hated herself for it. She didn't want to cry in front of Paul again. She didn't want to relive everything that happened with him.

'Liz, I'm sorry. That's not why I'm here.' He reached for her hand across the table, and she looked up, surprised at his touch. 'I didn't want to upset you.'

'Why are you here, then?' Part of her wanted to hold his hand, but she pulled it away nonetheless. It was too much, right now, having his familiar hand in hers. She knew his touch so well; the way that his thumb nestled into her palm when he held her hand. The warmth of his skin, and the black hairs on the back of his hand she always teased him about. He was one of those men who, if he didn't have a beard, he'd have to shave twice a day. He had a hairy chest and back, like a bear. She'd always liked it.

Beauty and the Beast, he'd always said. *That's us.*

But they weren't Beauty and the Beast anymore. Because life wasn't a fairy tale, and the Beast had broken her heart.

Liz took a sip of her glass of wine, which was sweet and full bodied, and helped settle her nerves a little.

'Straight to the point, huh. Just like always,' Paul sighed. 'I told you. I miss you, Liz. I wanted to see you. Check you were okay.'

'You've seen me, then. I'm alive. I'm okay.' She put down her glass and gave him a look. 'Now what?'

'Liz... please don't be like that.'

'Like what? You broke my heart, Paul. And now you turn up here, in the village where I came to get away from all of that. You. The IVF. Everything...' She didn't know whether to yell or cry. 'Please don't do this to me. I've just started to move on.'

'Do what? Liz, I...' he sighed. 'I just—'

'You just what?'

'I... I want you. I miss you.' He sighed, and looked down at the table. 'This couple of months has been agony. I think I want you back.'

'You want me back?' Liz almost choked on her wine and put the glass down hurriedly. She coughed, clearing her throat.

'Oh, God. I'm sorry.' He stood up and came to rub her back. 'I don't know what I'm doing. I just know that I've been miserable without you.'

Instinctively, Liz leaned back into Paul's touch. It was another thing he'd often done for her when she was upset, rubbed her back in soft, circular motion. She started to cry, just a little, knowing that they were in a public place, but unable to stop herself.

'Oh, Liz. Hey. Come on now.' Paul knelt down next to her chair and enveloped her in his strong arms. 'Hey. I'm here. I've got you,' his voice murmured, and Liz was overtaken by the familiar scent of him: his natural bearish warmth and the cedar-scented soap he favoured. She'd found it for him, years ago, and she'd always ordered it in for him so he had enough, stacked up neatly in his cupboard in their shared bathroom. She wondered if he'd run out yet, and felt an aching sadness once again. He wasn't hers anymore. She didn't have to do that for him now.

'Paul. Please.' She pulled away from his arms. 'This is too hard. I can't just turn it all back on for you. You know how much you hurt me when you left. And I've changed.'

He sat back on his heels, still crouching down.

'I know I did. I wish it had been different. But it just all got to be too much.' He exhaled, and hung his head.

There it was. The phrase that haunted her. *Too much.*

Liz's defences went up. She remembered what Gretchen had said: no good man would ever find a woman like her *too much.*

'I was too much for you?' she asked.

'Maybe. I thought so then.'

'And now?'

'I miss you. You were never too much. It was just... life stuff.'

'Are you telling me you've changed your mind? That you want a baby still?' Liz asked, her heart hammering in her chest. If he said yes, what would she do? She honestly didn't know. She still wanted a baby, but she didn't need Paul to have one anymore; in fact, she never did. She could do the sperm donation, if she wanted to.

'I can't say that for sure. But I want you.' He turned his eyes up to meet hers, and she saw the raw emotion in them. 'Please, Liz. It was never you and me that were the problem. I always wanted you. I still do.'

'I wanted a baby. I still do,' she said, carefully. 'That hasn't changed. And I'm not willing to be with someone who thinks I'm *too much*. Because I'm not.'

Paul got up and went back to sit opposite her again.

'I know you're not.'

Liz let out a long breath.

'That wasn't the only thing that was wrong in our relationship. You know that.' She met his eyes and refused to look away. 'You were hyper critical of me. You always wanted me to be someone else, just like you saying just now you want me to bake all day like some 1950s housewife. That's not who I am, Paul. It was never who I was. I don't know why you kept trying to make me into someone I wasn't.'

'I didn't!' he protested. 'All I was ever trying to do was try to get you to relax a bit. It wasn't healthy for you to work so hard. Everyone needs downtime. Hobbies. That's all.' He reached out and touched her arm. 'And it was always good between us. Physically. You know that.'

'Yes, it was,' she said, keeping her voice steady and ignoring the familiar frisson she felt at his touch. 'But you constantly tried to undermine my work, despite the fact that I explained to you hundreds of times how important it was to me. So, yes, it was good between us, in bed. But that changed for me too, over time, because I didn't feel like you really liked me anymore. You liked the *idea* of me. And I do still want a baby. That hasn't changed, either.'

Liz moved her arm away from his touch. He took his hand back, looking deflated.

'I thought, since you've had a break from everything, you *might* have changed your mind,' he said, lamely. 'You changed your job, and I never thought you'd do that. Where do you even work now? Is it as full time as before? You know you worked too hard. You have to admit that. It's nice to see you looking so rested, honestly.'

'At the local distillery. And, yes, it is as full time. Did you really think I would change my mind about something so important?' Liz stared at him, amazed at his apparent forgetfulness. 'You know what I went through to have a baby. What I was willing to do.'

'Yeah. I just... I don't know. Look, I'm not against having a family. But it was the IVF. The strain it put on us. In every way. If I could take you upstairs now and make love to you, and you got pregnant, then I'd be the happiest man in the world. Because I love you.' He leaned forward, reaching for her hand again. 'You have to know that. I love you. I always loved you, Liz. And I always will.'

Liz stared at him, feeling like her heart had stopped.

What? Her mind went blank. She hadn't been expecting *I love you*. The words were like a wrecking ball. It was almost as if she could see them ripping through her safe little cosy haven in Gretchen's cottage: vast, iron letters, shaped into a ball, hung on a chain and smashing through the cottage's thick walls.

'Liz? Did you hear me?'

She still didn't say anything, and the moment seemed to stretch out forever. How long had it been since she took a breath? She took in a sudden gulp of air and made herself cough again.

'Liz. Say something, for god's sake.' Paul looked worried. 'Here. Take a drink.' He handed her his glass of water.

She took a sip and regained some composure, though her heart felt as though Paul had just danced all over it in his heavy boots.

'I'm sorry. I just really wasn't prepared for you to say that,' she confessed.

'I understand. I know that it was a bit unexpected. But it's what I came here to say. So, I've said it.'

'What do you want me to say?' Liz felt completely blind-sided. 'How do I respond to that? You know that it's not just a case of taking me upstairs and making love to me.' She lowered her voice, saying the last part. 'I wish it was, Paul. I've wished it was that easy for the past five years! But it isn't. And that hasn't changed.'

'I know. But... I dunno. I guess I just hated how we left things. And I do still love you. I wanted you to know that,' he sighed. 'Where does that leave us now? I have no idea.'

Part of Liz still loved him. Of course she did: you couldn't turn love off, like a switch. But she'd spent more than three months mourning the loss of her old life; she'd moved away from her old flat, her old job, and Paul had left her. She had just started to feel hopeful again, and now, here he was, telling her that he loved her. That he wanted to make love to her.

Liz's heart felt like it was breaking all over again. She'd been so careful, working hard and distracting herself every time she thought about Paul. She had started to feel cautiously happy again, here and there.

And now, here he was, coming in and thinking he could tell her he loved her and it would all be all right again. He had no idea that he was wrecking the fragile happiness she had started to weave for herself in Loch Cameron.

'Paul. I could have been pregnant when you walked out. Do you know what that did to me? What it was like, sitting in that flat for a week until I had my period, and I knew I'd failed again – not just to be a mother, but to be...' Her voice broke. *To be someone's loved person. To be the one they were supposed to protect against everything.* 'You can't just come in here now and tell me you love me. That wasn't the action of a loving partner. You ripped my heart out!'

'I know. Liz, I'm so sorry.' His voice trembled, and she knew that he was upset. But she couldn't find any pity for him in her at that moment.

'Paul. I can't talk about this now.' She stood up. Every instinct in her body was telling her to run away. This was too hard.

'Liz, please...' he called after her, but she couldn't stay there for another moment. She grabbed her coat from the coat stand and dashed into the high street, pulling it on in the evening drizzle.

He loved her, so he said. Liz's heart was pounding. What did that mean to him? What he'd done to her wasn't what you did when you loved someone. Was it?

She started to cry, walking as briskly as she could away from the inn and up the high street.

'Liz. Liz! Wait!' Paul ran after her.

'Paul. Please, leave me alone,' she begged, hugging her coat around herself. She was aware that half her eye makeup was probably down her cheek – not that makeup was an important concern right now.

'I can't. I can't let you leave like this. Not again.'

He caught her and bundled her in his arms, towering above her.

'Paul! Let me go!' she cried out, but the pull of his body was too much for her, and she sank against his broad chest instead.

'Please,' she mumbled, not knowing whether she was asking him to release her, or hold her close and never let her go again.

'I know. This is hard.' His voice rumbled in his chest, next to her ear. 'I just know I love you. And I want you.' He tipped her chin up so that she looked up at him. 'Come back to Glasgow. Come back home with me.'

Liz was caught in his hazel green eyes, like she always had been whenever Paul looked at her. There was that connection, the indescribable *something* that was just there with some people, and you could never say why. And hearing Paul say *I love you* was a hammer to her heart. She couldn't stand up to it.

Did she want to go back to Glasgow, and leave behind everything she'd started in Loch Cameron? She didn't know. She didn't know what she felt, right now.

Slowly, he leaned in towards her, and kissed her, gently. Liz felt herself responding to him, just like she always had. The old magic was still there, despite all her mixed feelings. She kissed him back, all the dammed-up emotion of the past months flooding through her like a tsunami. She needed to be touched and kissed. She was human, and she had been so terribly lonely.

'Oh, Paul,' she murmured, as the kiss grew deeper. And, in that moment, she couldn't think about anything else but his lips on hers, and the way that Paul still made her feel like home.

TWENTY-FOUR

Liz stood in the muddy track at the bottom of the field, waiting for Ben to park his four-by-four.

It was a sunny March day, and Ben had offered to show her around more of Loch Cameron. In fact, he'd insisted that she come out with him this afternoon, even though she was knee deep in admin.

Don't make me play the boss card, he'd said when he opened the door to her office an hour earlier and asked if she wanted to come out to see a starling murmuration up in the hills. *Come on. It's beautiful, and I could do with getting out of here for a bit,* he'd added, frowning at his phone and putting it in his pocket. Had Liz imagined a haunted look on his face as he'd said that? She didn't know, but had reluctantly agreed to accompany him.

'So, is this connected to work in any way? Or do you really just like starlings?' she asked as Ben locked the car and pulled on his jacket. She was struck, again, by his remarkable good looks. Not that she was in the market for a man – Paul's reappearance was confusing enough, without adding another man to the mix. But Ben was undeniably hot, even just from a dispassionate assessment. Today, as he shrugged on his jacket, Liz noticed the width of his shoulders and the fact that his jumper fitted snugly against them, and the brief flash of his muscular midriff as his jumper rode up.

Liz was healing, and taking things slowly. But she wasn't dead. Still, hearing Paul tell her he loved her yesterday had blown her mind. She'd actually been grateful that Ben had interrupted her earlier and suggested they come out to watch the murmuration, because she hadn't been able to concentrate on work at all that morning.

'I really like starlings?' He grinned at her and handed her a sandwich wrapped in cling film. 'Here. Since I dragged you out during lunchtime, I picked these up from the café earlier. Myrtle's best cheese and pickle.'

'Oh. Thanks.' Liz accepted the sandwich, and as she did so, her stomach growled.

'Sounds like it came at just the right time,' Ben chuckled.

'I am a bit hungry,' Liz admitted. 'So, if you bought the sandwiches this morning, you knew you were going to ask me up here?'

They started walking along the muddy track and crossed a stile into a field by the road.

'I knew I was going to come up here, and yes, I fancied a bit of company.' He gave her an unreadable look. 'I took the chance you'd say yes. Frankly, I was willing to gamble a sandwich on it.'

'High stakes.' Liz tutted, grinning back. She had to admit that being out in the beautiful clean air of Loch Cameron in the middle of the work day was good for the soul.

'I'm a gambler, for sure,' he agreed as they walked along, companionably. 'So, how's life? How are you settling in, up here? Missing the big city?' Ben unwrapped his sandwich and took a big bite, wiping pickle from his chin.

'Yeah, okay.' Liz nodded. She must have sounded strange, because he raised his eyebrow at her. 'What?'

'You don't sound okay. And this morning, you were staring

out of the window like Elvis was doing his Las Vegas set out there when I came in. Penny for them?' Ben devoured the rest of his sandwich, catching her eye and looking guilty. 'Sorry. I too was really hungry.'

'Oh, you don't want to hear it,' Liz sighed.

'I do. But only if you want to tell me.' He wadded up the cling film the sandwich had been in and put it in his pocket.

Liz thought about it for a moment and realised that, actually, she really wanted to talk to someone. It wasn't so much Paul, as what his reappearance meant for her ambitions to have a family. Ever since Paul had kissed her, her head had been in a spin. He had said he didn't want a baby, still. But Liz still wanted Paul, and she still felt that he would be an ideal father, if she could only make him see it.

'I don't mind telling you,' she took a bite of her sandwich while she thought of what she would say, 'I ended a relationship. I needed a new start, somewhere else, which is why I applied for the job at Loch Cameron,' she began slowly. 'And, as well as that, my partner and I had been doing IVF for a few years. We were unsuccessful. Obviously,' she frowned, breaking off a corner of her sandwich and picking at it, 'it was really tough – physically, emotionally, mentally – doing my job at the old firm and going through that too. But I wouldn't quit. My work means a lot to me.'

'I can see that about you.' Ben nodded. 'You're very driven. That's why I gave you the job.'

'Yeah. Well, in the case of my ex, it also drove him away.' Liz raised an eyebrow. 'And, it didn't help me get pregnant. So, he left me, because of the stress that IVF was putting on our relationship.'

'I'm so sorry to hear that.' Ben's voice lowered. 'That's really difficult.'

'Yeah.' Liz half-laughed, feeling like she also wanted to cry. 'And, the thing is, that we broke up, and suddenly he called me up and wanted to see me again. So, we met up for a drink. He still doesn't want a baby. But he wants me. And wants me to move back to Glasgow. So he says.'

'Wow. It's... no wonder you looked distracted, earlier.' Ben raised an eyebrow.

'Ha. Yeah, you might say that.' Liz half laughed, though she also could have cried if she thought too hard about the Paul situation.

They reached the top of the gently sloping field and entered a wide meadow, bordered by trees. Liz recognised firs and yews, combining their deep green foliage with beech trees and oaks. In the wide, blue sky above, large birds Liz thought might be hawks circled slowly on the updrafts. When she looked down again, small flashes of brown caught her eye, and she realised that they were rabbits, frisking in the afternoon sun. She pointed them out to Ben, whose eyes crinkled up as he nodded, smiling.

'Bunnies!' Liz exclaimed, louder than she intended, then giggled self-consciously. 'Sorry. I sounded about five then.'

'Yes, bunnies.' Ben laughed. 'Don't apologise. I love them too, though so do those hawks.' They walked on a little further. 'This is where the starlings nest. They generally do their murmuration about now,' Ben added, holding out his arm to stop her going any further. Liz had the enjoyable sensation of contact with Ben's muscular arm against her body for a moment, and then he pulled away. 'Sorry.'

'No need to apologise,' she said. 'And yes, I am kind of distracted. I don't know what to do about the whole thing really.'

'I'm not sure that I have much wisdom to impart. But you should obey your instincts. If there's one thing I've learnt in this life, then always do what feels right to you. Not what you think you should do, or what other people think you should.' He looked at her thoughtfully. 'Do you love him? Do you want to go back to Glasgow?'

'I don't know,' Liz confessed. 'There are a lot of bad memories there. I did love him. But he broke my heart. I don't know if you can ever come back from that. And, he thought I was *too much*. You know I said that to you before. That I've been told that a lot in my life, in one way or another. And I don't want to be *too much*. I want to be... perfect, just as I am.'

'You did say that before, and I don't see it that way.' He nodded, seriously. 'You're a powerhouse. You're a funny, sassy, hardworking woman. If that's too much for someone, then they need to have a look at themselves, in my humble opinion.' He shrugged.

'Well, thanks. I appreciate that.'

'You're welcome. So, you needed somewhere to escape. Now I understand. I was amazed you took the job. I know it's nothing like what you had. You even took a pay cut.'

'Yeah. I needed somewhere quiet. Different. I think the slower pace here is good for me, anyway. Without wanting to sound lame, I think I needed somewhere to come and... heal, I guess. And the cottage – and the village, the people – are really sweet and friendly.' Liz watched as a small flock of birds started to fly from one tree to another. 'Is that it? Is it starting?' She pointed to them.

'Yes. They should all take flight soon.' Ben frowned, looking up at the wintry sky. 'Well, you won't find anywhere as quiet, probably. And, people are nice, on the whole. Probably a bit gossipy, but their hearts are in the right place.'

'That's no bad thing.' Liz felt vulnerable, like she had exposed too much of herself to Ben. She bit her lip, thinking that she shouldn't be so open. But there was something about him that inspired it.

'And do you still want a baby? Because if you do and he doesn't, then you've answered your question, surely.' Ben passed her a bottle of water. 'Here. Always best to stay hydrated.'

'I do. He doesn't. I suppose I just thought, maybe he might change his mind.' She took the water bottle and drank some, handing it back to Ben. 'Thanks.'

'He might. But generally, people do know what they do and don't want, in terms of having a family or not,' he said, looking inscrutable. 'Oh, look! Here they go!'

Suddenly, a cloud of black birds flew up from the trees in the meadow and met in the sky above Liz and Ben. There must have been thousands of them, Liz thought. And, as they flew, the overall impression was of a vast inkblot in the sky which shifted and flowed into new shapes every few seconds.

'Have you ever seen this before?' Ben watched her face as Liz watched the birds in wonder.

'No. Never,' she breathed. 'Wow. It's amazing. I had no idea it would be like this.'

They stood in silence, watching the birds for several minutes, until the flock started to disperse. Liz felt as though she had just observed a private miracle of some kind.

'So. What did you think?' he asked.

'It was amazing. Thanks for bringing me.' Liz stared up at the remaining birds that were still in the sky, thinking about Paul. She still didn't know what to do about him, but at least she felt a little calmer than she had before. 'It did me good to get out of my own head for a while.'

'I'm the same. Sometimes, it all gets a bit much, so I come out to the hills, or hike, or come here to watch the starlings. It helps.' Ben shrugged.

'I'm sorry about earlier. I kind of overshared a bit too much,' Liz confessed.

'Oh, not at all. I'm glad you felt like you could talk to me.' Ben looked surprised at the apology. 'I'd like to think we were becoming friends.'

'Sure. That would be really nice.' Liz felt suddenly shy, but she didn't really know why. Ben had been so kind to her, and she appreciated it. But it still felt difficult, opening up about everything that was going on, no matter how many times she did.

'Good. Well, we should probably head back, then,' he sighed and jammed his hands back in his pockets. 'Not that I want to. I'd much rather stay out here.'

'We do have work to do,' Liz said, gently. 'Well, I do. I assume you do too.'

'Ah, Liz. Ever the practical one.' He laughed wryly. 'You're right, of course. Let's get back, or Carol will wonder where we got to.'

They walked back to the four-by-four, across the meadow and then the field. Liz had the impulse to reach for Ben's hand as they walked, but resisted it: with everything that was going on with Paul, she couldn't handle any other entanglements with men, even if she and Ben were becoming friends.

There was just something about Ben: when she was with him, she felt safe and happy. He had a way of making things feel okay, even when they weren't. Holding his hand felt like a natural extension of that energy, somehow.

Instead, Liz put her hands in her pockets too, and they walked along in a companionable silence. As they approached Ben's four-by-four, a lone starling alighted on its roof, and cocked its head, looking at them both. They both stopped in their tracks, and Liz took in a breath.

'That's a lucky omen,' Ben said, under his breath so as not to startle the bird. 'Make a wish.'

'Is it?' Liz whispered. 'I don't know what to wish for,' she added, admiring the starling's green and blue plumage under its dark grey feathers.

'Well, then I'll wish for you,' Ben whispered back, and looked meaningfully at the birds for a few moments. As if it was listening to Ben's thoughts, the bird cocked its head again, and then flew off from the car, squawking loudly.

'What did you wish?' Liz asked as they got in the car.

'For you to have peace and closure. And to have whatever your true heart's desire is,' Ben answered, and then blushed. 'Come on. Let's get back.'

TWENTY-FIVE

'Muriel Peabody, Elspeth Anderson, Felicity Black and Evelyn McCallister.'

Liz stood at the front of the board room, her presentation on the four local women on the large screen behind her. Ben, Simon and the rest of the management team sat around the long, walnut board room table in front of her.

She swallowed a tic of nervousness. She'd done plenty of presentations before, but this one was more than a standard sales review. When researching Muriel, Elspeth, Felicity and Evelyn, Liz had really connected with their women's stories. She felt passionate about making them the focus of Loch Cameron Distillery's rebrand. This was the way that the business was going to reinvent itself, if she had anything to do with it: by celebrating the unsung voices of its community.

Liz had come into work this morning determined to put Paul out of her mind. And, now that she was in the board room, she was focused on what she was there to do. But, still, she knew that if she let herself, she could very easily start to obsess over him. What had that night meant? He'd told her he still loved her.

I love you, Liz.

Liz felt as if the rug had been pulled from under her. How was she supposed to cope with that? He'd asked her to move back to Glasgow too, which she could hardly believe. Why would she ever do that, when it had taken every bit of energy she had to leave?

For Paul. For what you had, her mind said. *You might be able to try for a baby again. Or, you could just let yourself be happy with him.*

He still doesn't want a baby, she thought, desperately wanting the peace and closure Ben had wished for her as they'd watched the starling murmuration a couple of days ago. *And he hasn't changed. He still wants you to be something you're not.*

But, the pull towards the comfort of Paul's arms was still there. Liz couldn't deny that it had still felt good when he'd taken her into his bear-like clasp.

Maybe it could be different. Maybe I should consider it, she thought, craving being held by someone again. But was she craving Paul's safe arms, or anyone's? She didn't know.

Liz cleared her throat. She couldn't think about Paul now, and Ben was watching her expectantly.

'Four local women buried at Loch Cameron chapel. Here are their gravestones.' Liz pressed the clicker in her hand, and photos of the four stones appeared on the screen. 'As you can see, we can't really tell much about these women just from their stones. Apart from the fact that the village, as it was then, thought OLD MAID was a just and fitting epitaph.'

She gave the room a smile, and was relieved to see smiles in return.

'So, I went up to the castle and did some research. I thought that there were probably some really interesting life stories behind these names, and I was right. Here's what I found out about the women.' She clicked onto a new slide.

'Muriel Peabody. Muriel was the schoolteacher at Loch

Cameron School from 1794, when she was eighteen, to 1833, when she retired from ill health. She died in 1834. That means that she taught at the local school for 39 years.' Liz flicked to a black and white image she had found of Muriel in Hal Cameron's archive. 'This is Muriel. She never married or had children, but she taught generations of local children in this village. I actually found a record that she wrote into the Parish records, also up at the castle. This is it.'

Liz flicked to another slide, showing faded copperplate handwriting and dated 1822.

'This is Muriel writing about the children in 1822. She records which children were given a prize for their exemplary school work throughout the year: a certain Jock McKenzie and Mary Spencer received a jar of jam each. And she's also written the names of all the children in her class that year. There were twelve of them.' Liz pointed to the list of names.

'I researched the school system in Scotland at that time. It was before there was national free education for all, but many small communities like this one would have something called a "Dame School" which was what Muriel ran. It was called a "Dame" school as it was usually run by a local woman, or "school dame" who the locals paid a small fee to educate their children. I don't know what Muriel taught the children, but it would probably have been sewing and knitting with some maths and reading.'

'I had no idea.' Ben was leaning forward on his elbows. 'Fascinating.'

'I think so.' Liz smiled at him, grateful for his enthusiasm. 'Okay. Elspeth Anderson.' She moved to the next slide. 'Elspeth, like all four of these women, was recorded as an "old maid". But I found out that she too had a much more interesting life.' She flicked to the next slide.

'Elspeth was a midwife. In fact, she may have been the only midwife for the village, and indeed many villages around here.

We know that she was, because she signed various birth certificates Hal has on his records, and her occupation is listed in the Parish record of 1860. I couldn't find a picture of her, sadly.'

'Another skilled job,' Ben mused.

'Difficult job in those days, I bet,' Simon agreed. 'When were painkillers invented?'

'Ether was used in surgery from about the mid-1800s.' Liz was prepared for the question, having looked it up herself out of curiosity. 'But I have no idea if Elspeth would have used it in childbirth. More likely, she would have used the old methods learnt from a local wise woman or herbalist. It would be fascinating to know.'

There was general nodding and murmurs of assent from around the table. Liz was enjoying giving the presentation. She loved thinking on her feet, being the focus of the discussion and making everyone smile. She felt her old spark again: this was who she was, and she loved it. This was what she wanted, not to be stuck in a house somewhere, baking cakes for Paul.

'My dad always told me that women were the best distillers. All that old knowledge was handed down, mother to daughter,' Simon said. 'That's that old wise woman knowledge, too.'

'Yes. Ben told me all about that too. That's kind of where I'm going with this.' Liz grinned, glad that Simon seemed to get what she was thinking. She hoped the rest of them would, too.

'Felicity Black.' Liz moved to a new slide which showed a picture of a young woman sitting at a weaving loom. 'This isn't her, I'm afraid, but it's a picture of another female weaver taken at approximately the same time. Felicity worked as a weaver. Now, there isn't much detail about where she worked or what she made, but textiles were important in Scotland in the nineteenth and early twentieth century. Felicity was born in 1880, so a bit later than Muriel. She was hard to find in the records at all, but, again, she was a skilled worker. She might have made all sorts of fabrics. The Industrial Revolution was happening around then, so she may have worked by hand at more traditional methods, or used a mechanised loom. We don't know.'

'And what about the fourth one?' Carol, the receptionist took a shortbread biscuit from a packet and offered it around the table. 'I have tae say, this is all very interestin' but I'm wonderin' what it has tae do with whisky.'

'Evelyn McCallister. Yes, I'm getting to that.' Liz gave Carol a purposefully twinkly smile. 'Evelyn is probably the one I'm most excited about. Because Evelyn, as well as being an old maid, was also for a brief time a Master Distiller, right here at Loch Cameron Distillery.'

This was Liz's big moment, and she let the information settle with her audience for a few moments before starting to explain.

'A woman Master Distiller?' Ben asked. 'That's unusual; I'm not sure I've heard of that before. Not in those days, anyway.'

'Well, Simon almost beat me to it just then, by reminding us that, traditionally, distilling was regarded as women's secret wisdom. But, yes. Evelyn McCallister was trained as a distiller here in the village in the early 1900s. This is actually something I found out by looking in the records up at the castle, but also in those records in my office, Ben,' Liz noted. 'She was the daughter of the Master Distiller at that time, Tommy McCallister. You might remember that name.'

'Agh. Maybe. My dad was the one with the encyclopaedic memory.' Ben screwed up his face, trying to think.

'Well, Tommy was the Distiller from the late 1890s until the start of World War One, which is when he joined up in the Black Watch,' Liz said, showing a picture of a fit-looking man in a kilt and smart uniform on the screen. 'You know, in World War One, the Germans called the kilt-wearing Scottish soldiers the *Ladies from Hell*.'

There was a rumble of laughter from around the table.

'Aye, an' I bet the Germans *were* terrified,' Carol said, proudly. 'Nae more of a man than the one that goes intae war in a kilt. I wouldnae want tae face them on the battlefield either.'

'Indeed. Apparently, also, the women in France were quite enchanted by our Scotsmen in World War One,' Liz remarked. 'Anyway, the point is that Tommy trained Evelyn to take over when he went to war. He must have realised he was going to be conscripted at some point. According to the records in my office, Evelyn was Master Distiller for three years while Tommy was away. He actually survived the war and returned to work at the distillery, but she helped him after that, too. I wonder whether the war may have changed him.'

'Plenty o' lads came back wi' the shakes, an' worse,' Carol reminded them all. 'I bet she did have tae help her faither.'

'Well, I don't know all the details,' Liz said. 'But I think it's cool that Evelyn became a distiller, if only for a short time. So that was what brought me to the concept for our new launch, and our new product. Ladies and gentlemen, I give you...' She paused for dramatic effect, and changed the slide to a mock-up she had made of four new whisky labels.

'... the Old Maids: Evelyn, Felicity, Elspeth and Muriel. Each a limited edition Loch Cameron Distillery ten-year-old single malt, but each one with its own flavour, depending on the cask. I know that you have malts currently finishing in sherry, plain oak, bourbon and wine casks, Simon, so that's doable.' She shot Ben a smile, hoping he liked the idea.

'I thought that, if we used the women as a focus, then each whisky has its own story. The story of the women of Loch Cameron, and how they supported the community, enabling it to thrive. And enabling the distillery to thrive, too.' Liz took a breath. 'It would appeal to the newer whisky drinkers because of the focus on women. But also to the traditional demographic, because of the historic focus on tradition, the war, that kind of thing.'

There was a silence around the table. *Come on, guys. Say something,* Liz thought, taking a drink of water and trying to retain her composure. She had stayed up late the night before, getting the presentation ready and rehearsing it. She really wanted it to go well. Ben had hired her for her reputation as someone who got results, after all. But it was more than that.

Liz cared about these women. She really wanted the Old Maids range to revive the business, but she also wanted to tell these women's stories. She wanted them to be heard.

'Liz, I don't know what to say.' Ben frowned, leaning forward, his hands steepled in front of him, like a judge. 'This isn't what I expected.'

Simon, sitting next to Ben, was looking at Liz with an unreadable expression. *Oh my god, they hate it,* she thought. *They don't like the Old Maids thing. Maybe they don't like the local women theme at all. Maybe I totally misjudged everything.*

'You don't like it?' Liz kept her voice steady.

'No. I love it.' Ben broke into a smile.

TWENTY-SIX

'So. Where do we start?' Liz asked as she, Simon and Ben stood in the main distillery hall, among the tall, gleaming copper stills. She loved being in here. A distillery was part science lab, part witch's lair, turning ordinary ingredients into something magical that brought communities together.

She'd been working hard on the Old Maids concept as well as planning for the big presentations she had to make to the three supermarkets she had appointments booked in for. Plus, she'd been in touch with all of her favourite contacts at off licenses, cafes, restaurants and all manner of other stockists, telling them that they should be buying Loch Cameron whisky too. There hadn't been time for her to think about Paul much, and that was one hundred per cent fine with Liz.

They hadn't seen each other again, though they had messaged a little, back and forward. Paul wanted to come and see her again, and take her out for dinner. She had answered,

Paul, I don't see what that will achieve. Nothing's changed between us. You know that.

I know. But you can't deny what's between us. Let's just enjoy some time together. I think we need that. To heal, he'd replied. *And you haven't answered me about coming back to Glasgow.*

Paul, you can't ask me to do that. I'm settled here now, in Loch Cameron. We can see each other a little and be gentle, see where it goes. Maybe. But I'm not just going to up sticks and move back because you want me to, she'd replied.

Okay, okay. Baby steps.

Not dinner. A casual drink, she'd replied.

Fine. Drinks.

I'm organising a launch party for the distillery's new product. Why don't you come to that? she'd replied. It was a perfect no pressure date: the party was already happening, and she had to be there anyway. Plus, it was a way for her to show Paul what she'd been doing since she'd been in Loch Cameron.

Okay, sounds good, he'd replied.

Part of Liz had wanted to reply that no, they shouldn't see each other at all. But being in Paul's arms was too difficult to say no to. She yearned for that comfortable feeling it gave her, even though he was the one who had damaged her feelings of safety before; even though she still suspected he felt that she was *too much*. It was a complicated set of feelings.

As well, in the background, there was the fact that she had some confusing feelings for Ben too. Their time together watching the starlings hadn't helped; there had been several times now when they'd had... *moments*... that had felt both electric and comforting at the same time. Clearly, Ben was her boss, and nothing was likely to happen there. But Liz still knew that there was something between them, and she'd caught herself daydreaming a few times about what it would be like to kiss Ben. Was it Ben she wanted, or Paul, or in fact neither of them? Perhaps she just needed a hug. Perhaps she just needed some basic human contact because she was lonely. She didn't know.

'Well, we've agreed on the four varieties for the new range. So, we need to differentiate them,' Simon said, crossing his arms over his chest. 'I suggest we go with the different casks, like Liz said. Then we just use the normal malt. Minimal disruption, and we already have all four in cask. So, we'd be able to launch them in the next six months, if you got all the packaging ready.'

'I was thinking we could actually change the barley in some way. Add in a small secret ingredient for each one, based on traditional herbs. Like in *uisge beatha*,' Ben suggested.

'That's a lovely idea,' Liz agreed. 'It's got real local appeal, and people would like the herbal element. The thing is, whisky isn't like gin. You can be a lot freer with the botanicals with gin.'

'Agreed.' Simon tapped the copper still next to him, checking its temperature. 'You cannae just start addin' whatever ye like intae the mash. It willnae be whisky if ye do.'

'We can if we want to,' Ben argued. 'And, of course it would still be whisky!'

'Not in the traditional definition,' Simon raised an eyebrow. 'Yer faither would never've done somethin' like that.'

'Yeah, well. I'm not my dad,' Ben answered, shortly. 'I think we should look into it. Okay? We'll do the four different casks as well. That's the appeal for most buyers. I just like the idea of each one having a small, important difference. The local herbs and those traditions are important to preserve.'

'Whatever ye say. Yer the boss.' Simon shrugged, though he was clearly not in agreement.

'Yes, I am,' Ben replied, an aggressive tone in his voice.

There was an uncomfortable silence.

'Right. Well, I better get back tae it. No rest for the workers.' Simon smiled at Liz. 'Liz, always good tae see ye.'

'Thanks, Simon.' Liz felt uncomfortable. Mostly, she either talked to Ben or Simon separately, or they were both there in the management meetings with her and the rest of the team. It was quite unusual for the three of them to meet about anything, and now Liz knew why. Clearly, there was some kind of problem between Ben and Simon.

'Fine.' Ben looked like he wanted to say more, but instead he took out his phone and frowned at it.

'I've got to take this, sorry. Liz, come up to the office when you're ready. I want to go through some branding options with you.'

He walked off, slamming the door to the room loudly behind him.

'What was *that* all about?' Liz stared at the door that Ben had just stalked out of.

'Ah, ignore him. Ben and I don't always see eye to eye.' Simon adjusted a switch on a control panel and peered into a small glass panel on another.

'That was obvious,' Liz retorted. 'Why don't you get on?'

'Dunno. Two stags lockin' horns, maybe.' Simon shrugged.

'You mean, you're competitive with each other?' Liz rolled her eyes inwardly. *Save me from the battle of the egos,* she thought. She thought about what Gretchen had said about working in the male dominated books world, all those years ago, and how hard she'd found it. *Fifty years later, and here I am, stuck in the middle of a who's-bigger-than-who's testosterone fight,* she thought. *Time might as well have stood still.*

'Aye. He's the boss, but I'm the expert. It's a fine line to tread in a relationship, Master Distiller and boss. My dad and Jim Douglas had a respect for each other, but I wouldnae say they were friends.'

'And you and Ben aren't friends?' Liz probed.

'I wouldnae say so, no,' Simon admitted.

'Do you respect each other, though?' Liz could see a problem emerging with the new range if Ben and Simon were going to lock horns over every single decision.

'Hmm. Ask me when I've had a dram or two.' He frowned.

Great.

'It's no secret we dinnae always see eye to eye.' Simon sighed. 'I tell ye, if I'd had the luck tae inherit this place, I wouldnae be caught dead messin' anythin' up. Still, it's no' my business.' He shrugged dismissively, but Liz could see in his eyes that Simon was anything but casual about the distillery.

'I know you care about this place,' she said, carefully. 'You might not own it, but your family are invested in it. There's history here.'

'Aye. An' for lots o' us,' he said, seriously. 'We like Ben. He's a nice guy. But this place doesnae just belong tae him, ye know? It belongs tae the community. An' we've all got a lot ridin' on it bein' a success.'

Liz wondered how much Simon knew about how badly the business was doing. As Master Distiller, he sat on the board, so he would have seen all the reports that she had. She guessed that he understood pretty well that the business was in bad shape. However, he didn't currently know that Ben had an offer on the table from a large multinational distillery to buy the business.

Buyouts like the one that Ben had been offered were fairly common. Drinks companies based in America or Japan or Europe kept an eye on the smaller, family-run whisky distilleries in particular, because they were always looking for bespoke brands that could add cachet and heritage to their more corporate image. Sometimes, companies like those – and she'd worked for one of the biggest, so she knew how they worked – would buy a distillery and keep everyone on staff. But, often, there would be redundancies following a buyout. There were no guarantees.

'I understand,' she replied. 'All I can say is, now that I'm here, I'll do my absolute best for you all. You have my word.'

'I appreciate that.'

'So. What's his story?' Liz asked, nodding in the direction of the door. She might as well utilise Simon's knowledge for something, at this point.

'Ben? What d'you want tae know?' Simon turned on a tap

connected to a pipe and released some amber liquid into a glass. He swirled the liquid in the glass and held it up to the light.

'I don't know. General stuff...' Liz trailed off. She was curious to know more about Ben, and that included his private life. But she realised as soon as she said it that it just made her sound like she was personally interested in Ben.

Which I am not, she told herself firmly.

'Oh. Ye got designs on the man in charge, eh?' Simon raised an eyebrow.

'Oh, no. Nothing like that. I was just...' She searched for what she was trying to say. 'I'd have thought that he'd be a good catch for someone. Not me, obviously. But, you know. Owning a business. He seems a nice enough guy. I just wondered.'

'Hmm. Well, aye, he's single. He wasnae, mind, for a long while. Married his childhood sweetheart, a girl from the village, would ye believe. His faither didnae like it, but Ben wasnae gonna be persuaded oot o' it.'

'Why didn't his father want him to marry his childhood sweetheart?'

'She wasnae good enough for the Douglas inheritance, in his eyes. Bein' a simple village girl.' Simon shook his head. 'Snobbery, o' course. Ben was sent away tae boardin' school most o' his young life. That's what the toffs do, aye. Send their young uns away. But Ben mustae met Alice when he was back in the village for a holiday or somethin', when he was still a teenager. Or even before that, I dunno. Anyway, he insisted an' they got married when they were eighteen. Too young tae know any better, I guess. My faither told me how mad auld Jim was. He wouldnae speak tae Ben or Alice for a year, even though they lived in the big hoose with him. He wouldnae see them on the streets.'

'The big house?'

'Aye. Not far from here. It's been the family hoose since the distillery's been here. Perhaps longer.'

'So, Ben married Alice and his dad didn't approve. How come he's single now?'

Simon exhaled.

'Would ye not rather talk aboot somethin' else?' he met her gaze with an unexpectedly charming smile. 'I can think of other things I'd prefer to be doin' than wastin' my time talking about Ben Douglas.'

'Oh. No, it's fine, I was just curious,' Liz replied, politely.

'Aye, well, curiosity killed the cat, as they say,' Simon sighed. 'Well, all I can tell ye is that he left Alice, a year or two ago. No one knows what went on between them, exactly, but I do know one thing.' He paused for dramatic effect. 'She was pregnant.'

'Pregnant?' Liz's heart sank into her belly. Just the word alone revived so much trauma for her: all the times that she and Paul had held hands, hoping that this time would be the time that the embryo would take. The two times that she had got as far as a week or two of morning sickness before she had miscarried: how she had prayed and hoped for the sickness to continue, but, instead, a loss.

'Aye. Never seen her back here again, with a baby or withoot. I dunno how anyone can be so cold as tae turn away his pregnant wife, whatever came between them.' Simon shook his head. 'Just goes tae show, eh. All the money in the world doesnae give ye basic decency.'

'That's terrible!' Liz was shocked. 'How could anyone do such a thing?'

'Dunno. But that's the nature of the man, since ye asked.' Simon walked along the stills, checking them, with Liz following. 'Not surprising that the business's gone tae hell since he took over. If ye want my opinion.'

'It would certainly seem that way,' Liz said, slowly. Ben had seemed for all the world like a friendly, gentle guy when they'd spent time together. How could someone who could be that gentle also do something so heinous? 'I just can't believe he would do that.'

'Aye, well. Ye never really know people, I suppose. Never know what they're capable of until they do it.'

'I suppose not.' Liz felt awful. She had trusted Ben, and now she felt betrayed in that trust. She checked herself. *What your boss does in his personal life is none of your business,* she reminded her inner voice. *All that matters is your work relationship.*

But it did matter to Liz, because the subject was so personal to her. How could she continue to work with a man that she knew had – what? Abandoned his wife. His childhood sweetheart, the woman that he had disobeyed his father to marry, just when she needed him the most.

Liz felt a bolt of rage rip through her. *Do you know how hard I tried to get pregnant?* She wanted to run over to Ben's office right now and yell at him. *Do you know how much it took from me? I lost everything. I lost my partner of six years. I lost two babies. How dare you. How dare you disrespect another woman who was lucky enough to be pregnant. To do you the ultimate honour of carrying your child, and to have the gall to leave her.*

Her feelings were already sensitive because of Paul. Seeing him again had churned everything up within her, and this revelation threatened to drive her into even more confusion.

'You all right, Liz? I hope I haven't upset you?' Simon put his hand on her arm, looking concerned.

'What? Oh. No, I'm fine,' Liz lied. Her heart was pounding. She knew this was a trauma response; it wasn't really about Ben, though she was disappointed that he wasn't the man she thought he was. No, this was about her. She knew that. 'Excuse me. I should head back to the office.'

'All right. See you later. And I'm sorry if that was a shock.' Simon looked like he regretted saying anything. 'Maybe I shouldnae have said anythin'. My mouth can run away with me, sometimes.'

'It's okay, Simon. But I have to go.' She tried to sound normal.

Liz fought the impulse to run back to the safety of her office, making herself walk and smile to the people she passed as she did so. Running with a tear-streaked face to her office and slamming the door behind her would have seemed odd, and she wasn't looking for a reputation as the newbie involved in some kind of workplace drama.

She made her way to the small corridor where her office was, and let herself in, leaning against the inside of the door once she was inside. Fortunately, she didn't see Ben: he would be inside his office, possibly feeling aggrieved at his run-in with Simon.

You came here to get away from stress, she warned herself, before she felt the tears well up in her throat and her chest. It felt as though they were burning; she let them go as quietly as she could. Even trying to be quiet, there was no way to stop some loud, hiccupping sobs that leaked out. *This was supposed to be a clean break. A new start. Somewhere you could leave the drama behind.*

Liz wiped her eyes with a tissue. The thing was, she realised, that she could move to the North Pole but the emotional drama would come with her. Her feelings weren't something she could take off and leave somewhere. *More's the pity*, she muttered as she slowly stopped crying, and wiped her eyes again. If there was some amazing business idea for a place people could leave their feelings in a locker somewhere and get on with their lives, she'd apply to be Sales Director of that company in the blink of an eye.

I guess that does already exist, though, Liz thought. *It's called a pub.* Only, there weren't lockers for rent where you could leave your feelings. Instead, a pub was somewhere you could come with your friends – or even alone – and drink a magical potion that made it easier for you to express your feelings. All the while, the bar staff were there, like underpaid therapists, to listen to your woes if you didn't have a friend to tell them to – or to kindly yet firmly tell you when you needed to go home and sleep it off.

Liz felt like she could do with a dram of something right there and then, but it was the middle of the afternoon. She'd never been tempted to drink heavily: perhaps it was because she worked in the drinks industry, and had to consider the dark side of where it took some people as part of her work. She had been to so many conferences and seminars about addiction and alcoholism that even if she had been that way inclined, it would have put her off for life.

Ben Douglas might be a rat. But he would have no way of knowing that whatever happened between him and his wife would be so personal to you. First, he doesn't know that you know any of this. And, second, the fact that this has upset you so much means that you still have a lot of healing to do. You're only this upset about it because of what happened between you and Paul.

'It's still too raw,' Liz murmured under her breath. She slumped into her office chair, got out her compact mirror and looked at her mascara-streaked face. She sighed, and opened her handbag. She cleaned away the black streaks around her eyes, reapplied her lipstick and rubbed a little of it onto her cheeks as well.

There wasn't much Liz could do about her eye makeup, but she never wore much anyway –mascara and a little eyeliner on her top lid. Probably no one would notice.

Makeup done as best she could, she stared at herself in the mirror.

'Now. You're going to get on with your day, and be pleasant. And at the end of the day you can go home, and if you need to cry again, then you can do it there. You need to make a good impression on these people.' She took a deep breath and then let it out again. 'You got this, Liz. You're a winner. Pull it together.' She pep-talked herself, adjusted her high ponytail, and left her office, knocking at Ben's door.

He wouldn't upset her. She wouldn't allow it.

That was one thing she was sure of.

TWENTY-SEVEN

Now that Simon had clued Liz in to Ben's real character, organising a launch party for the Old Maids whiskies was less appealing than it had been before. Liz had no real desire to spend any time in Ben's presence now, and she'd been avoiding him as much as she could ever since her and Simon's conversation. Yet, she'd promised the crochet coven that they'd have a fundraising event, and it seemed the perfect opportunity to make the small local launch for the whiskies all part of the same thing.

The whole thing had put her in a bit of a spin. On one hand, Ben Douglas' private life was none of her business, and it shouldn't have any effect on their work relationship.

In all other ways, Ben and Liz worked well together, despite the fact that Liz was finding him increasingly unreliable. As well as that time a week or so before, when he'd been late to her meeting because he claimed to have a last-minute emergency but had plainly been in his office five minutes beforehand, talking to Henry the dog, and the time that he'd stormed out of the distillery shed after talking with Liz and Simon, Ben had started disappearing at odd times in the day. There had been a couple of times Liz had walked into his office, expecting to have a meeting, and he hadn't been there; not even Carol knew where he had gone.

However, Liz still walked into the bar of the Loch Cameron Inn, feeling better than she had for months.

When she'd first suggested having a launch party for the Old Maids whiskies, Ben hadn't seemed that keen. But, with the help of the crochet coven, Liz had turned the bar into a haven of Easter delights. It was still a few weeks before Easter, but the village seemed to be one of those places that was always up for a festive celebration: the girls in the crochet coven had helped Liz cover the bar in blue, pink and yellow streamers, twinkly lights with stuffed toy bunnies, cardboard cut-out bunnies and baskets of chocolate eggs all over the place. Eric had set up his vinyl turntable and speakers, and was playing a dubious selection of party hits from the 80s.

Pre-sales for the Old Maids range were looking very healthy, and there was interest from one of the major supermarkets she'd met with. Liz was feeling pretty positive, not least because she'd checked her work email just before the party and seen the new bottle label had come back from the designer. It looked perfect.

And, she'd managed to get her hair done at the village's one and only hair salon, Curl and Wave, which was only open two half days a week, though *which* two half days was apparently random.

For the party, she had treated herself to a new dress from Fiona's Fashions, the boutique in the village. Fiona had been only too happy to help her choose a flattering little black pencil-skirted dress which also flattered her neckline.

All in all, as she took a glass of champagne from a waiter, she was feeling good.

'Liz! You look lovely, dear.' June from the crochet coven

tapped her on the shoulder. 'What a gorgeous dress! You put the rest of us to shame!'

'Oh, June. Shhh. You look wonderful,' Liz replied, giving the older woman a hug. In fact, June always looked glamorous and tonight was no exception. Despite the fact that all of the crochet coven had been hard at work with Dotty and Eric from the Loch Cameron Inn, setting up the bar to look so welcoming, June was dressed in a lovely long purple silk skirt, a matching jumper covered in rhinestones, and her grey hair was curled in a perfect style. Liz waved to Kathy, who was a few feet away, chatting to Eric behind the bar, and she saw Bess and Sally on the other side of the room, laughing with a group of villagers.

Liz saw Ben across the room, who waved at her. She went over, noting the bags under his eyes. He looked tired. Washed out, as if something was bothering him. It was so pronounced that it took Liz a few moments to notice how good Ben looked in his suit for the evening. He had dressed rather like James Bond, Liz thought, in a sharp black suit and white shirt with the top button open. It was such a smart, streamlined look that Liz really could imagine him as a spy for a moment. Despite her confused feelings about Ben, she couldn't deny that the thought gave her a frisson of excitement.

'This all looks great, Liz, Thanks so much for organising it.' He leaned in, as if he wanted to kiss her, but she stepped backwards, avoiding the contact. There was an awkward moment.

'I had a lot of help from the girls in the crochet group,' she said, politely.

'Oh. Well, do thank them from me,' he replied, stiffly.

'I will.'

There was another silence. Ben frowned. 'Look, Liz, if I've done something to offend you—'

'So. Do you want me to make a little speech?' she interrupted. 'I'm happy to. Just thank everyone for coming, formally announce the range, invite everyone to have a taste. That kind of thing.' She gave Ben her dazzling, professional smile which she knew brooked no argument.

'Sure. Of course.' He nodded. Liz detected a resigned tone in his voice.

'Perfect. I'll do it now, and then everyone can enjoy the evening,' she said, briskly, and went to stand by the bar, at the centre of the room.

'Everyone! Can I have your attention, please?' She used a spoon to tap on the side of a nearby whisky tumbler until everyone had quieted down. 'Thank you. Welcome to the launch of Loch Cameron Distillery's new Old Maids range of four whiskies, and also, our joint Easter fundraising event for the mother and baby group! You've been so kind to buy tickets to tonight's events, and the money we've raised is going towards a trampoline for the kids, and, if we earn above our target, we'll also be able to buy them some other much needed play equipment. So, cheers to you!' She raised a glass and toasted everyone in the room, who returned the gesture.

'So, please enjoy the free samples of our four new whiskies, enjoy tonight's entertainment from the children, who I believe are going to sing us some lovely songs before the Easter egg hunt which will happen in the garden outside. Please do tuck into the delicious food, all supplied by Dotty, Eric, Bess, Mina and Kathy. Thank you, everyone!'

There was a round of applause, and Eric turned the music back on.

'Liz. You look beautiful tonight.' Paul turned around from where he was standing by the bar and gave her that slow, appreciative grin she had fallen in love with, once. 'That's some dress.'

'Oh, you came. Thank you. It's new.' Liz did a little twirl, and then felt horribly self-conscious. 'You look very nice too,' she added, shyly.

Paul, in fact, looked very handsome in a sharp navy-blue

suit and a crisp white shirt underneath. Liz hadn't told him it would be a dressy event, and there was a mix of people here already, some dressed up in cocktail dresses and suits, some in jeans and sweatshirts. Some of the children sported Easter jumpers and bunny hats.

'Thank you. Wanted to make an effort for your big launch.' Paul smiled, clearly pleased at the compliment. 'Great party! You organised this?'

'Oh, well, partly. I had a lot of help.' Liz sipped her champagne. There was an awkward pause. 'It was kind of you to come,' she added.

She didn't know how she thought about seeing Paul again. Did she really want to go back to what she'd had with him, even if their chemistry was still there? Nothing had changed. He'd asked her to go back to Glasgow and she'd refused. He didn't want a baby. They were at an impasse.

It was comforting, being around him, and knowing that she was welcome in his arms and in his bed. But she wasn't sure if that was enough.

'Would you like to dance?' Paul gestured to the dancefloor, which was already busy. A popular song from the 90s was playing.

'Oh, you know that I don't really dance.' Liz blushed, feeling like she'd been caught off guard.

'Come on. It isn't like you have to know the steps?' Paul held out a hand for her. 'Not these days, anyway. I think back fondly to the 1940s and the 50s. You know, when there were actual dances to learn.'

'I know what you mean.' Liz laughed, raising her voice to be heard above the music. 'You know I've never gone to a dance class, though. No tango or foxtrot for me.'

'I took a Lindy Hop class recently. If you want me to show you.' Paul took Liz's hand gently. 'C'mon. It'll be fun.'

'Oh, no. I couldn't,' she protested.

'C'mon. I promise, you'll be great.' He took her champagne glass from her and set it on the nearby bar.

'Oh, what the hell!' Liz relented. It was a party, after all.

'That's the spirit.' Paul led her to the dance floor, and they found a space among the dancers.

'Okay. What do we do?' Liz held Paul's hand as they stood among the dancers. His touch was warm and familiar.

'Right. You hold my left hand. Then, look, I'm going to do the basic triple step. Then you copy it. Okay?' he asked, and she nodded, watching his feet. 'All right, then.'

The beat of the song playing was fast, so Paul took a moment, and then gave a surprisingly smooth demonstration of a forward and back step, followed by three steps to the left, accompanied with a half turn. He did it again, and then held his hand out to her.

'Okay. That's what it looks like. So, follow me: forward, back. Then step-step-step to the side, with a turn. Right.'

They practiced the steps for a few minutes, laughing as Liz stepped on Paul's feet. Slowly, Liz got the hang of it.

There was something lovely about being together again and having fun. For a few minutes, Liz allowed herself not to think about the impasse they were at, and just let herself focus on enjoying Paul's company.

'That's good. Okay, now, we're going to hold hands. I take your arm back like this.' He demonstrated, pulling her arm gently, and making her turn by doing so. 'And when I do that, you do step-step.' He demonstrated a slightly different step and positioning of his feet.

'Okay.' Liz frowned, trying to make her body remember what to do. Concentrating, she made a passable attempt at the basic steps. 'Oh! I'm doing it!'

'Good! You're a natural,' Paul laughed. Unexpectedly, he picked her up off the ground and swung her effortlessly to one side, landing her expertly on her feet.

'What was that part?' she cried, above the music. She felt slightly taken aback by the sudden move, but she could feel that Paul knew what he was doing with the dance. Clearly, he'd taken more than a few classes. She felt sad that they hadn't done more things like dance classes when they were together. It would have been fun.

It was nice, now, having fun with Paul.

'That was a lift. I got a bit ahead of myself,' Paul shouted back.

'It was fun, but maybe I need to practise the basics a bit more?' Liz raised her voice just as the song came to a sudden end, and the people dancing near to them laughed good-naturedly as they overheard.

'Ah, well. If you can't swing a beautiful woman now and again, what's the point of life?' Paul shot her that same, disarmingly slow smile. Liz felt slightly awkward – wanting that smile, but knowing what she and Paul wanted was basically at odds. A slow song came on, and she stepped away from him, not wanting to smooch with Paul on the dance floor.

'Thanks for the dance,' she said, intending to go back to find a drink and chat to the rest of the people and their families who had come along. She wanted to keep this light, with Paul.

'Where're you off to?'

'Oh, well, it's a slow song, so...' Liz trailed off, feeling a little uncomfortable. 'I don't think we're quite there yet!' she said quietly.

'What? We were having a nice time.' Suddenly, Paul's expression changed.

'I just don't want to do a slow dance. That's all.' Liz took a step backwards. 'I told you I needed to take this slowly.'

'Christ, Liz.' He looked annoyed. 'I thought we were having a good time.'

'We were. Like I said to you before, if anything's going to happen between us again, I just need to take it slowly. I'm not going to move back to Glasgow with you. This is my life now. So, we can maybe see each other casually and see where it goes, but...' She trailed off. 'I can't say I love you. Not now,' she added in a low voice. 'It's too much. Too soon.'

'A dance is too much? Come on, Liz. We've done so much more than this together.' He gave her his warm smile and held out his hand. 'It's like a hug, but with a slight shuffle. That's all.'

'That's sweet, but I don't want to.' She smiled patiently. 'I've got a lot of people to talk to: this is a work event, after all. Why don't you mingle a bit and get to know people? You were quite keen on the idea of hanging out in the local, after all. Now's your chance.'

'Same old Liz.' The affable expression disappeared from his face. 'Work, work, work.'

'I told you that this was a work event, Paul.' Liz started to get annoyed. 'And I've told you I need to take this slow. I don't want to slow dance with you right now, in front of...' She happened to glance up and catch Ben Douglas' eye. She knew that he was wondering who Paul was – probably, everyone was. She hadn't introduced him to anyone yet, because she didn't know what to say. *This is my ex-partner, who I thought I was going to have everything with and then it all disappeared, one rainy afternoon when he told me he didn't want me anymore.*

Not exactly what you told people at a fundraiser-slash-launch event.

'In front of who?' Paul followed Liz's gaze. 'That guy? Why? Who is he?'

'No one. My boss,' Liz corrected herself.

'I see.' Paul's eyes narrowed and he stared at Ben.

'What do you see?' Liz asked as quietly as she could and still be heard over the slow song that couples around them were swaying to, slowly.

'Nothing.' Paul nodded. 'That's fine. I'll go and make nice with the locals. Leave you to lover boy.'

'Lover boy?' Liz followed him off the dance floor and caught his arm, smiling at Bess who caught her eye across the room with an inquisitive look. 'He is not my lover. He's my boss. I just told you that,' she said in a low voice. 'There's nothing going on between us. And even if there was, it wouldn't be any of your business. You left me, remember,' she added.

'Oh, it's like that, is it?' Paul replied sulkily. 'Are you ever going to let me forget? Is that going to come up every time we have a falling out?'

'Oh my...' Liz swore under her breath. 'I can't believe you'd say that.'

'I'm saying it because that's how I feel. You're not going to forgive me. That you're going to trot that out, every time we have an argument...' Paul rammed his hands in his pockets. Liz led him to the side of the room so that they weren't in the middle of everything.

'I'm not going to *trot it out*, as you so charmingly put it, but, sure, if you want to talk about it now, I am going to take a while to forgive you. Because you broke my heart!' Liz kept her voice level, but she felt the anger wash over her. 'How *dare* you complain that I've mentioned it! Damn right I'm going to mention it! I'll mention it every time I please, thank you. I didn't walk out on *you* when *you* could have been pregnant!'

'Liz. I love you.' Paul reached out for her, but she pulled away.

'No. This isn't right.' She felt the tears that wanted to come, and she heard the crack in her voice. 'I loved you, Paul. But I can't do this.'

Finally, she had the closure Ben had wished for her, in the field, watching the starlings. She knew it was over with Paul.

'Liz. Please.' Paul looked broken hearted. 'I'm sorry for everything I did. But you have to understand why I did it.'

'I do understand. I know. We're just people that want

different things. And I've changed. I've moved on, Paul.' Liz blinked back tears. 'Just go. Okay? Please.'

Paul took in a deep sigh, and let it go.

'All right. I'll go.' He nodded, picked up his coat from the overloaded coat stand, and gave her a wan nod. 'All the best, Liz. You deserve it.'

'Liz. Are you all right? Who was that?' Sally appeared at Liz's elbow and looked at Liz in concern. 'Bess just told me you seemed to be having words with that guy. You're shaking. Come and sit down.' She guided Liz to a table and made her sit down at one of the chairs. 'Here.' Bess handed her a shot of whisky from a table nearby where Carol had arranged a help yourself display.

'My ex,' Liz said, taking it thankfully and swallowing it in one shot. 'He just reappeared recently after quite a difficult breakup. I wasn't sure if I should go back with him, but there was an attraction still. I don't know... I wanted comfort.' Her voice cracked a little and Bess handed her a napkin.

'We've all been there, love. Don't worry.' Sally patted her back and handed her another shot of whisky. 'Exes can stir up all kinds of emotions. Here. This'll help.'

'Oh, well, I don't really drink that much...' Liz protested, but Sally insisted.

'Get it down you. Good for shock.'

'Whoa! What's up?'

Ben walked up to the table, a concerned look on his face; Liz thought that she must look terrible, apparently downing shots of whisky for no reason. 'Liz? You okay?'

'Umm. Sure.' Liz smiled brightly. Ben frowned at her.

'That looks like a fake smile.'

'No, I'm fine,' she insisted.

Ben set the drinks he was carrying down on the table and sat down next to Liz.

'Come on. You look awful. What's up?'

'Thanks.' Liz tried to laugh it off, but she was really upset. 'Just a misunderstanding. That was my ex. He ... well, it doesn't matter.'

'Oh. That's your ex? Who you were talking about the other day?'

Liz nodded. Sally put a protective arm around her shoulder.

'Exes are toxic sometimes. You're best far away from him, love. You've got a good thing going here, remember. New job. New life.' She frowned at Bess. They both looked concerned.

'I know. I'm okay, really,' Liz assured them. She took some deep breaths. 'That was just hard. But it was the right thing to do.'

'Are you sure you're okay?' Ben looked concerned.

'I'm fine,' Liz repeated, feeling mortified that her private life had been on display for all of Loch Cameron to see.

'You don't look it,' he said, frowning. 'And I agree with Sally. We've all got bad exes. Doesn't mean we should go back to them.'

'I'm not sure you're in a position to talk about exes,' Liz snapped. His comment had reminded her about what Simon had told her, and she said it without thinking. Her feelings were raw.

'What does that mean?' Ben gave her an odd look.

'Nothing. Forget it.' She closed her eyes. 'This has just been a difficult evening.'

'Liz. Please. I'm sorry if I said anything to upset you.' Ben sighed. 'I just... I wouldn't want to see you get involved with a bad guy. That's all.'

'Wow. It's literally none of your business.' Liz felt herself becoming angry. 'You're my boss at work, Ben. My life outside work is nothing to do with you.'

She didn't say it, but she wasn't interested in Ben's opinion of her love life, since he was the one who had abandoned his pregnant wife.

Oh, hell no.

It had been traumatic, earlier, with Paul. But now, Liz felt annoyed, and it was something connected to the fact that she had trusted Ben to be a good guy, and now that she knew he had something less than exemplary in his past, she felt betrayed. *Are there no good men at all?* she wondered.

'You know what? I've had enough. I'll see you in the office on Monday. Or, maybe I won't, seeing as you seem to disappear as and when you want to, these days.' She stormed out before Ben had a chance to respond, grabbing her coat from the rack by the door. 'Thanks, Sally. Bess,' she added.

So much for a pleasant work party, she thought. *I should have just stayed at home.*

TWENTY-EIGHT

Liz was in Ben's office, having their weekly catch up, but her mind was somewhere else.

Since the launch party – where, fortunately, no one apart from Sally, Bess and Ben seemed to have noticed what happened with Paul – she'd been thinking more and more about sperm donation. She kept taking the leaflet from the fertility clinic out of her handbag and reading it, thinking about making an appointment at the clinic to talk it through, and then folding up the leaflet and putting it away again.

This morning, she was thinking that she should call the clinic and make an appointment. She didn't have to commit to anything, but it would be good to just go along and find out more.

It's definitely not going to happen with Paul. So, if you want a baby, this is it, she thought to herself. *Surely if you want it as much as you think you do, you should make the call. All that hard work shouldn't be for nothing.*

'What?' She looked up from where she'd been doodling on her notepad. 'Sorry. Can you say that again?'

'I was just telling you that we've been given a prime slot on the National Beverages Conference agenda this year to present Old Maids ahead of launch. Did you even hear me say that?' Ben frowned.

'Sorry. I was somewhere else.' She made herself focus. 'We've been asked to present? That's great!'

'Yeah. I mean, that's going to be up to you, pretty much, if that's okay. Obviously, I'll come and deliver the presentation with you. But it's your baby.'

'My baby?' Liz felt a slight discomfort at the phrase, though she knew Ben didn't mean anything by it.

'Yes. I mean, as Sales Director, you'll need to write and make the presentation. Old Maids is your concept. And you know how to do these things. The kind of top line stuff people want to hear.' Ben gave her an odd look.

'Oh. Right. Yes.' She nodded, realising she was just jumping at shadows.

'Liz. I realise we haven't known each other very long. But if you have a problem with me, I want you to know you can tell me.' Ben tapped his pen on the desk, then stopped, obviously realising it was irritating. 'And, if this is about what happened at the party... I'm sorry about that. I wasn't being rude. Or, at least, I didn't intend to. If I offended you, I'm sorry.'

'It's not the party.' The evening had played on Liz's mind since it happened, but she was at least glad she'd come to some closure with Paul. He'd texted her a few times since, but she hadn't replied. She knew it was for the best.

Now, at least, she could look ahead. But, now, she had the new quandary of following her fertility dream, or leaving it forever. It should have been an easy decision, but somehow, it wasn't. And that was killing her.

Was it just the idea of being a single parent? She didn't know. She wasn't opposed to being one, though the ideal would have been to have a baby with a loving partner. She could still win the baby game show; she didn't need a partner, necessarily. The prize had always been a child.

It was just... scary, she thought. Unknown territory. And she'd been enjoying her job and her new life and not thinking about getting pregnant for the first time in what felt like forever.

'What is it, then?' Ben leaned forward, his voice soft. 'It's not like you to be so distracted. I can tell something's wrong.'

Liz felt tears welling up in her eyes unexpectedly at Ben's kindness. It was always when people were kind that this happened. She thought she would have preferred Ben to be harsh or tell her off for not listening, almost.

'I'm sorry. Nothing's really wrong.' She wiped her eyes. 'Just... I don't know. Stressful things.'

'It's clearly not nothing,' Ben replied, still softly. 'You can talk to me, you know.' He reached out and touched her arm, and she stiffened. His touch did things to her, but she was too confused and distracted to want that, right now. She pulled her arm away.

'I don't want to talk to you about it.' Liz sniffed, blowing her nose. This was the man who left his own pregnant wife, after all. As much as Ben's kindness touched her, she couldn't forget that. How could she trust a man like that with her own problems around fertility, or indeed anything personal? What would he be able to tell her that wasn't tinged with his own bad behaviour? His betrayal of that poor woman?

'Sorry. I shouldn't have...' he stammered, and looked away.

'It doesn't matter. Let's just focus on work, okay?' She fought to get her voice under control. 'Let's talk about the conference presentation.'

'Well, if you're sure. But I'm here if you need me.' Ben looked uncomfortable.

You often aren't here, actually, she thought, but she didn't say it. If she was honest, Liz thought that Ben's disappearances were him not-so-subtly removing himself from the business. He was probably off playing golf or something; he'd made it more than clear that he never wanted to be CEO. Which was fine: he could quit at any time. But, as long as he was head of the company, then he had responsibilities – not least supporting Liz in the launch of the Old Maids campaign.

'Thank you,' Liz said, a little stiffly. She opened her laptop. 'Let's get down to it, then, shall we? Let's talk about what we should say in the presentation.'

'You're the boss.' Ben sighed, and looked down at his notepad.

* * *

'Now, ladies and gentlemen. If you'd like to follow me, we'll head into the Loch Cameron Distillery Archive.' Grenville tipped his hat – a grey fedora – to Liz as she walked into the main distilling shed and found herself at the back of a group of tourists. Liz gave him a little wave and mouthed *carry on* to the shopkeeper, who was evidently enjoying his new role as distillery tour guide very much.

'However, before we do so, I'd like to point out that we have the distillery's very own Sales Director with us, Liz Parsons! Say hello, Liz,' Grenville called out in his jolly baritone. Liz gave the group a shy wave.

'Hi, everyone! Hope you're enjoying the tour?' she asked. There was a happy murmur of assent, and more than a few smiles and nods.

'Miss Parsons. Did you want me, or did we just impede your no doubt busy and productive day?' Grenville trilled.

'I just wanted a quick word, Grenville.' Liz caught up with him and walked along as Grenville shepherded the group through the door and out into the courtyard, which was in full bloom.

'Of course,' he murmured. 'Seems to be going well, by the way. Second tour this week, and both have been fully booked.'

'That's so great.' Liz grinned. 'Word's going to get out, and people are going to be lining up to listen to you. I knew you'd be fantastic.'

'Ach, flattery will get you everywhere, my dear one.' Grenville chuckled. 'And how are you? I hoped I'd see you at the shop again, but I expect you've been far too busy whipping this place into shape.'

'Yes. It's been a little frantic, what with the launch party, rolling out the new range, and having meetings with stockists,' Liz admitted, not wanting to add that she felt like her life had been blown apart again recently. 'Did you enjoy the party, by the way?'

She'd spoken to Grenville a little at the launch, but the unpleasantness with Paul had ended up with her leaving early.

'Oh, yes. It was marvellous.' Grenville opened the door to the archive and led her through, ushering the group in and warning them to be careful on the stairs. 'Still, I missed you. You left before I could ask you to dance.'

'Oh. I'm sorry,' she replied, evasively. 'Anyway, I just wanted to check in and see how the tour was going. Are you talking up the Old Maids range? And you're taking their email addresses, right? So we can let them know when it's available to buy?'

'Yes, dear. All on my little clipboard.' Grenville tapped his pen on the board he held in his hand. 'I have, of course, mentioned my shop, too. If that's all right.'

'Of course. We want them to invest in the village as much as possible.'

'Oh, good. Now, that reminds me, dear. I did want to say something to you, as a matter of fact. About Evelyn McCallister, one of your Old Maids. Just wait a minute. I've got to do my thing.' Grenville held up a finger to Liz and marched to the front of the group of tourists.

'Now, then. Here we are in the Loch Cameron Distillery Archive, the largest whisky archive in Scotland,' he began, his sonorous voice filling the cavernous space. Grenville had flicked all the lights on, but the way that they were arranged down in the cellar was that they faced upwards, lighting up the vaulted ceiling and casting the rest of the space into shadows. Liz liked the spooky feeling she got down there: it was old, and it felt authentic. It *was* authentic, she reminded herself.

'Rumour has it that the archive is haunted by the ghost of the distillery's first ever owner, Iain Raymond Douglas. He started the business, selling whisky locally in 1785, and began importing whisky to England a few years later. Thirsty Englishmen wanted Loch Cameron whisky, because it was among the best in the world! In fact, the whisky gained a Royal Warrant from King Edward VII in the early 1900s.' He winked at Liz, who nodded.

The Royal Warrant would be a huge feather in her cap if she could get it back. She'd looked at the old records, and it seemed that Ben Douglas' father, Jim, had had a good relationship with the Royal Household Warrants Committee for many years. The Warrant had consistently been in place from 1908 to 1995, meaning that King Edward VII, King George V, King Edward VIII, King George VI and then Queen Elizabeth II had all actively supported the brand. However, Liz wasn't sure what had happened in the 90s. It seemed that the Royal Warrant had ended, and all she could find was a brief official letter from the Committee citing "operational difficulties" as the reason.

Liz had also discovered that it took at least five years of supplying goods to the royal family before a company was eligible to have its application considered for recommendation. That meant that regaining the Royal Warrant was a long game and not something that could be achieved quickly. She was absolutely going to do her best to contact the palace and see if they would take bottles of the Old Maids range when they were ready, to try and see if they liked it. She was confident that anyone would, but she also knew that she was up against some stiff competition from all the other whisky brands on the market that were either already supplying the royals, or had plans to.

Still, at least Loch Cameron Whisky had a history with the Royal Warrant. She had that on her side, though she was currently out of ideas about how to make a new relationship with a member of the Royal Family. Liz had researched it, and even if you could get your product to be used by the palace for five years, then the Warrant grantor – the king, or possibly one of the dukes – had to personally sign off on the Warrant when they received the recommendation from the Warrant Committee.

The grantor was empowered to reverse the committee's decision, and therefore the final decision to accept or withhold a grant was a very personal one. They had to like it, personally. And the king or one of the dukes had to approve wholeheartedly of your company, the product itself and have faith that you really were the best in the business.

All in all, Liz wondered how in the world Jim Douglas had ever managed to get a Royal Warrant in the first place.

'It's said that old Iain Raymond Douglas can be heard at night, at the time of the full moon, rattling the bottles down in the archive. He's looking for the lost vintage: a whisky he only ever made ten bottles of, and which, legend says, were lost when the cellar flooded in 1806. Wait! What was that noise?'

Grenville turned his head, his eyes wide, as the faint noise of tinkling glass could be heard in the background. Liz suppressed a laugh: she could see that Grenville had a cloth bag in his hand, and was shaking it behind his back. It was, no doubt, full of broken glass, but it certainly added an atmosphere to his tall tale.

Liz could see that the tourists were loving this piece of outrageous theatre from Grenville; there were delighted squeals and murmurs as they stood there, listening raptly to him. Liz, again, congratulated herself on having the idea of putting Grenville on show in the first place. He clearly loved the spotlight.

She waited a few more minutes until Grenville had finished talking about the archive, and began walking the group around the different tunnels that made it up.

'So. What did you think, Miss Parsons?' He reappeared at her side, grinning.

'That was remarkable. I had no idea you were going to throw in a ghost story.' Liz grinned. 'Is it true? About the archive being haunted?'

'Oh. Well, not really. It is true that Iain was the one that founded the distillery.' Grenville placed both of his hands on his heart. 'Don't tell anyone, but I made the rest up. About the lost vintage. People love that kind of thing.'

'I won't tell a soul,' Liz whispered. 'And it is quite spooky in here. You're not wrong about that, though I did see you shaking whatever's in that bag.'

'Ha! You have a sharp eye, Miss Parsons. Nothing gets past you, does it?' he chuckled. 'Anyway, look, before I have to be wonderful again, I was wanting to tell you about Evelyn McCallister.' He tapped his temple. 'Must remember, I thought, if I see you. And now, here you are.'

'Okay. What did you want to tell me?'

'Well. I hear that Evelyn is going to be one of your new whisky poster girls,' Grenville began. 'And you know about her being a Master Distiller, back in the day?'

'Yes. I found that out at the castle.'

'Ah, Hal Cameron's records. Yes, the Camerons have always been very good at that.' Grenville nodded. 'But what I doubt you know is that Evelyn was my great aunt.'

TWENTY-NINE

'Evelyn McCallister was your great aunt?' Liz was taken aback. 'Are you sure?'

'Oh, yes. She's the reason I have the shop,' he continued, as they walked around the archive with the tourists as they took photos and peered at the barrels and dusty bottles. 'Evelyn worked up at the distillery all her life. Her father, Tommy, trained her up when he went into World War One. Thankfully, he lived through it and returned home in 1918. However, he wasn't really up to the job when he got back, and so Evelyn more or less took over until she passed it onto Simon's father in the 1950s. Tommy was always the titular Master Distiller apart from those three years he was away, but Evelyn was really the one doing the work.'

'So, her sister was your grandmother?' Liz asked, amazed at the connections that existed in tiny communities like Loch Cameron.

'Yes. Isabel. Bel, she was called in the family. Bel had four children that lived: my mother, and my three uncles. But she died when I was still quite young, and Evelyn used to help my mother out with me and my brothers and sisters when we were small. We were quite a handful: five of us.'

Liz nodded, thinking about how hard it must be to have so many children, but also feeling her heart twist just like it did every time she thought about children at all.

'So you were quite close to your great aunt?' she asked, instead.

'Oh, yes. She was quite a character. Never married, as you know: that's how she ended up an old maid, as you noticed from the village graveyard. She was dedicated to her work, and she loved us kids. Many was the day she brought us up here to the distillery to watch us. I loved it up here, as a child. Running around the mash tuns. The smell of the grain.' He looked wistful.

'So, how did the shop come about?' Liz prompted him.

'Well, I grew up fascinated with whisky, because of Evelyn.' Grenville shrugged. 'When I was a young man, there was a system in the village where you could make a proposal to the Laird – that was Hal Cameron's father, at the time – to take over one of the commercial properties when they came available. The shop was sitting empty, and I said, what about a whisky shop? He liked the idea. I've been there ever since.'

'Wow. I had no idea,' Liz mused.

'Indeed, indeed. But the really interesting thing is that I own some of Evelyn's things,' Grenville continued. 'And, one of those things is her diary. I thought you'd like it. For your launch of the new whiskies,' he added. 'There might be something in there you and Ben could use. I've flicked through it and it's mostly whisky notes. But there are some other quite... interesting things there, too.' He gave her a curious look. 'Ben would probably be quite keen to hear about what's in there. I've often considered sharing the diary with him, over the years, but it never seemed like the right time. Somehow, you feel like the catalyst.'

'Oh, my goodness! Grenville, this is amazing!' Liz took the small book from him and opened it, peering in the dim light at the handwritten pages. 'This is absolutely invaluable! Are you sure you don't mind me borrowing it? I'll give it back, of course.'

'Not at all, dear. I'm happy to help, and happy that Evelyn's getting some of the attention she deserves after all this time.' Grenville patted Liz on the arm. 'You'll let me know if you use anything from it? In publicity or something? Or...' He looked thoughtful. 'Ben might like to talk to me about what's in there. Let him know that I'm here when he wants me. Okay?'

'Oh, of course!' Liz was flabbergasted. This was such an important find.

'Good, good. Right. I'm going to lead this lot into the gardens now and get back in the fresh air,' he said, raising his voice to call out to the group. 'All right, everyone! Follow me now back up the steps, we're going outside. Be careful of your feet, it's slippery! This way.'

Liz waited for the group to go ahead of her, following them out of the cellar with its many cubbyholes and corridors. She couldn't wait to read Evelyn McCallister's diary, and she felt somehow honoured that she held it in her hand. It was a link back in time to another woman that had worked here and made a success of her work; it was also more of a clue about Evelyn's life. More proof that she wasn't just an Old Maid.

THIRTY

Diary, 1921

March 21st

*Papa coughs all the time. His lungs have never recovered
from the war, and I worry about him. It seems to be
getting worse. Mr Douglas says that Papa shouldn't be
around the stills for fear that he will infect the brew, but
that is ignorance talking. Whisky is alcohol, and alcohol
is sterile. It beggars belief that a man such as Mr
Douglas, with an education at Eton, should think such a
thing. I benefitted from the ministrations of the local
school and fared much better.*

*Still, I know that I should keep such opinions to myself.
Mr Douglas entertains me under sufferance, which I
know. However, it worries me that when Papa finally
dies (may his life be long), I may lose my standing at the
distillery.*

April 2nd

*I have not written for some time since we have had an
outbreak of flu at the distillery, and though I have not
caught it, I have been covering the work of many of my
fellow workers to cope with their absences.*

*We have had a few new people start as temporary work-
ers, which has helped in the menial work at least:
sweeping the floors, washing the windows and sifting the
grain. One of them is a fellow called Sandy Crowley,
who has been most attentive to me.*

*Sandy says that he wants to learn the whisky business as
much as he can, and he asks me questions all the time.
He is fair with piercing green eyes, and clearly fit from
working in the fields in summertime. It is a welcome
change to talk to Sandy, compared to the others here who
treat me like an inferior. Sandy enjoys books, as I do, and
I have lent him my book of poems by Longfellow, who he
admires.*

April 9th
*An interesting day! Sandy returned by book of Longfel-
low. Inside, he had left me a note, asking me to meet him
at Queen's Point, up by the Ross family cottage. I felt
some trepidation, but as it happened, Papa was sleeping
and Bel and the children did not need me, so I went last
night.*

*I hardly know how to write what happened. We walked
along the lochside and talked about poetry. The moon
was almost full, and the light played on the water. Sandy
was a perfect gentleman, but asked to hold my hand, to
which I assented.*

*He has asked if I would join him again on Sunday
evening.*

April 13th

*Another walk with Sandy. He is so interested in my
work! I have never known a man be so fascinated with
what I do, or even accepting that I am a working woman
in the first place. I told him all about how whisky is
made, and what I do to control the distillation. He did
want to know about the business side of things, but I
confessed that I know little about that. All of Mr
Douglas's ledgers are in his office and he is the one that
manages everything.*

*We discussed poetry again, and Sandy asked if he could
kiss me. I said yes.*

April 15th

*An odd day. Sandy came to find me while I was at the
stills and tried to get me to hide away in the unused
office next to Mr Douglas's one. I suspect that he
wanted more kisses, and perhaps more than that: I
might be unmarried, but I know how babies come
about because of Bel. I was shocked that he should
approach me in the daytime, and among everyone else
at the distillery. I sent him away, but there were some
looks. I hope that this will not affect my standing at
work.*

April 20th

*Sandy apologised for the event at work last week; I had
been avoiding him after that to ensure that my reputation stays intact. He asked me to meet him at Queen's
Point again, which I did, despite my better judgement.
He won me around again, however, and our kisses led a
little further this time. I believe that it is not wrong of me
to engage in the activity that most others do, even though
I am unmarried: one must try a little first before one
agrees to marriage, after all.*

> *I don't know what Sandy is thinking, but I would be*
> *accepting of a proposal from him, if this continues.*

Liz sat back in her leather chair and looked at the cracked ceiling of her office, thoughtfully. Evelyn's diary was more detailed than Grenville had suggested, and this whole story with Sandy Crowley was a fascinating insight into the life of a woman in the post-World War One period. She turned the page, expecting more updates about Sandy, but the entries that followed seemed to detail Evelyn's work: tasting notes were recorded in Evelyn's neat handwriting, but nothing more about Sandy.

Liz flicked the pages of the small notebook until she found the next personal entry.

> July 28th
> *I know, finally, what this sickness is. Bel told me her*
> *suspicions yesterday, and I had to admit that I had had*
> *relations, out of wedlock.*
> *She is not shocked. Bel says that we have lived through a*
> *war, and being with child is nothing in comparison.*
> *Perhaps this is easy for her to say, because she has four*
> *children and is married. It is certainly not easy for me to*
> *accept that I will become a pariah in this community*
> *when the baby comes.*
> *I never set out for this to happen.*

Oh, no, Liz thought, her eyes widening. She had assumed that Evelyn had enjoyed a flirtation with Sandy Crowley, but nothing more: Evelyn seemed so straight-laced. But Liz knew as well as anyone what could happen when passions took over. Not that she had been in that position for a long time. She turned the page.

August 15th

I can hardly write this. He has abandoned me. Refused me. Though it is his child.

I don't know what to do. I live in fear that Papa may discover the truth, which he certainly will soon.

'No!' Liz exclaimed, out loud. There was a knock on the door, and Ben poked his head into her office.

'All right in here?' he asked, cordially. 'I thought I heard something.'

'Oh, sorry. I was just reading this.' Liz held up the diary. 'Grenville gave it to me yesterday. It's Evelyn McCallister's diary. You know, one of the old maids? Get this: she was actually his great aunt! Can you believe that?'

'Wow. I mean, I can, because it's Loch Cameron, and everyone's been here forever. But I didn't know that specifically.' Ben came into the office. 'That's fascinating.'

'It is. Grenville also said you'd be interested, and you should talk to him about it.' Liz shrugged. 'I guess that's just because she worked here, it's part of your family history. And because of the Old Maids launch, of course.'

'Hmm. Is there something good in there, then?'

'Yeah. Evelyn was seeing some guy, a temporary worker that came to work at the distillery in 1921. I guess she was in her late twenties at the time. She was working with her dad as Master Distiller then, but he was off with ill health a lot. So, it was mostly Evelyn running the show.'

'Okay.' Ben sat down in the black leather chair on the opposite side of Liz's desk. 'Who was this guy?'

'Sandy Crowley. He wooed her with poetry, by the sounds of things.' Liz looked back at the diary. 'The reason I shouted was because he got her pregnant, and then refused to acknowledge her or the child. That's where I'm up to.'

'Oh my goodness. Read on.' Ben leaned forward, his head on his hands. 'What happened?'

'Hang on. Let me go back to the page.' She flicked the pages of the book. 'Here it is.

D is angry with me. He says I am a common hussy for seeing Sandy and deserve everything I get.

'That's it. The entries end here. She goes back to work notes for pages and pages.'

'D? Who's D?' Ben frowned, looking at his phone, which had lit up.

'Do you need to get that?' Liz asked, but he shook his head and turned it to mute, then turned it face down on the table.

'No, it's fine. Carry on. You were saying. Had she mentioned "D" before?'

'No. This whole thing was mostly a work notebook, I think, and for whatever reason, she decided to start writing in more personal entries for a brief time. But, look.' Liz flicked slowly through the pages of Evelyn's meticulous, copperplate hand-writing. 'All tasting notes, ordinary stuff. I mean, it's still amazing to have – and we can use all that stuff for the product launch. But it kind of leaves us on tenterhooks as to what happened to Evelyn and her baby.'

'No kidding. But if she was buried as an Old Maid, what does that mean? That she didn't have it? Or that she did, but she never married?'

'I don't know. But I want to find out.' Liz put the diary down on her desk. 'Maybe D is for Dad? Her father disapproved?'

'Maybe. But she'd be more likely to call him Father, wouldn't she? And why just the initial if she was talking about her dad? That would be innocent enough.'

'Hmm. I don't know.'

'It's a mystery, all right. Maybe Grenville knows. You should ask him,' Ben suggested.

'I will.' Liz looked up at Ben, taking him in, now that she wasn't as preoccupied with the diary. Today, he wore smart black trousers and a light blue shirt, open at the neck. He was clean shaven, but he was that kind of classic Celtic black-haired guy who had a shadow of a beard by mid-afternoon, even if he'd shaved in the morning. His black wavy hair looked like he had raked it back in haste with his fingers: a slight curl had escaped at the front and gave him a boyish look. She always liked looking at him. Liked his presence, which was warm and safe and exciting at the same time. But he was also a man that she couldn't trust; she had to remind herself of that. He was her boss, nothing more. 'He's doing really great with the tours, by the way. I saw him in action earlier.'

'I bet. It was an inspired idea to ask him to do them.' Ben nodded. 'I'm going to go along to the next one. I'll probably learn a lot.'

'You probably will.' Liz smiled neutrally. Ben held her gaze for a moment and, despite her wanting to keep things neutral, a pleasant frisson of energy passed between them. She looked away, knowing that she didn't want to encourage that. *You are not the man I want to do that with,* she thought, firmly. *Men like you don't deserve my attention.*

'I've sorted our accommodation for the conference, by the way. We're on the same floor, but not next door to each other, or anything,' he said, looking down at the office carpet. Was that a bashful look on his face, or was Liz imagining it?

She didn't care if they had rooms next to each other; she'd done that with work colleagues for years and never thought twice about it. It was just what you did when you had presentations to practice, or if you wanted to hang out and have a drink at the end of a long day but couldn't face networking at the hotel bar. But, perhaps the idea of them sleeping near to each other – even if separated by a wall – was too much for Ben.

'Great. I'm almost done with my presentation, by the way. I'd appreciate your eyes on it soon, so we can tweak it with your suggestions,' she replied, smoothly.

'I'm sure it doesn't need any tweaks, but of course.' Ben flashed her a sudden, warm smile. 'I'm around, if you need me.' He stood up and gave her a little wave, then immediately looked mortified. 'Sorry. I don't know why I did that. I'll be next door. And let me know what you find out about Evelyn's baby.'

'I will.' Liz watched him go, wondering how this Ben Douglas – the one who embarrassed himself by giving her child-like goodbye waves when he was just leaving the room – could be the same Ben Douglas as the one who heartlessly abandoned his pregnant wife. It seemed odd, but, if life had taught her anything, it was that you couldn't trust people. They could seem to be one thing, and actually be something else.

And, now, there was Evelyn. Another woman who was abandoned while pregnant by the father of her child.

Liz felt the weight of sadness in her heart for this woman who had been dead for many years already, but had had to endure that most terrible of betrayals. How had she coped? What had happened to her in Loch Cameron? Had she been ostracised by the rest of the villagers, like she herself had feared?

Evelyn had worked as Master Distiller for those three years while her father was at war and into the 50s when she'd handed over to Simon's dad. So, if she'd had the baby, people would have known – and if she hadn't, what had she done?

Liz felt a cold sense of dread in her heart, knowing that Evelyn's story probably wasn't a happy one. Typically, women who had babies "out of wedlock" in the early part of the twentieth century – and perhaps especially in small, remote locations like Loch Cameron – had little support from the community, who would be far more likely to demonise them than sympathise for their impossible situation. Yes, Evelyn had been tempted by Sandy, and contraception hadn't been readily available to unmarried women in the 1920s. But she was a flesh and blood woman, and she had spent her life working and looking after her family.

When Sandy came along, quoting poetry and wooing her, was it so wrong that Evelyn let herself have just the tiniest bit of fun? Liz didn't think so. But it broke her heart that Evelyn had – possibly – paid such a heavy price for her brief happiness.

Had Evelyn had the baby? And what had happened to it, if so?

It was more than curiosity for Liz: she had to know, for her own peace of mind.

Liz got the letter from the fertility clinic out of her handbag and unfolded it once again. She didn't need to read it again: by now, she knew it by heart. She had been mulling it over and over again, but for some reason, reading Evelyn's diary had made her feel more decisive. Evelyn had had terrible choices when it came to having a baby, but Liz had the power to take her destiny into her own hands. Just like Gretchen had: Gretchen Ross had not wanted to be married, but she had wanted a child, and so she had adopted one. Gretchen's story gave Liz hope.

Going to the clinic meant that Liz was making a positive choice. She still wasn't sure if this was a path she wanted to go down, but she had realised that she should at least make an appointment and have the conversation.

If she pursued it and if it worked? Sure, she'd be a single mother, but millions of women did it and their kids turned out just fine. Gretchen had raised her daughter.

Evelyn had been forced into whatever circumstances she'd ended up with, and she'd been labelled an Old Maid. That didn't have to happen to Liz. The outcomes of sperm donation were as ambiguous as everything she'd done so far, because she was battling her own fertility issues. But she could try. She could give them a call.

Liz tapped the clinic's number into her work landline and listened to the phone ring at the other end. It felt good to be taking another small step forward; slowly, she felt as though she was taking back control of her life. And that was good.

THIRTY-ONE

'So, Liz. You understand the process?' The doctor handed her the same leaflet that had been sent in the post, and which she'd already read and re-read obsessively. 'You can choose a sperm sample from the bank we hold, and that sperm can be used to fertilise your last egg. You had a number of viable eggs, I believe.' The doctor frowned, looking at her computer screen.

'Yes. They've been used in the last rounds of IVF.'

Liz sat opposite the doctor in the clinic office, gripping the handle of her handbag tightly. *Take deep breaths*, she told herself. *In, out, In, out.*

Visiting the fertility clinic hadn't always stressed Liz out. When she and Paul had first visited, when they'd decided to start IVF, they had been full of enthusiasm and excitement. Paul had held her hand through that first appointment when a different doctor had talked them through egg viability and all the stages of what was going to happen.

That first time, Liz had felt like she was stepping into her new life. She had *known*, deep in her heart, that she was getting her baby.

That picture she thought about – the gaudily-lit prize in the baby game show she felt she was a contestant in – the one of her as a happy mother, seemed so close that she could hold it.

But she had been wrong. And it had broken her heart.

'So, this is...' the doctor trailed off, politely.

'Probably my last chance with my own eggs. Yes,' Liz answered, more curtly than she'd intended. 'Sorry. This is just quite stressful.'

Every time that Liz had come to the clinic after that first unsuccessful round, she'd felt worse and worse. Paul had tried to cheer her up after the appointments: he bought her flowers, cooked her dinner, talked her round. *It would work this time. It would be all right.*

Liz knew that she couldn't have asked for a better, more committed partner than Paul when it came to IVF. But, eventually, Paul's – patience? enthusiasm? love? – had just run out.

So, now, despite the fact that the clinic was a tranquil place, with vases of fresh tulips in the waiting room, clean white walls with tasteful art on the walls and you got a nice cup of coffee while you waited, Liz's legs turned to jelly whenever she walked into it. Because, no matter how nice the décor, this was the place that reminded her of her two miscarriages, and of Paul leaving, and of every time she'd had to sit down in the doctor's office and talk about whether she wanted to try the process again.

'Not at all. I quite understand how difficult this all is,' the doctor replied kindly. 'You have endometriosis and polycystic ovaries, it says here. So that's the reason for IVF so far.'

'That's right.'

'Do you get a lot of pain with the endo? I know it can be very difficult for many women.'

'Some. Not debilitating. But when I had my scan, it showed that it's messed up my fallopian tubes. And the PCOS is messing up my ovaries.'

'Hmm. Both conditions are so common, too. I wish there

was more medical research being done.' The doctor shuffled the papers on her desk. 'So, have you looked at the donor catalogue?'

'Yeah,' Liz sighed. When she'd looked at the letter from the clinic again, she'd seen that there was a link to an online catalogue of 500 sperm donors. She'd looked through it, but come away strangely uninspired. 'Look, I haven't decided, as yet. It's all a bit strange, looking at these anonymous descriptions. Like dating, but for bodily secretions.'

'Yes, it is a little odd, in its way.' The doctor smiled. 'It's not for everyone. But, if you no longer have a partner who wants to go forward in the process with you, then it's an alternative.'

'Hmm.' Liz made a noncommittal noise. 'I'm just not sure. I mean, I thought I'd come along and talk about it, but I'm not ready to proceed just yet.'

'Of course. I'll do an examination while you're here, and you can go away and think about whether you want to go with a sperm donor. Some people prefer to go with a known donor – a friend, perhaps, someone they feel comfortable with.'

'I don't have anyone like that.' Liz thought about Paul, and it was painful to do so. 'I was with a long-term partner. But, he... he decided he didn't want to carry on with our fertility journey,' she added.

The doctor nodded.

'It's not uncommon. There can be a lot of pressure on couples to conceive. From family and friends, but people also put a lot of pressure on themselves. And, of course, there's the social pressure to have children, especially for women. You know that we do offer counselling here? I'd be happy to book you in. I don't know if you were ever offered it before?'

'I was. We were. But we never did.' Liz felt the stress of remembering assail her again. Paul had said, that day he'd left her, *I constantly feel like I've... failed. Because I can't give you what you want.*

Perhaps if they'd gone to counselling together, Paul never would have left. But they'd thought they were strong, together. That all they needed was each other.

She knew that she'd been wrong to think that. But it was too late now.

'Do you want to have counselling? I think it might be a good idea.' The doctor gave her a penetrating but kind look. 'You've been through a lot, Liz. Even if you don't go ahead with any more treatments, then it would still be worth talking to someone.'

'Yeah. Okay. I'll think about it.' Liz took the leaflet that the doctor held out and folded it up in her bag.

You know what, Liz, you're not made of steel, she thought to herself. *Maybe accept some help, now and again.*

She found that she didn't entirely hate the idea of talking to someone about everything that had happened on her fertility journey so far. Being a part of the crochet circle had opened Liz up to the fact that talking about your feelings and experiences could be helpful – and that she wasn't the only person in the world that difficult things had happened to. She was a natural loner when it came to dealing with problems, but maybe that wasn't always the best way to be.

She had believed, once, that Paul was all she needed to get through the ups and downs of IVF. Deep down, though, she'd also always believed that the only person she could rely on was herself.

But what if that wasn't true? She had made a new life for herself by moving to Loch Cameron and taking the job at the distillery, yes. From that point of view, she'd relied on herself to make the changes that she needed.

But though the choices had been hers, the new friendships she'd made, the sense of belonging she was starting to have in the Loch Cameron community and even her renewed relation-ship with her body was something that she couldn't have predicted. Liz's life was slowly falling into a new pattern, and many of the new things she took pleasure from were her relationships with others – the crochet coven, chats with Carol on reception, Gretchen's stories, researching the Old Maids. She had merely found these people, and they'd enriched her life so much already. Loch Cameron was forcing Liz to re-evaluate the way she thought about herself, and she found that she liked it.

THIRTY-TWO

'Ah, Miss Parsons. Always a pleasure.' Grenville broke into a dazzling smile as Liz walked into the whisky shop. 'Please excuse me for a moment? I must have a quick word with this lovely young lady.' He bowed to the customers that he had been talking to when Liz came in; she could tell they were tourists from their American accents.

'Hi, Grenville. Business doing well?' she said, as the shop owner enveloped her in a bear hug.

'It certainly is, all thanks to you. These people attended the distillery tour and are very enthusiastic about taking an authentic piece of *auld Scotland* home with them.' Grenville winked, dropping into a broad Scottish accent mid-sentence.

'That's great. One hand washes the other, as they say. Wait, was that a Mafia thing?' Liz shook her head. 'Anyway, you know what I mean.'

'I don't think we're quite the Cosa Nostra of the whisky world just yet, dear, so don't trouble yourself.' Grenville chuckled. 'What can I do for you, anyway? Or is this just a social visit? In which case I'll pop the kettle on.'

'Hmm. Well, I'm happy to stay for a cup of tea, if you're

making one. But it's about Evelyn's diary.' Liz lowered her voice. 'I had some questions about it.'

'Ah, I thought you would. The baby, I expect.' Grenville raised his eyebrow. 'Let me finish up with these customers, and then we'll have a chinwag.' He ushered her to the back of the shop, where there was a small kitchenette. Hastily, Grenville pushed a pile of magazines and catalogues off a threadbare dining chair and motioned for her to sit down. 'You sit here, and I'll be right back, okay?' He flicked the kettle on to boil, and ambled back into the shop, where Liz heard his voice assume its theatrical boom.

A few minutes later, the shopkeeper returned.

'Thanks for waiting. I had an inkling those Americans would be a big sale, and I wasn't wrong. Two bottles of the vintage Loch Cameron, and a case of the ten-year-old. They can't wait for the Old Maids to come out, too.' He reached for a couple of chipped mugs from the shelf in the kitchenette, added in tea bags and poured in the hot water. 'Milk?'

'Yes please.' Liz took the mug Grenville proffered.

'Come and sit in the big chair.' He led her back into the cosy shop front. 'That one'll do your back in. I know, I tried to do my accounts out there last week. Goodness knows why.'

Liz took the leather chair behind Grenville's spacious desk, and Grenville pulled up a low stool.

'Now then,' he began. 'I expect you want to know what happened to Evelyn's baby.'

'Yes. Exactly.' Liz sipped her tea. 'That was such a surprise. Among all her work notes – which are invaluable, by the way – there it was. This heartbreaking story. Completely out of the blue.'

'Hmm. Indeed. My mother told me some of it when Evelyn passed away. I would have been in my twenties by then.' Grenville sighed and picked up his mug. 'A very sad event. I don't know that she ever got over it. Evelyn, I mean.'

'What did she tell you? I mean, Evelyn was buried with a gravestone that said OLD MAID. So I assumed from that that she never had children or got married.'

'Well, you'd be correct. Mother said that Evelyn got pregnant with her baby, but she went away to have it. The family didn't want her to get a reputation, so it was all kept very hush-hush. Of course, my great-great grandfather was also not the kindest of men. He didn't want Evelyn's pregnancy to tarnish the reputation of the family in the village at the time.' Grenville sighed. 'Times were very different then.'

'Okay. So Evelyn had the baby? Where did she go?'

'She went to an aunt that lived in Inverness. Very remote, up there. She had a little cottage in the middle of nowhere. My mother said that she was a skilled midwife, so I suppose she cared for Evelyn in her pregnancy, and helped her with the delivery. But the deal was that Evelyn had to give the baby up. So, she came home alone.'

'What happened to the baby?' Liz felt dread clench her stomach. She had been desperate to know Evelyn's story, but she also knew that it wasn't going to be easy for her to hear.

Yet, she also felt that she owed Evelyn her truth. Someone needed to know what had really happened to Evelyn and her baby, and Liz had the sense that Evelyn herself needed a kind of closure too. Perhaps Liz piecing her story together was one way to give her that.

Even if Liz couldn't give the same closure to herself.

'It was adopted, my mother told me. Local family took her. I know that much, but not a lot else.' Grenville sighed. 'It's sad, because she would have been my cousin. I do think about her often. What we missed out on, not knowing each other.'

'That's terribly sad.' Liz felt the tears in her eyes and blinked them away. 'And Sandy Crowley? Did Evelyn see him any more? They could have got married.'

'She never married. But, dear, I think you need to know that Sandy wasn't the baby's father.'

Liz did a double take.

'Yes, he was. Evelyn was dating him. Those diary entries. She even says something about how she doesn't think it's a sin to have sex outside marriage.' She frowned. 'He must be the father.'

'But he wasn't. That was part of why Evelyn was sent away to have the baby,' Grenville explained. 'Evelyn's baby was John Douglas's. The head of the Loch Cameron Distillery at the time. Ben's ancestor.'

THIRTY-THREE

'What?' Liz was completely floored. 'John Douglas?'

'That's what my mother told me.' Grenville nodded sagely. 'It's been a family secret for years, but I think enough time has passed for us to be able to talk about it.'

'But she never mentioned him once!' Liz protested.

'She does, actually. D. That's her code, I think. Pass me the diary, I'll show you.' Grenville held out his hand, and Liz reached into her bag and passed it to him.

He opened the pages, trailing down a few of them with his finger before pointing at a D in the margin of one entry, then several others.

'Here, see? And here. I think she noted when she saw John. She never wrote about their affair – if that's what it was. But I personally believe that it was less of a torrid affair than, likely, he was taking what he could from her. And they both knew she wouldn't say anything.'

'You mean... he forced her?' Liz was aghast.

'I hope he didn't. But he knew that Evelyn desperately wanted to keep working at the distillery. She was the only one supporting the family during the war and then after her father came home: he clearly wasn't able to work, so she took over. And she did love her work. John Douglas had a reputation as a bit of a bastard. You can ask Simon; his dad had a lot of stories about Old John Douglas that he heard from his father. Apparently he had an eye for the ladies and didn't like to be refused.'

'Oh, no. Poor Evelyn,' Liz breathed, her heart breaking. 'I can't believe it.'

'She told my mother it was John's baby. Apparently, she and Sandy never got quite as far as consummation. But she loved Sandy. You can tell that by the fact that she writes about him. She never writes about John.'

'She could have found Sandy again when she got home. They could have been happy,' Liz said. 'Why didn't she?'

'I don't know. Perhaps he'd moved on already; he was a casual worker, remember. He wouldn't have known why Evelyn disappeared so suddenly, and she would have been away about a year, all in all. Maybe he never came back to Loch Cameron. Or, maybe Evelyn didn't want to pursue it when she got home. She could be forgiven for not wanting to have anything to do with a man again, after that.'

'I can understand that.' Liz sighed, feeling Evelyn's heart-break as her own. It was an awful situation.

'Also, Mother told me that Evelyn always said after that, she felt dirty. Used. Like she was less of a person,' Grenville sighed. 'Even if Sandy had found her again, I don't know that she would have allowed herself to be happy. She was a great lady. But she always had that self-doubt in her. Always stayed in the background. I don't remember her ever talking to a man, not even my father. She was great with us kids, though. I guess we were safe to be around, in her eyes.'

'Poor Evelyn.' A tear rolled down Liz's cheek. 'I wish I could have known her. Helped her, somehow.'

'Indeed. However, she and Mother were always close. I think Evelyn gained some comfort from that, and from us when we came along. I was the youngest – a late baby for Mother. Rather a surprise, from all accounts.' Grenville looked nostalgic. 'Anyway, my brothers and sisters were into their teens when I was born, so Evelyn stepped in again to look after me. She must have been approaching sixty by then but we were very close.'

'I'm happy to hear that. It sounds like she would have made a great mum.'

'Oh, she would have. She was, in a way. A brilliant great-aunt, anyway.'

'D'you think there's any way to trace her daughter? The baby she gave up?' Liz sipped her tea.

'I don't think so. No records were kept that I've been able to find. And, anyway, I think it's better to let sleeping dogs lie.' Grenville sighed. 'That girl would have had a claim to the Douglas estate if she could prove her parentage. I imagine that's why Mr Douglas was so keen for Evelyn to be sent away to have the baby. I don't wonder that some money might have changed hands with Evelyn's family.' He raised an eyebrow. 'I can't prove it, but Mother did tell me that after Evelyn went away, the family moved house from one of the small cottages into the one I live in now. It's much bigger.'

'Wow. Really?'

'Well, I don't know for sure. But it's something of a coincidence, and the family didn't have any money to be moving house before then.'

'Have you ever told Ben any of this?' Liz put her mug down and frowned. If Ben didn't know, then she felt weird that she did.

'No. It seemed better to just let it go. No reason to rock the boat, and he's a nice fellow. I've never seen the point in upsetting him. But, now I've told you, I suppose I have to tell Ben.' Grenville sighed.

'I think he needs to know,' Liz agreed. 'Especially since

we're putting Evelyn front and centre in this new campaign. It's going to be weird if we don't tell him.'

'You're right, of course, Miss Parsons,' Grenville said. 'I should have said something years ago. But you know how places like this are. Well, perhaps you don't,' he corrected himself. 'Anyway, Loch Cameron's full of old family secrets. It's just what happens when the same families have lived somewhere for generations.'

'I know. I'm learning that,' Liz said. 'It's good to unearth the truth, though, isn't it? For Evelyn's sake? I wanted there to be more to her story – and the rest of the women – than just two words on a gravestone.'

'Well, there's certainly a story there,' Grenville said with another sigh. 'The problem with unearthing stories, though, is that sometimes you realise they were better off forgotten. Especially if unravelling one story leads to others that nobody wants to remember.'

'Do you think that's what we're doing?' Liz had a moment of doubt. Was it right to air out Evelyn's dirty laundry in public? Would Evelyn have been mortified to know what happened to her, all those years ago? And what good would it do to Ben to know that his ancestor had treated one of his female employees with such disrespect?

But the truth is important, said a voice in her head. *What happened to Evelyn wasn't fair, and I owe it to her to set the record straight. Even if that just means a conversation with Ben Douglas.*

'Maybe. But I trust your judgement, dear.' Grenville took her hand. 'And I owed you a favour, too. You've given me and this little shop a new lease of life since you've been here. And, I loved Evelyn. We should do right by her.'

'All right. In which case, we need to talk to Ben as soon as possible.' Liz sighed. 'I don't know how he's going to take it.'

'He might surprise you, dear.' Grenville looked thoughtful.

'That young man's seen his share of problems. I trust *him* to do the right thing, too.'

I wouldn't say that I do, Liz thought, frowning. If Ben's previous performance leaving his pregnant wife when she needed him most was anything to go by, then he couldn't be trusted at all. But it had to be done.

THIRTY-FOUR

'Ben? Can I have a word with you?' Liz peeked into Ben's office. He was striding around the office, on the phone to someone. 'I'll come back,' she mouthed, but he shook his head and pointed to the seat in front of his desk.

Liz sat, watching him pace. He was listening to whoever was on the other end of the call, and it clearly wasn't a pleasurable experience. His brow was furrowed and a palpable sense of tension sat in the room, like smoke.

'All right. I've got to go. Bye.' He ended the call abruptly. Liz waited for him to speak.

Ben returned to his desk, opened a drawer and took out a bottle of whisky.

'Too early?' He held out the bottle to Liz.

'It's lunchtime.' She watched as he unscrewed the lid. 'Not for me, but you go ahead.'

'Right.' Ben took a crystal tumbler from a tray on the side cabinet and poured himself a generous measure, then gulped it down in one go.

'Stressful call, I take it.' Liz watched him with some alarm.

Was this a regular occurrence? If it was, it might explain Ben's less than optimal leadership of the company over the past years.

'You could say that,' he muttered.

'Um, look. This clearly isn't a good time, so I'll come back later. Maybe tomorrow.' Liz got up. She'd been planning to talk to Ben about Evelyn McCallister's story, but it was something she really had to catch Ben in a good mood for. Neat whisky at 11.45am didn't scream *good mood* to her.

'No. Stay,' he said, abruptly. 'What was it you wanted? We don't have a meeting, do we?'

'No. It was something else. But it's not urgent.' Liz got up to go. 'Really. I'll catch you later.'

'Liz. Please.' There was a sudden, desperate tone in his voice that made her look up in surprise. 'I mean...' He looked away from her, down at his hands holding the glass. 'I could do with some distraction. I'm okay. Please, stay.'

'Well, it's really fine, but... all right.' Liz had mixed feelings, but she had come in to tell Ben about Evelyn, and it was better to tell him sooner rather than later. 'Is it work-related? The call.'

'No,' he said, shortly. 'Personal.'

'Oh.' He clearly wasn't going to say any more, and Liz wasn't going to press him. She took a deep breath. 'All right, then. I had a chat to Grenville recently, and he told me something about Evelyn McCallister I thought you should know.'

'What?'

'Well, there's no easy way to say it. But, if you recall, she was Tommy McCallister's daughter, and she took on the role of Master Distiller for a few years. Unofficially, by the way, she probably did it for about fifteen years.'

'Right. I remember.'

'Yeah. And if you recall, in the diary she says basically that she's fallen pregnant?'

'I remember.'

'Agh. I really hate to tell you this, but if what Grenville told me is true, then it was John Douglas – that's your ancestor – who was the father of the baby she had.'

'What?' Ben frowned.

'He says it's true. Apparently his mother told him. It's something they kept within the family. He never told you because he didn't want it to come between you as friends. But I guess with us making a big focus on Evelyn now, he had to say something.'

'But he told you and not me.' Ben got up again and started pacing around.

'I know. But that was because I read the diary and went to speak with him about it. He did say that there was information in there he thought you'd be interested in. I just thought he meant general history of the distillery. But this is what he meant, I think.'

'This is kind of a bombshell.' Ben swore under his breath. 'Sorry. It's just...' He shook his head.

'I know. I'm sorry.' Liz watched him as he circled the office.

'So you're saying... they were having an affair?' Ben frowned, sitting on the edge of his desk and facing her.

'Not exactly. Well, we can't know. But Grenville says that Evelyn told her sister – that was his mother – that it wasn't a consensual relationship.' Liz bit her lip, hoping that she didn't have to explain further.

'Not consensual? What does that mean?'

'You know what that means, Ben.' Liz gave him a resigned look.

'Oh, god.' Ben put his hand over his mouth, his eyes wide. 'You mean he—'

'It seems that way, yes,' Liz said, interrupting him so that he didn't have to say the words.

'Oh, no.' Ben looked shocked. 'So...'

'So, she had the baby, but it was adopted,' Liz said. 'That does mean that, somewhere, there's someone else who has some claim on the Douglas estate. But they probably have no idea that they do.'

'Jeez. This is a lot to take in.' Ben stared at her. 'So, that would be, like... I'd have a half aunt or uncle somewhere? Kind of?'

'Kind of, yes. Your ancestor's illegitimate son or daughter. They might not be alive anymore, of course. But they might also have had children. And you'd be related to them still.'

'Wow. That's intense.'

'Yeah.' Liz nodded. 'I'm sorry to be the bearer of bad news, but as soon as Grenville told me, I had to tell you.'

'Of course. I'm glad you did.' Ben took in a deep breath and let it go. 'It's more troubling to think about what happened to Evelyn at that man's hands, though, to be honest. That poor girl.'

'I know. It's terribly sad. But Grenville says that he remembers her as a fantastic aunt to him.'

'That's good,' Ben sighed. 'My dad was a difficult man. I never knew my grandfather or anyone else before him, obviously, but there were stories about the Douglas men. Not about things like that, but some of them were cruel. My dad told me once that his father beat a maid in front of everyone with his riding crop for spilling his cup of tea by accident. He broke her arm.'

'Oh, my goodness. That's terrible.' Liz was honestly shocked.

'Yeah. But the thing was, my dad told me that story as a kind of amusing anecdote. He wasn't that horrified by it. He just said, that's how you teach the lower orders respect. He even laughed about it.' Ben shook his head in shame. 'That's what I come from. Someone who uses the phrase "the lower orders". Someone who genuinely believed he was better than other people, just because he had the luck to be born into having money and a nice house. And I hate it. I hated him.'

Liz didn't know what to say.

'I'm sorry, Ben. That must have been awful,' she said, levelly. She was wondering, though, if Evelyn's story was making Ben reflect on his own experience with Alice. What did he think, hearing this? Was he making some kind of connection to his own actions? Liz couldn't imagine that it didn't make him think of Alice, and she wondered if he was reflecting on his connection to that strain of cruelty that seemed to run through the Douglas family.

'It was not great, no,' Ben said, shortly. 'But it means that, sadly, I believe Evelyn's story.'

'Yeah.' Liz nodded. 'Me too.'

'So, what does this mean for Old Maids?' Ben asked.

'Nothing, really. I mean, I think we should still feature Evelyn. It would be awful not to. But we don't have to share this piece of her story, in terms of your family, anyway. That's personal, to you and Grenville and Evelyn.'

'Agreed. I'd prefer not to do that.'

'Right. But Evelyn's story is still important.'

'Yes. It is.' Ben tilted his head back and looked at the ceiling, letting out a long sigh. 'Ugh. This morning is not a great one, so far. I feel like I need another whisky.'

'Don't stop on my account.' Liz met his eyes without a smile. She was still unsure how to be around him, knowing what she knew about his past. Yet, when they were together, Ben was nothing but good company. 'What's up?'

'Oh. Nothing. Personal stuff.' He shook his head.

'Coffee, instead? Let's go and get one from the kitchen.'

'All right.'

What personal stuff? Liz wondered. As far as she was aware, Ben wasn't seeing anyone – not that it was any of her business.

Perhaps Ben's got someone squirrelled away somewhere. A secret relationship. Maybe a married woman, she thought,

following him out of the office and into reception, where Carol
was on the phone at her desk. Maybe he did have a dark side
that was just very well hidden. That would explain how he
could be so charming and nice to her, but also have done such
terrible things in the past.

Hmm.

It wasn't something she should be thinking about now, at
work. It was pure conjecture on her part, but Liz wondered, just
the same. What was it that made Ben disappear all the time in
the working day?

'Listen, as another thing, I had another thought about the
Old Maids,' she said, waving at Carol, and watching as Ben
went to the cupboard to get two mugs, and then started the
gleaming coffee machine.

'What thought?' he said over his shoulder as he poured
coffee beans into the grinder and flicked a switch.

'Well, you know that we had trouble coming up with much
history for Felicity Black,' Liz began. Felicity had been the hardest
Old Maid to research, and most of what Liz had for her was based
on generic information about female weavers of their time and not
Felicity herself. 'I've been worried about presenting inauthentic
information for her. The other women, we have those compre-
hensive, personal stories for. You know? She doesn't quite fit.'

'Hmm. I see what you mean, yes.' Ben got some milk from
the fridge and poured it into the milk frother. 'I have to say, by
the way, that I've been a bit worried about Evelyn McCallister,
too. I had a chat with Grenville about it. He seems very sure
that my great-grandfather... or my great-great grandfather – I
can't remember which one it was – forced himself on her.'

'Hmm. That's what he said to me, too.' Liz watched Ben's
face, trying to read his emotions, but he was obviously keeping
his feelings purposefully under control.

'It's... difficult.' Ben frothed the milk, keeping his gaze

studiously away from hers. 'Awkward, you know? I want to commemorate Evelyn as much as you do. More, in a way, because I know that it's my relative that treated her so badly. But... if the information got out, it wouldn't look good for the distillery. That's my worry.'

'I can understand that.' Liz thought about it for a moment. 'But I don't think Grenville would want that part of Evelyn's history shared, either. He told us because he trusts us. So I think we keep it between ourselves, and we celebrate Evelyn's achievements as Master Distiller. That's the best thing we can do for her.'

'Hmm. You're right, I know. I just feel terrible about it. As if my ancestors weren't crappy enough, you know? Now I know that one of them was a rapist.'

'It's not great,' Liz admitted. 'But it's not your fault. We can't control what our ancestors did. All we can do is try and make the best of it from where we stand.'

'Hmm.' Ben flicked the dials on the coffee maker; it hissed. 'So, what's your solution about Felicity?'

'Well, I thought we could swap her for Gretchen Ross.' Liz stood next to Ben at the kitchen counter and folded her arms over her chest. 'What d'you think?'

'Gretchen Ross? The Gretchen Ross that's still alive?' Ben frowned. 'Doesn't that mess up the whole concept?'

'Not really. Gretchen is an Old Maid. In fact, she's proud of it. I actually like the idea of having someone still living be a part of the selection. That way, we capture a selection of local women from Loch Cameron across a longer time period, bringing us into the present day. And Gretchen's got some amazing stories.'

'Oh, I know. She's such a character.' Ben smiled, looking thoughtful. 'But haven't you already got the labels and boxes on the way? They're done already.'

'No, they're still with the designer. I can make changes, and we can still change the sales information for the ordering.'

'Hmm. And you really like this idea? What does Gretchen think? Have you mentioned it to her?'

'No, I haven't. She gave me the idea, though she was only joking. I think she'd like it, though.'

'Well, I'm not opposed to the idea, if Gretchen's okay with it. So, why don't you ask her, and see what she says?'

'Okay. That would be great. Thanks, Ben.' Liz took the mug of coffee that he handed her and took a sip. It was strong and chocolatey, and just the right level of bitter. 'Wow. That's good.'

'I do make a mean cup of coffee. I like to think that's as much mean as I have in me, though. Not like the rest of the Douglases,' he said, seriously, as he sipped his. 'I don't want you to think that I inherited... all that toxic stuff from the men in my family. Everything we were talking about,' he said, giving her a serious look. 'I've worked really hard to try and let go of all of that, you know? It's been hard, but...' He trailed off. 'Sorry. I don't know why I'm telling you all this. Just ignore me.'

Liz was about to reply when Carol bustled in.

'Now then, I see nobody asked me whether I wanted a coffee, aye,' she teased, tapping Ben affectionately on the arm and reaching up to the cupboard to get a mug out. 'Ach, if ye want anythin' done, do it yerself, eh.'

'Sorry, Carol. I would have made you one, but you were on the phone,' Ben protested.

'Ach, away with ye. I'm only pullin' yer leg.' Carol beamed at them both. 'What's up wi' ye both? Ye look like ye lost a pound an' found a shillin'.'

'We're fine. Just the Old Maids stuff. The big conference is coming up,' Liz filled in, quickly. 'Anyway, I've got a lot to do. I'll see you both later.' She shot a smile at Carol, and avoided Ben's eyes as she left.

It seemed that Ben had wanted to open up to her; that he

was keen to tell Liz that he wasn't the bastard that some of the men in his family had been. But how could she square that with what she knew about Ben and Alice, his ex-wife? Surely Ben could see that he'd done a terrible thing to his wife. If that was true, he wasn't so different to the other Douglas men, and Liz wasn't going to help him pretend that he was.

Liz just couldn't balance the two Bens: the one she knew, and the one Simon had described. That version of Ben didn't tally at all with the one who took her to see starlings swoop across the evening skies or the one who knew the names of all the local plants, and seemed to want only the best for her. But Simon had no reason to lie – did he? He'd seemed genuine when he'd told her about Ben's past. Sure, the two men didn't see eye to eye about the running of the distillery, but that was no reason to concoct such an elaborate lie, if it was one.

It bothered Liz. Plus, there was this nagging thought in her mind, now, that Ben might be having some kind of illicit relationship with someone. Not that it was any of her business, of course.

How could he be two such different people?

THIRTY-FIVE

'Hallo, dear. I didn't expect to see you today.' Gretchen looked up from her bed and gave Liz a weak smile. 'How are you?'

'Oh, Gretchen! Never mind how I am. What happened?' As soon as she'd walked into Gretchen's room, Liz knew that something was wrong. For one thing, Gretchen was never in bed in the daytime, as far as she knew; when she'd visited before, her friend had been in the lounge, and whenever they'd spoken on the phone, Gretchen always seemed to be running between bridge games, canasta competitions and the beauty salon.

'Ah. A bit of angina, that's all.' Gretchen coughed, and Liz went to her and reached for her hand. She looked so small, tucked into her bed. 'Don't worry, please. I can't stand the fuss.'

'Angina? That's your heart, isn't it?' Liz sat in the chair next to Gretchen's bed. 'Have you had it long?'

'A few years. Yes, my heart. I'm in my mid-eighties. It's just what happens.' Gretchen patted Liz's hand. 'I told you: don't get old. Stay thirty-seven forever. That's my advice.'

'What does the doctor say?' Liz asked, squeezing Gretchen's hand very gently.

'Oh, doctor, schmoctor. He can't tell me anything. Just to rest and take my medicine.' She rolled her eyes. 'You know, these GPs look everything up on the internet. He's about fourteen. They make anyone doctors these days.'

'I don't think that's true, Gretchen.' Liz smiled, relieved that Gretchen seemed her usual self, although she was plainly weaker than she would have liked. 'He's just trying to look after you.'

'Hmph. A stiff whisky would look after me much better,' Gretchen complained. 'You haven't got any, have you? Sneak me in some next time you come. They wouldn't suspect you. Though I wouldn't put it past the nurses to frisk you on your way in. They're no fun.'

'I will if it's allowed, but not if it would make you more poorly,' Liz offered. 'I don't have any on me, though.'

'Eh. It was worth a try.' Gretchen closed her eyes for a few moments, coughing again. 'You'll have to forgive me, dear. The angina makes me very tired.'

'That's all right. Please don't apologise. I'm just sorry you're not well.' Liz looked around at Gretchen's cosy room. A vase of tulips stood on the table by her bed, and a couple of packets of biscuits accompanied a fruit basket next to it.

'They're from Alun. Help yourself. I can't abide bananas.' Gretchen sniffed.

'Aww. That's nice of him.' Liz remembered Alun from when she'd visited the care home before. He'd been the one that had offered her his hanky when she'd cried. She took a banana.

'Yes, he's kind.' Gretchen smiled faintly. 'Now. What can I do for you? Something about the cottage? Is everything all right there?' She sat up a little and reached for an extra pillow that lay at the foot of the bed. 'Prop me up a little, would you, dear? There. That's better.'

'No, the cottage is lovely.' Liz peeled the banana and bit the top off. 'I was actually coming to ask a favour for the distillery.'

'Oh? What?'

'Well, you remember that you helped me do some research, up at the castle? For the Old Maids?' Liz asked.

'Of course I do. I'm not senile.'

'Ha. No, you're definitely not,' Liz chuckled. 'Well, the thing is, you might remember that we couldn't find out an awful lot about Felicity Black. She was the weaver, if you recall.'

'Hmm. Yes, I remember. A shame, because that was a very interesting profession.'

'Yeah. Well, I thought it would actually be nice to have someone in the range that was a modern woman, and someone who had lived in Loch Cameron most of her life, but also technically an Old Maid. And I couldn't really put myself in the range. So, I wondered if you wanted to be the fourth woman?'

'What do you mean, dear? I don't understand. You want me to be one of your Old Maids?' Gretchen frowned. 'For the whisky?'

'Yes. I mean, you know we settled on Old Maids as a name for the range, but we're very much about reclaiming the term. I don't want there to be negative associations with it. I'm not being mean to you, or anything. I want to celebrate your life. As a career woman, a single mum by choice, someone who adopted a daughter. Everything you did and everything you are.'

'Oh, Liz.' A tear rolled down Gretchen's cheek. 'That is so kind. I honestly don't know what to say, apart from I mustn't seem like a very strong woman to you just now.'

'As if you could ever not be amazing, Gretchen. You're a force of nature. I'm inspired by you,' Liz said, honestly. 'And I want the world to know about you.'

'Oh, you're being kind. I hate that.' Gretchen cry-laughed. 'Look at me. I'm a mess.' Liz handed her a tissue, and Gretchen blew her nose. 'Of course you can have me in the Old Maids. If you really want me. I'd be honoured.'

'Oh, I'm so happy! Thanks, Gretchen. This is going to be

awesome.' Liz leaned over and kissed her friend on the cheek. 'Listen. When you're feeling a little better, I'm going to get some label designs over to you. And some copy. You can let me know what you're willing to share, about your life. I was wondering if you had some old pictures of you we could use on the packaging. Maybe in the 80s? Or now?'

'Look over there, on the shelf. Above the novels. There are my photo albums.' Gretchen pointed to a cabinet on the other side of the room. 'Take them out. Yes, those.' She nodded as Liz got up and went to where Gretchen had indicated. 'Bring them over here,' she added, and Liz carried a number of the white leather-covered albums over to Gretchen's bed.

'We can do this another time, Gretchen,' Liz said, setting the photo albums down gently on Gretchen's thick quilt. 'It's no trouble.'

'No, let's do it now. Strike while the iron is hot, as they say.' Gretchen waved at the albums. 'Look at that one on top. There are some pictures of me when I worked in publishing. Shoulder pads and hairspray.' She smiled, weakly.

'Oh, wow. These are amazing.' Liz opened the album and was instantly plunged into a world of Gretchen in a series of 80s power dresses and suits.

'That's me with Salman Rushdie.' Gretchen reached across and tapped the page. 'That's Danielle Steele. Oh, and that's Shirley Conran. You probably don't remember that name. But she was huge in the 80s.'

'Wow. Gretchen, look at you with all these celebrities!' Liz turned the pages, smiling. 'Oh, look. I love this. You in your office.' Liz peered at the slightly faded picture of a coiffured Gretchen with shiny red nails wearing a white double breasted power suit. In the picture, she was sitting at a wooden desk in an office with appalling orange and brown wallpaper and a huge vase of white flowers next to her.

'Ah, that's a good one. And there's one of me with Andrew,

my secretary.' Gretchen pointed to the next picture, clearly taken on the same day, because Gretchen was wearing the same outfit. In this picture, she stood somewhat stiffly next to a very good looking young man in his twenties who wore a pink shirt and an orange tie.

'I remember you telling me about him. Are you still in touch?' Liz smiled at the picture. 'I really love this one of you at your desk.'

'No, we lost touch. A shame. He was a lovely boy.' Gretchen coughed a little. 'I think he ended up living abroad. You can take that one, if you want. Use it.'

'Well, I don't want to deprive you of the original. Let me take a picture of it,' Liz said, getting out her phone. She took some close-up shots of the original.

'Would you like to see Stella? My daughter?' Gretchen turned a few pages and pointed to a very different picture. 'Here she is.'

In this picture, Gretchen was cuddling a little girl who might have been five or six. She had black, curly hair and dark skin, wearing a blue flowered dress. In the picture, Gretchen wasn't in her formal work wear, but had a scarf tied around her hair and wore blue jeans and a plain white T-shirt. She and Stella were laughing at something and looking into each other's eyes with what looked like a profound sense of joy.

'Oh, Gretchen. What a lovely picture,' Liz breathed. It was almost exactly the picture she had always imagined in her mind when she had visualised having a child, if she had been in Gretchen's place. The same moment of joy, caught unawares. The same togetherness that Liz had always yearned for.

She felt a lump in her throat and looked away as her throat tightened. 'I'm sorry. That's... It's just such a lovely picture,' she said, unable to explain what it reminded her of. That same, glittering, lit-up imaginary picture of herself and her child that she'd thought of, like a prize to be won in the fertility game show she'd tried so hard to keep up with.

'I still can't look at these without crying either.' Gretchen touched Stella's little face in the picture with so much tenderness that Liz thought she might bawl. 'I still miss her. I always will. But it's funny, how I miss her most from when she was this age. And, even when she was alive, she hadn't been six for a long time.'

'She was so beautiful.' Liz looked at the little girl in the photograph.

'Yes, she was.' Gretchen smiled sadly. 'She was so sweet. When they're little, they're so innocent. It's hard to describe. But such a blessing to have experienced.'

'I can imagine,' Liz said, quietly. 'Can I take a picture of this one, too? I'd love to use them both, if that was all right with you.'

'Yes. That's all right.' Gretchen blew her nose and let Liz take the shot on her phone. 'It was a very happy time. And I don't think Stella would mind.'

'Thank you, Gretchen.' Liz closed the album and gave her friend a gentle hug. 'It really means a lot that you're willing to share her memory with us.'

'You know, since I had a child, that doesn't technically mean I am an Old Maid.' Gretchen wiped a tear from her eye. 'Have you thought about that?'

'I know. But you never married, and you're a shining example of an independent woman who lived by her own rules,' Liz said. 'So, from that point of view, you fit. Is that okay with you?'

'Of course it's okay. I'm absolutely honoured, as I said.' Gretchen nodded. 'Come on. I think this calls for a celebratory chocolate.' She reached down to the other side of her bed slowly, and brought up a large box of chocolates that were still unopened. 'Here. Get these open. I rather fancy something naughty.'

'Alun again?' Liz grinned as she tore the cellophane off the box. 'And are you supposed to be eating chocolates?'

'A few won't kill me, dear.' Gretchen winked. 'And, no. Not Alun. These were from Mike.'

'Mike? Who is *Mike*?' Liz laughed.

'He's new.' Gretchen smiled back, and took a coffee cream. 'Oh, lovely. My favourite.'

THIRTY-SIX

Liz had been to more than her share of conferences in her life, but she was dreading going to the National Beverages Conference this year.

For one thing, it was still a little awkward with Ben. Liz knew that he'd been struggling with the ramifications of Evelyn's story, and she understood why. In a way, it was good that he was uncomfortable with it. If he wasn't, Liz thought that she'd worry more. Ben's horror at what his ancestor had done to Evelyn was a normal reaction. He'd also agreed that they should add in Gretchen as the fourth Old Maid, which Liz had been scrambling to put into effect before the conference.

Liz was glad that Ben hadn't asked her to take Evelyn out of the Old Maids range; she hadn't presented him with that option, but of course he would have been perfectly within his rights to do so. Ben was the CEO: ultimately, he was in charge of everything.

But Ben hadn't said that, and by keeping Evelyn in the Old Maids range Liz felt that it was a way for the distillery to make reparations to Evelyn – or, to her memory at least.

Still, there was a certain uncomfortable-ness about the fact that Liz and Ben now both knew that John Douglas had forced himself upon Evelyn. Liz had also wondered whether Evelyn had been the only one – she hadn't mentioned it to Ben, but she thought it had probably occurred to him too. John Douglas was clearly not a good man, and neither was Ben's father, Jim. Liz wondered what it must have been like to grow up in their shadows.

Even before Liz had found out about the whole Evelyn story, she had been finding it increasingly awkward around Ben. Even though she'd told herself a thousand times that Ben's personal life was none of her business, and neither was his past, she couldn't help thinking about it. It was so personal to her: that was the problem. What Ben had done to Alice was like a worse version of what had happened between her and Paul.

Arriving at the hotel the night before, Liz had steeled herself for two solid days of nonstop networking. Networking wasn't something she usually disliked: with a career in sales behind her, she was used to making nice with people she wouldn't necessarily have chosen to socialise with in her private life. That was a necessary evil, and quite often it turned out to be a perk of the job. Sometimes, she did meet interesting people, and sometimes, they even turned into friends.

Usually, she looked forward to the conference. It was a place to catch up with everyone, gossip and see what was happening with the industry at large. Plus, there was always a nice formal dinner on the second night, and many a year, Liz had found herself dancing on the tables in the bar into the early hours afterwards.

This year, though, she wouldn't be dancing on the tables. She was delivering one of the main presentations, for one thing, thanks to the organiser and her old friend Nigel agreeing to her proposal to do a soft launch of the Old Maids range as part of it. So, she wasn't going to drink, or stay up late. She'd be practising her delivery in her hotel room with a healthy dinner and a bottle of mineral water. Secondly, she really didn't feel up to her usual level of jolly sociability, and it wasn't just because of Ben Douglas and the Evelyn McCallister situation.

Last year, even though she'd been part way through a fertility cycle, she had pushed herself to be the sparkling, lovely Liz everyone expected to see at the conference. Despite the fact she was feeling awful with morning sickness, despite the fact that she had recently conceived as part of the fertility cycle and should have been taking it easy, she had gone to the dinner, stayed up late and made sure she spoke to everyone she wanted to. She had made new relationships, established new leads and made everyone believe she was at the top of her game.

Liz had been at the top of her game. But it came with a heavy cost. The night after she had got back from the conference, she had miscarried.

Paul had held her as she'd sobbed her heart out, that night. And she knew, in her heart, that was the night that Paul had decided to walk away from their relationship.

He hadn't done it then, of course. He had done everything he could to reassure Liz that what had happened hadn't been her fault. That the miscarriage was outside of anyone's control. But she knew it had been her fault. It was her defective body that hadn't been able to carry the baby. Her messed up insides. Her lack of ability to mother, to nurture, somehow.

Liz judged herself for staying up late that last time at the conference. She should have gone to bed earlier. She shouldn't have attended all the presentations, or stood on her feet for so long, making new leads and establishing new sales relationships. She should have stayed home. Maybe she should have given up her job altogether, just like Paul suggested.

Later, when she'd had a chance to start recovering from the miscarriage and the stress it brought, she had started to accept that the miscarriage wasn't her fault. It was just bad timing with the conference, and, even more sadly, it wasn't the only miscarriage she'd had. That was why she had been undertaking the fertility treatment in the first place, after all. Because her body needed help.

She had forgiven herself at least a little, though there was still a way to go for Liz in feeling any sense of peace with her fertility journey so far. But, as she had arrived with Ben in the taxi at the same London hotel that the conference was always held at, she had felt like throwing up.

Being at the same hotel as the year before, knowing what had happened just after, made her feel like curling into a ball and crying.

Liz had got to her room with a degree of relief, saying hello to the people she knew as she made her way through the lobby but not stopping to chat. She was also stressing about whether to take the next step at the fertility clinic. She'd been back and forth, in her mind – part of her wanted to try again, and thought that a sperm donor wasn't such a bad idea.

But there was a large part of Liz that wasn't sure about the sperm donor route. It wasn't so much that she was scared of being a single parent: Gretchen had done it, she thought to herself again, which was inspiring, and she knew that women – and men – did it all the time. It was more that Liz just didn't know whether to try again for a baby at all, or to draw a line under her fertility journey completely and call it a day. Whatever she did, though, she knew she was in control, and that felt good.

Her and Ben's presentation was the next morning, and she wanted to stay relatively closeted until then, making sure she was happy with what she was going to say, and feeling as confident as possible.

Confidence is an interesting concept, she thought, as she adjusted the font on the presentation slides. She knew how to project an image of confidence. And she was confident in the

Old Maids. It was something that had become very close to her heart.

But, inside, she was a mess. She wouldn't let it show, tomorrow. Or for any of the time she and Ben were at the conference. But this whole time was going to be an endurance test, not least because she had to keep everything hidden from Ben, too, who was booked in the seat next to her on the flight back and had flown down with her.

A knock on her door distracted her from her thoughts. She went to the spyhole and looked out: Ben stood on the other side. She sighed, and opened the door.

'Hi, Ben. I'm just finishing up on those last notes we talked about,' she said, hoping her voice didn't betray her weariness.

'Oh, right. Well I thought I'd come and escort you down to dinner.' He held out his arm in a mock-gentlemanly way. 'You must be hungry.'

'Oh, I'm just going to have something in my room,' she demurred. 'You go. I'll see you at breakfast.'

'Oh. But everyone will be there.' Ben looked surprised. 'You've been really quiet all day. Are you all right? Not worried about tomorrow?'

'No. I've presented here before,' she said, which wasn't a lie. She was confident in the presentation. It was just the being here at all which was difficult.

'You're not hungry, then?' He frowned.

'Not very.' Liz gave him a wan smile. 'Anyway. Better get back to it.' She went to close the door, but he rested his hand gently on it.

'Liz. What's wrong? Please tell me. Is it the job? Is it me? Have I done something wrong? Because I'll fix it. Whatever it is.'

'There's nothing for you to fix,' Liz said, tiredly. She was tired of feeling awful about her past. She was tired of thinking about it, remembering it. The dread that she had felt when she had approached the hotel in the taxi had almost floored her; it had been all she could do to keep a normal expression and not start sobbing. 'Just go to dinner without me.'

'I don't want to. I don't know anyone, really. I was looking forward to you going with me. So you could introduce me to everyone.' He gave her a shy smile. 'That's one of the perks of having employed one of the top Sales Directors in the industry, after all.'

'Well, I'm sorry you won't be getting your money's worth,' Liz snapped. 'Anyway, won't you need to disappear during dinner? You've hardly been around recently. I wouldn't want to cramp your style, whatever it is you go off to do. Golf, or whatever. You clearly don't care about whether we're successful here or not.'

As soon as she'd said it, she regretted it, but the words hung between them in the air like a curse.

'Liz. Is that what you think?' Ben looked devastated.

'It's none of my business what you do, Ben. But you asked me to come on board and help you rebuild the company. That's what I'm doing; it's what I've done, and I've had to do it almost single-handed, because you keep disappearing on me. It's fine if you don't want to be CEO. But be straight with me. Be straight with all of us. Because at the moment, we don't know what's happening, and it's not fair,' she said, angrily. She'd been wanting to say something about Ben's disappearances for weeks, but she'd been too polite to do so.

However, now, she'd lost her temper, and all bets were off. Being here, at the same hotel where she'd miscarried her baby, was affecting her more than she'd realised it would.

'That's not what's going on,' Ben protested.

'Well, what is it, then?'

'I can't.' He looked away. 'Please believe me. I'd like to, but I can't.'

'Oh, how convenient.' She rolled her eyes.

'No. Actually it's not convenient at all,' he argued. 'But... sure. I'll see you tomorrow. Let's have time to cool down, and we can refocus on the presentation tomorrow.' He turned away, then turned back towards the door, obviously having something else to say.

'What?' she demanded, desperately trying to stay composed. She could feel herself breaking down rapidly, and if she didn't close the door soon, she was going to dissolve into a puddle.

'I don't know what's going on here. But if this is because of some gossip you've heard about me...' He trailed off. 'You shouldn't listen to it, if so.'

Liz stared at Ben, not quite believing the words that were coming out of his mouth.

'What? Are you kidding me?' she yelled, anger finally coming to her aid. She'd read somewhere once that anger was the protector of hurt, and she understood that now. Liz was hurting badly, but she was almost grateful for the surge of anger that overtook her now because it could be the thing that protected her when she most needed it.

Ben took a step back, obviously surprised at her sudden shout.

'All right. I guess it isn't.' He looked shocked.

'No. It isn't.' Liz's voice was staccato. 'If you must know, since this is so important to you and you can't just leave it alone and leave me alone: Being here, at the hotel, is really hard for me. Okay? because last year, when I came, I got home and I had a miscarriage.' Her voice wavered on the last few words; it was difficult to say them. 'So, no. I don't give a toss about you and whatever random gossip I may or may not have heard about you. And the very fact that you think I would be upset about that as opposed to something real and important, like the loss of an actual life, just shows me exactly what kind of man you are.'

Liz tried to slam the door, but Ben strode through it and closed it from the inside.

'I'm not leaving after you've said that. Liz, listen to me. I'm so sorry.' He looked terrified, but Liz's anger was in full swing. She didn't want to stop being angry, because she knew that sadness waited for her like a nightmare, like a monster, threatening in the darkness.

'No. Go away,' she yelled, but she could feel the sadness coming, and there was nothing she could do to stop it. 'Please. I can't...'

'Oh, Liz.' Ben wrapped her in his arms and held her more tightly than she thought she'd ever been held. 'Liz. I'm so sorry.'

She cried then: big, screaming gulps of pain that felt like they swallowed all the air in the room. This was the type of behaviour that Paul might have found *too much*, perhaps; Liz rarely showed her emotions, but when she did, they could be stormy.

But rather than leave her, Ben held her and didn't let go.

Liz sobbed her heart out. She felt herself letting go of all the hurt she had held onto for all this time. It was like every single terrible analogy she'd ever heard of: the floodgates opening, water crashing through a dam, tsunamis, waves crashing onto beaches. But it was true. There was a relief in letting go of her emotions, finally, at last, in the safety of Ben's arms. She knew, because he'd told her, that Ben didn't think she was too much. He admired her strength, and she was grateful for that.

After some moments, her breathing started to slow, and she could feel her body relaxing. Instinctively, she leaned into him. There was something indescribable about his physical presence – something so soothing. Familiar, even, though they were only work colleagues.

Ben handed her a tissue from his pocket, but his grip around her stayed firm.

'Thank you,' she sniffled, wiping her eyes. 'I'm sorry.'

'Don't apologise,' Ben murmured, his voice resonating in his chest, where her head still rested. 'I'm just glad I was here for you. I can't imagine what you must have gone through, and I'm so sorry.'

She frowned, thinking of what Simon had told her about Ben's ex-wife. It just didn't make sense that Ben would turn his own pregnant wife out on her ear and be so sweet to Liz about her failed pregnancy. Okay, she wasn't his wife. Maybe it was different.

She had a sudden thought. Was Ben faking all this sympathy? Maybe he was just being polite because he wanted to keep Liz sweet ahead of the big presentation tomorrow. It was important for the company, after all.

'Ben. I don't understand you.' She untangled herself from his embrace. 'How can you be like this with me? When you left your own wife when she was pregnant? Don't you understand what a vulnerable time it is for a woman? I just...' She shook her head. 'If you're comforting me because you're worried I'll crack up at the presentation, you don't have to. I'm a pro, okay? You can save your pretences.' She went to the hotel door and held it open.

Ben stared at her for a long moment.

'If that's really what you think of me, then you don't deserve an explanation. I'll see you in the conference room tomorrow,' he said, coldly, as he walked out. 'Don't worry. I'm a professional too.'

He slammed the hotel door behind him, and Liz heard him stalk off down the corridor.

She rested her head against the door, her heart heavy.

Why did she feel like she'd just made a terrible mistake?

THIRTY-SEVEN

'According to a recent study, about forty percent of whisky drinkers are women.' Liz began her presentation to the room of hundreds of representatives of the beverage industry: boutique gin makers, sales reps, master whisky distillers, master tasters, journalists for food and drink magazines and buyers for all of the big chains looked at her expectantly from the floor.

'For a long time, it was considered taboo for women to consume alcohol at all, but we've come a long way from those rather... limiting views,' she added, smiling, and was relieved to hear a few chuckles from the audience. 'Marketing efforts are no longer just focused on men, and that's something we're really running with at Loch Cameron Distillery. Women hold the purchasing power; we are the ones driving the whisky category, and that's what's inspired our new range: Old Maids.'

Liz clicked onto the slide that showcased the new range of whiskies. She was so happy with the way that the design for the new labels, boxes and bottles had worked out: they looked fantastic. The designer had managed to change Felicity Black over to Gretchen Ross without too much effort, also.

'Muriel Peabody, Elspeth Anderson, Gretchen Ross and

Evelyn McCallister.' She read the now-familiar names aloud, winking at Gretchen who sat in the first row. 'Four women that have been integral to Loch Cameron's present and past.'

Ben had suggested they invite Gretchen to the conference. Liz hadn't been sure that Gretchen would be able to come, but her friend had informed her that she would be there with bells on. In fact, her grandson had come with her, and Ben had sent a car to ferry them there and back to Gretchen's retirement home. Liz suspected that Gretchen was loving the opportunity to see her long-lost grandson again, and she certainly looked as pleased as punch about being made a fuss of – despite her claims that she hated it.

Liz caught Ben's eye as she started to relax into her spiel. He was standing next to her on the stage, waiting for his cue as they'd rehearsed in the office.

He smiled encouragingly at her as she started to describe the sales strategy she had developed for the Old Maids campaign, discussing her entry points into major supermarkets for the standard Loch Cameron Ten Year Old, and following that up with the limited edition Old Maid range as a way to revive their market share.

Focused on their shared task, Liz forgot about her misgivings concerning Ben. She put aside all of her worries about the fertility clinic and about everything else, and made herself think only about what she was doing in that moment.

Liz had always excelled at this; no matter what was going on for her, she had always been able to put normal life aside and concentrate on presenting well. But it was more than that. As Ben started speaking, detailing the history of Loch Cameron Distillery and his family's ownership of it, Liz felt the chemistry between them bloom and fill the space between them.

They fed off each other well, like performers; she'd missed a note, just earlier, and Ben had filled it in effortlessly. They were formal in the presentation, making sure they said everything they needed to, but they were also having fun.

'Back to you, Liz.' Ben smiled at her, finishing his first few slides.

'Okay, thank you, Ben.' Liz shot the crowd a dazzling smile. 'Now, I'd like to tell you all a little more about our four cover girls.' Liz talked through Evelyn, Elspeth and Muriel's stories and then flicked to the photo of Gretchen at her desk with the blinding white 80s power suit that she'd snapped from Gretchen's photo album.

'Last, Gretchen Ross. Gretchen was born in 1937 in a workman's cottage in Loch Cameron. Here's a picture of that. Coincidentally, it's where I live now.' Liz showed a recent picture of the cottage with its whitewashed walls and blue door and window frames.

'Gretchen's family lived in the cottage for generations. Gretchen herself, though, didn't always live in Loch Cameron. She was a studious girl, attending the local primary school in the 1940s, then going off to a girls' school a few villages away after that until she finished school in 1954. Gretchen was always a keen reader, and after school she went to secretarial college. From there, she got a job at the library – as was, sadly it's closed now – in Loch Cameron, where she worked for many years.

'In the 1960s, Gretchen wanted to spread her wings, and so she moved away from the family cottage and went to live in Edinburgh, where she started working for Dunne's Books, a publisher of popular fiction. Publishing was very much a man's game in those days, but Gretchen rose through the ranks and became an editor in 1970. She honed her editorial instincts and worked with a variety of well-known authors.

'Between 1980 and 1990, Gretchen was promoted to Editorial Director at Hatch Publishing. While she was there, she adopted a baby daughter, Stella. She remained staunchly single, refusing to marry, despite several offers. She became the only female Editorial Director at Hatch, and was known in the publishing industry at that time as a formidable editor and then publisher. She promoted and developed the careers of several of her female colleagues, and set an example for including more women in the publishing workplace.

'Gretchen is technically an Old Maid, since she never married, but I hope you can appreciate just how strong and inspiring she is – and why her name very much deserves to be celebrated as one of Loch Cameron Distillery's new whiskies. Celebrating women, and our heritage,' Liz finished. 'And, I'm really delighted to say that we have Gretchen with us in the audience today. Give her a round of applause, everyone.'

Gretchen, in her seat at the front of the auditorium, turned and waved grandly at the crowd, who gave her a huge round of applause. There were even a few whoops.

'So, we hope you enjoyed our presentation, and we're available for any questions afterwards,' Liz rounded off. 'Thanks for listening, everyone.'

She stepped off the stage and handed over to the conference organiser, who announced a break for coffee.

'Hey, Gretchen.' She leaned in to greet her friend, who was looking much better than she had last time Liz had seen her, looking so small and frail in her bed. 'You look great! Thanks for coming.'

'Thanks for making me an Old Maid,' Gretchen countered. 'This is my grandson, Eric.'

'Hi, Eric. Really nice to meet you.'

'Same.' Eric was in his early twenties and reminded Liz of an athletic dog – tall, rangy and with a bouncy gait. He was dark haired like Stella and wore jeans and a shirt with a black suit jacket over the top.

'What did you think of the presentation?' Liz asked. 'And, did the doctor really say it was all right for you to come today?'

'Pffft. You know I don't believe in doctors. But, yes, he said it was all right.' Gretchen gave Liz a stern smile. 'As to the presentation, I believe the phrase is: you smashed it! It was great.'

'Awww, thanks. I've been really nervous about it,' Liz admitted.

'Excuse me. I'm so sorry to interrupt, but I just wanted to say congratulations on the Old Maids project. It's really impressive.' Liz turned around to find a middle-aged woman standing politely to one side. She was dressed smartly in a skirt suit and a pearl necklace and wore carefully coiffured hair. 'Simone Ballantyne. I work at the Royal Warrant.'

Simone held out her hand, and Liz shook it.

'The Royal Warrant! Wow. Lovely to meet you. I've actually been trying to get in touch with you guys for a while now,' she said.

'I know. I'm so sorry not to have come back to you sooner. As you can imagine, things are hectic.' Simone smiled warmly. 'Anyway, I just wanted to say that I've got your paperwork and I'll be in touch. You and Ben should come in for a meeting soon. We've actually been reviewing past providers including Loch Cameron Distillery recently, and we wanted to follow up with you and see if we could reconnect.'

'Oh, amazing! That's great news. We'd love that.' Liz beamed.

'Perfect. I'll email you. I just wanted to say hi.' Simone nodded, and walked off.

'Eh! That was good,' Gretchen whispered loudly. 'Ben's going to love that!'

'What am I going to love?' Ben interrupted, and swept Liz into an impromptu hug, actually lifting her off the ground. 'I think it might be Liz, whatever you're talking about! Liz, that was amazing!'

He set her back on the ground, kissed Gretchen on the cheek and pumped Eric's hand in greeting.

'Happy, then?' Liz asked, the wind a little knocked out of her, and discomfited with Ben's sudden display of affection. She just couldn't work him out at all.

'Ecstatic. I've just been talking to loads of people, and they all loved the Old Maids. You're a genius. A lifesaver.'

'No, I'm just good at my job,' Liz replied, stiffly.

'A lady from the Royal Warrant just spoke to us,' Gretchen interjected. 'It looks like you've got an in there, thanks to this one.' She inclined her head at Liz. 'I'd say she deserves a raise.'

'She certainly does,' Ben agreed, cheerily. 'She can have it! She can have what she likes, after that. It was brilliant!'

'That's not necessary.' Liz looked away. Yes, she and Ben had had amazing chemistry onstage, but that was over now, and Liz felt oddly deflated.

Ben took a step back, and his face changed from joyful to guarded.

'What's wrong?' he asked, quieter. Liz shrugged.

'Nothing. Just tired, I guess. There was a lot of anticipation leading up to this. I probably just need some time to myself.' She knew she was making excuses, but she didn't know what else to say. He regarded her quietly for a moment.

'Listen, can we talk? Alone?' He took her arm, and she nodded.

'All right.'

THIRTY-EIGHT

'That went well,' Liz said, politely. Eric, obviously sensing that Ben and Liz needed to talk, had taken Gretchen outside for a cup of tea and a cake, supporting her as she walked slowly, holding his arm.

Now that the presentation was over, Liz was unsure how to talk to Ben, after their argument the night before. It hadn't even been an argument, really: she had been upset, Ben had comforted her, and then she'd ruined everything by insulting him.

'Yeah. Thank you. I mean that. For all your hard work.' Ben cleared his throat.

The crowd around them had dissipated because of the coffee break between sessions, and Liz and Ben were left standing together at the front of the conference hall. Liz started packing up, taking her memory stick out of the laptop drive and gathering up some of the props she'd used: Carol had mocked her up some whisky bottles with the new label on them and she had some promotional boards she'd shown.

'You're welcome. It's my job,' she said, levelly.

'Well, you did your job very well.'

'Thank you,' she replied, curtly.

'Look. I need you to listen to me for a minute, and not interrupt. Is that okay?' Ben looked uncomfortable: he wrung his hands, and then seemed to notice what he was doing and put them behind his back. 'Agh. I don't want to do this here.' He looked around at the people milling at the back of the room. 'Meet me outside, okay? There's a balcony.'

'Do what? Okay...' Liz followed Ben to the side of the room where there was a door she'd never noticed before. He opened it and she followed him through onto a narrow balcony that overlooked the red roofs of the British Library, which was next to the hotel. 'Wow. This is some view. I didn't know this was here.'

'No. I discovered it two years ago when I was looking for somewhere to escape the conference.' He gave her a shy smile.

'Why are we here?' Liz folded her arms over her chest. 'Are you going to sack me? I suppose you'd be within your rights. Things got kind of heated last night. But I would say, I think I've done a very good job on the Old Maids project and I'd expect to see that reflected in a separation agreement.'

'Sack you? No. Why would you think that?' Ben let out a frantic-sounding laugh. 'Goodness. That's the opposite of what I want. I couldn't run this company without you.'

'Well, what then?' Liz frowned.

'Okay. Here goes.' Ben gripped the metal rail of the balcony they stood on and gazed out over London for a moment. 'Last night, you mentioned my wife. Alice.'

'Yes. I'm sorry. It's none of my business,' Liz sighed. 'It was just that... I couldn't understand why you were being so kind to me about my struggles with fertility, when that had happened.' She hedged around saying something more specific like *I heard you threw your pregnant wife out on the street. What've you got to say about that, you heartless bastard?*

'It is your business. At least, I'd like it to be.' Ben ran a hand through his hair. 'Agh. This is all coming out wrong. I mean, I

don't want Alice to be your business. But I want you to understand what happened between us.'

'Why?' Liz studied his face. She could see he was struggling
with something difficult. 'Why does it matter what I think?'

'Because I don't want you to think I'm a monster,' Ben
sighed. 'Because you mean a lot to me. More than I've told you.'

Liz's heart quickened as Ben took her hand.

'I'm listening,' she said, trying to keep some composure in
her voice.

'All right.' He took a deep breath. 'The first thing you
should know is that I loved Alice. And I would never hurt
her.'

Liz said nothing.

'We met as teenagers. She lived in the village. One summer,
I was home from school. I met her in one of the fields outside
the village. It was near her family's farm. I was there, looking for
dragonflies and moths, because I was... a massive nerd, I
suppose. Still am.'

Liz allowed him a smile.

'You are, when it comes to nature. I've noticed that.'

'Yeah. Well, I pretty much fell in love with her straight-
away. She was beautiful, and she understood me in a way that
no one else ever had. My dad always wanted me to be something else, you know? More like him. He hoped boarding school
would change me, but it didn't. I was never good enough for
him.' He took a deep breath. 'Alice wasn't like them. We...' He
chuckled, remembering. 'Well, it doesn't matter. We were in
love, anyway. When I was old enough, I asked her to marry me.
Dad disapproved. But we did it anyway. I was eighteen, she was
twenty.'

'Did your dad ever approve of Alice?' Liz leaned in to him a
little.

'Yeah. We lived at the family house, where I live now. Dad
was tough, but he wouldn't let us go homeless, and there was no

room for us at Alice's family's farm. Over time, he got fond of Alice and he forgave me. I think, anyway.'

'So, what happened? It all sounds okay so far.' Liz frowned.

'What happened was that Alice had always said she didn't want children. Remember that we were pretty young when we got married anyway; it's reasonable that a girl of twenty doesn't want a family just yet. But time went on and she got to thirty and she still didn't want any kids. She was happy just with me, she said.' He raised his eyebrow. 'But then, she fell for someone else. I don't know why. Maybe I wasn't enough for her.' He swallowed.

'Anyway. The long and short of it is that she got pregnant by this guy, who then left her. I was pretty angry, as you can imagine.' He let out a long breath. 'But I still loved her. And I'd do anything to keep her. When Dad found out, too, he told me that there was no way in hell that he was going to allow his grandchild be brought up by someone else, so I went to Alice and I told her I'd still support her, and I'd bring the child up as my own.'

'Oh, my goodness! Ben!' Liz was aghast. 'I can't believe that! It's...' She struggled to think of something to say. 'It's like something from one of those terrible TV talk shows!'

'Yeah. It's right up there.' He nodded. 'DNA test on national TV territory.'

'So, what happened then? Simon said that you threw her out when she was pregnant.'

'I might've known Simon would be behind all this,' Ben muttered, darkly. 'He's always been jealous of me inheriting the distillery. I think he's always thought he could do a better job of running things than me. He's probably right, too. And he was fond of Alice. I always thought he liked her. Maybe he would have asked her out if I hadn't been there.'

'Well, anyway,' Liz prompted him. 'What happened?'

'She refused. She said she couldn't bear to be with me a

moment longer, and she didn't want her child to grow up a Douglas. She went off to try and make it work with the baby's father, and I didn't see her again, not for years, until recently. I didn't tell anyone what had really happened because I was ashamed. She'd cheated on me, left me, and she didn't even love me enough to let me bring the baby up. Another man's baby, at that.'

'Oh, Ben. I'm so sorry.' Liz wrapped her arms around him and gave him a hug; hugging Ben felt completely natural, like she should always have been hugging him. Before, she'd been so guarded around him, but that feeling had disappeared. 'That's horrible. I'm so sorry it happened to you.'

'It's in the past. I didn't tell you so that you'd feel sorry for me,' Ben said, quietly, hugging her back. 'I wanted to explain, since you asked me about it last night. And I could see you were so upset about the miscarriage, and everything you'd been through. I just couldn't stand the thought that you'd think... I don't know. That I would knowingly hurt any woman, but especially do anything as heinous as what Simon said I did.'

'I understand,' Liz replied, hugely relieved. 'Thank you.'

'I'm just sorry I walked out. I should have explained to you then, but I was angry with myself.' Ben let go of her and took both of her hands instead. 'There's something else.'

'What?'

'Last night you said you thought I wanted to leave the company. Because I keep having to go out. I know I've been terrible – missing meetings, being unreliable. The thing is that Alice has been back in touch with me recently. And...' he took in a deep breath, 'she needed my help.'

'She ... she'd had the baby, but it had been taken away by social services. It's – she says it was a girl, that's all I know – it was taken up for adoption. Alice... had a kind of breakdown. She was always fragile, when I knew her. When I was younger, I thought I could be the one to keep her together. I took a kind of pride in that idea, I suppose.' Ben sighed, and ran his hand over his face. 'Pride goes before a fall, though, doesn't it?'

'What kind of breakdown?' Liz could see the worry etched in Ben's face, and she kicked herself for not seeing it earlier. Of course Ben wasn't off playing golf, being the irresponsible person she had thought he was. He had been suffering, worrying all this time, and she hadn't known or helped him.

'Some kind of dissociative episode. That's what the doctor called it,' he said. 'Anyway, she's in a place where they can look after her. At least I feel that I can help her that one way.'

'You're paying for it?'

'Yes.' He looked away. Liz didn't know if he was embarrassed, but he shouldn't have been. It was an incredibly caring thing to do for anyone, never mind someone with whom you had a difficult past.

'So, it was Alice calling you?'

'Yes. I met up with her a few times over the past months. She'd call me in a state, and I'd go and try and bring her back to earth, I guess. She wasn't eating or really looking after herself: she seemed much worse than she ever had been before, but she wouldn't let me get help until a week ago I found her unconscious on the floor of the flat she was living in. I called the hospital and they came and got her. I suppose I still felt guilty about how I left things with her when we separated, even though I know now it wasn't my fault: that's why I kept going when she called. Alice... she was a sweet girl. I did love her once. But not anymore. I need you to know that.'

'Ben. I'm so sorry. I don't know what to say.' Liz hugged him. 'Of course I understand.'

'You've got nothing to be sorry for. I should have explained what was going on. I shouldn't have left you in the lurch, coming up to this big presentation. I knew how important it all was. But... I was just ashamed, and I also had to help Alice. I just had to.' He rested his head against hers. 'Can you forgive me?'

'Of course. There's nothing to forgive,' she murmured.

'Thank you.' He took a deep breath and held her close to him. 'And the reason I'm saying all this is... that I really like you. I mean, I *really* like you.' He pressed her hands to his mouth and kissed her palms. 'And I've wanted to do something about it, and not known how. I kept thinking, *you can't get involved with your co-worker.* And then you told me about Paul and the IVF, and I thought, *Liz just really doesn't need a man in her life now, messing it all up again.*'

'And now? What's changed?' Liz breathed, her heart racing. She felt filled with nerves.

'You. Me. This, whatever it is between us. I don't know.' Ben stroked her hair. 'I just feel like, you came along and changed everything. After Alice left, I'd sworn I was done with women. I was going to concentrate on the business, be a hermit, wait for death. You know. That kind of thing,' he chuckled. 'And then you walked into the distillery that day and I just knew. You lit a fire under me – with the business, with every-thing – and...' He shrugged. 'I just knew. I know. You're the one.'

THIRTY-NINE

'Wow. This is all very unexpected.' Liz blinked. *That was a less than romantic response,* she chided herself. But she didn't know what to say. Today, when she'd woken up, she'd thought that Ben hated her and she might well have lost her job. Now, he was professing some pretty big feelings for her.

'You don't feel the same?' Ben asked, his eyes vulnerable. 'It's okay if you don't. I can cope. I just had to tell you.'

'No, it's not that, at all.' Liz had been attracted to Ben from the start. She knew as well as he did that there was something there. 'I just... didn't see this coming, I guess. But, yes. I've always felt something between us. You always felt... right, to me. Somehow.'

'Oh, Liz. I couldn't bear to see you cry, yesterday.' Ben took her in his arms again. 'It broke my heart. I want more than anything to make you happy. As much as I can. I don't know where this is going... I mean, I know where I'd like it to go.' He smiled, bashfully, and Liz's heart melted a little more. 'But... I guess what I'm saying is... Can I kiss you? And, perhaps, after that... take you for dinner?'

Liz laughed.

'Yes. As long as we go somewhere that isn't the hotel. I don't want our first romantic dinner to be interrupted with questions about the presentation, or shop talk.'

'That's fine. I agree.' Ben leaned his head a little closer to hers. 'And the kiss?'

Liz kissed him, a gentle sigh escaping his lips as she did so. It was a soft kiss: just a brush of her lips against his, but she knew that he wanted more by the way that his hands gripped her waist and drew her to him. She didn't mind the intensity of his touch at all: in fact, she loved it. She loved the solidity of his body and the smell of his skin, which was something hard to describe. She couldn't say exactly what Ben smelt of – it was nothing fragranced or artificial, but rather a comforting, warm sense of manliness that made her mind and body melt.

'You feel so good,' she murmured, pulling away just long enough to look up into his deep brown eyes.

'You do too,' he breathed. 'I've waited to hold you for so long.'

His lips met hers softly, and, this time, the kiss deepened. Liz felt the heat rising between them instantly, and her body reacting instinctively to his.

'Hmmm. I'm not sure that I can wait until after dinner.' He grinned wickedly, and pulled her in towards him.

'I never said there was anything planned for after,' she murmured back, knowing that she would be unable to resist the pull of his body on hers if he kissed her like that later, and if they were alone, in a hotel room. There was something between them that was so electric and connected, and yet she'd never felt as safe with anyone else as she did in Ben's physical presence. Not even Paul.

'You blaze fiercely compared to everyone else around you,' Ben murmured, stroking her hair. 'I don't know if you know that. But you do. And I've always thought you were so... *disturbingly* beautiful.'

'Disturbingly?' She chuckled a little, secretly floored at his description. 'No one has ever said that to me before.'

'Well, you are. I haven't been able to concentrate on work for months, knowing you were in the office next door. Well, that, and everything else.' He kissed her again. Liz felt the tough stubble of Ben's top lip brush her lip; she traced the new, unfamiliar shape of his mouth with hers.

'I'm happy to have disturbed you, then,' she murmured, between kisses. 'You don't think I'm too much. I love that about you.'

'God, never. I can't get enough of you. You could never be too much,' he replied, his arms circling her waist, holding her firmly. 'I never want to let you go.'

'I don't want you to, either,' Liz whispered in his ear. 'But I think we should probably find a cab. It's getting cold out here.'

The view over the city from the balcony was amazing, but Liz was right: the evening was approaching, and the temperature had dropped a little. Not that Liz thought she could ever really feel the cold if Ben was holding her.

'All right,' he sighed, letting her go. 'But I just want you to know that this is temporary. The you-not-being-held-by-me stage of the evening, that is. I want to hold you a lot more.'

FORTY

Ben stood behind her, his arms wrapped around her as they stood together on the top of the mountain, looking out at the stunning view.

'What d'you think?' he murmured, holding her tight.

'Breathtaking,' Liz said, honestly.

It was a Sunday afternoon. The wind was chilly, but the view made up for it. That morning, as they lay in bed, Ben had suggested that they come. *It's so romantic, up there,* he'd said, propping himself up on his elbow and gazing at her. *I want to share my favourite place in the world with you.*

Liz had demurred; it was so cosy in bed, but Ben had promised that they'd stay warm.

But we could just stay here, she'd giggled, wrapping her arms around his neck and looking up into his eyes. *It's warm here. Let's save the mountain for another day.*

That, my darling, is incredibly tempting, Ben had murmured, as he kissed her softly, tracing his fingertips on her neck and collarbone. *But this means a lot to me. I want to take you up there. It was somewhere I'd always go, when I was a kid.*

It's where I went when I wanted to get away from Dad, from school, everything.

So, after waking up in his warm bed at the manor house he had inherited from his family, they had wrapped up in their coats and got into Ben's four-by-four.

It was all still very new between them. After Ben had taken Liz out for dinner in London, after the conference, they had ended up in bed together. Liz hadn't thought she was ready – there had been a point where she had never thought she'd want another man. But Ben had been tender, sensitive, and incredibly patient with her that night. They had slept together, but it had been slow and sensual, and for what seemed like hours before that, Liz had just laid in his arms. He'd held her, and they'd talked as he stroked her hair and told her how beautiful she was, and how he was the luckiest man on earth to be there with her.

And passionate, Liz thought, casting a shy glance at him under her eyelashes. Ben had always struck her as a gentle soul, and he was always nothing but a gentleman. Yet, when he had picked her up in his remarkably strong arms and thrown her on his bed last night, she'd seen the lust in his eyes and realised that, under the sweetness and sensitivity, there was a man who knew how to pleasure a woman.

She shivered with delight, thinking about the night before.

'Are you too cold, sweetheart?' Ben murmured in her ear, and Liz shook her head.

'No. Perfect,' she replied, and nestled in towards his body.

She had to admit that the view was stupendous. By the time Liz and Ben had hiked to the top of the mountain, it was past eleven, and though it got colder the higher they went up, the sun had come out and there wasn't a cloud to be seen in the crisp blue sky. Liz could see all the way across the loch, with the village spread underneath them like toy houses and then, beyond Loch Cameron, to other, heather-covered hills in the far distance. There was a fierce majesty in the green lushness of it all that took Liz's breath away.

'So.' She undid the thermos and poured hot chocolate into the cup, offering it to Ben.

'No, you have it.' He smiled, watching her. 'So, what?'

'So, how often do you come up here?'

'I used to come a lot. It was my special place, but I haven't been up here for a year or two. I stopped wanting to for a while.' He hugged her to him tighter. 'You made me feel like coming here again.'

'Do you really mean that?' she asked, feeling slightly breathless.

'Of course I do. More than anything.' He kissed her. 'I can't believe I'm here with you. You're like a beautiful fairy that came into my life and turned everything from grey to golden sparkles. And, yes, I'm aware how corny that sounds.'

It was such a romantic moment, but Liz's internal voice was trying to spoil it: *he won't love you, he'll want a baby and you probably can't give him one, you should end this now and save yourself the heartbreak later,* it whispered.

'Ben. You know that I probably can't have children, don't you?' She reached for his arm, feeling anxiety unfurl in her belly. She didn't want to push him away, but she knew she had to say it. 'I told you, about the IVF. It ruined my previous relationship. If you want a baby... I mean, I understand that you probably do, based on what happened between you and Alice...' She trailed off, avoiding his eyes. 'I can't give you a family. I need you to know that before this goes any further.'

There was a silence. *He doesn't really want me,* Liz told herself. *It's just physical attraction. Now that he realises what he'd be giving up by being with me, he'll walk away.*

'Liz. Look at me.' Ben tipped her chin up gently with his fingers, meeting her eyes with his. 'Liz. I don't care about all of that. Okay? That isn't why I'm here. I understand what's happened. I understand a baby might never happen. I mean, it's kind of early to be having this conversation.' He paused, and smiled. It made Liz smile too, and a weight started to lift in her heart.

Maybe this would be all right. Maybe there was a way forward.

'But I know this is important to you, so I'm telling you here and now that I understand why you've brought it up. And, sure, I did always kind of see kids in my future, when I was with Alice. But it didn't happen. And if that whole experience taught me anything, it's that you don't know where life is going to lead you. Okay?'

Ben kissed Liz again, gently. 'Liz, you are unlike any other woman I've known. I want to be with you. And, if you want to try IVF again, I'll support you. Later down the road, if you want to adopt, I'll support you. I want to be with you. Whatever that involves. And if it ends up being just the two of us, then I'll still be the happiest man on earth.'

'Do you really mean that?' Liz was overwhelmed.

'Yes. I've been waiting for someone like you. I don't want to mess around, this time. I'm too old for that now.' He smiled, ruefully. Liz shivered, but it wasn't the wind up the mountain that was causing it this time. 'I want you. And...' He trailed off.

'What?'

'You'll think this sounds hasty, but it isn't. I've been thinking about it for a long time, and then when you joined the firm, it solidified my idea.'

'What idea?' Liz stood back a little from Ben, looking up at his handsome face. His eyes twinkled at her. She kissed the end of his nose, playfully.

'I wanted to put a plan in place so that I could eventually either step down as CEO altogether, or share the role. I want us to run the distillery together. If you want that.' He smiled soppily at her kiss. 'Aww. That was nice.'

'Wow.' Liz was speechless. 'That was... not what I was expecting you to say.'

'What were you expecting me to say?' He smiled, and brushed a stray hair away from her face.

'I don't know. Not that.' She laughed nervously. 'You want me to be joint CEO? With you?'

'Yes. If that doesn't feel too forward.'

'It's diabolically forward.' Liz let out a laugh.

'Too much?'

'Yes. No. I mean... obviously, I do want that,' she said, feeling a little giddy. 'Would you still have asked me if we weren't... you know.'

'Sleeping together? Yes, I'd still ask you. You could really run the show without me. I think we both know that.' Ben laughed. 'But I enjoy us working together. We've got great chemistry, as lovers and colleagues,' he murmured, kissing her again.

'Mmm. I know.' Liz kissed him back. 'But what does that mean, in practice? I'm already a director.'

'You taste like hot chocolate. How does partner CEO sound?' Ben murmured. 'You've earned it. And it would allow me to step back a little from the stuff you know I hate. I could concentrate more on the craft and the creative side of things.'

'I think that sounds amazing, if you're serious.' Liz stood back, looking up into Ben's open face. 'You mean, I'd take over... operational control? Financial control? Sales?'

'Yep. All that stuff. I mean, obviously, we'd still run everything together. But you're so much better at the business than I am. I admit that.' He chafed his hands together against the cold.

'It's your family business,' Liz argued. 'I wouldn't want you to give that up.'

'And I wouldn't. But I see us going forward with it together.' He took her hand. 'Come on. Let's go back down, and talk it over a bit more.'

'I can't believe this is all happening.' Liz took his hand.

'It's happening.' Ben held her hand to his mouth and kissed her palm. 'Are you ready? Because I'm ready for you.'

'I am.' Liz's heart fluttered with excitement.

If anyone had told me four months ago that I'd have fallen for my new boss and just been made CEO of a family business, I'd have laughed in their faces, she thought, marvelling at how quickly life could change, sometimes, when you made yourself open to the possibilities. *But here I am. And, more than that, I didn't think I'd ever feel like things on the baby front were ever going to be hopeful again. But they are.*

Trying for a baby had been such an integral part of Liz's life for so long now that, for her, it was part of any conversation that was worth having.

And Ben was definitely a conversation worth having. Ben could be a lifetime of talking, laughing, working and all the other, physical, less easy-to-describe things that made him so irresistible.

And Ben understood that Liz needed to have the baby conversation now. He wasn't frightened of it; he knew everything Liz had sacrificed to have a child, so far, and how much it meant to her. And, having had the conversation, he hadn't run away. She was so grateful for that.

Perhaps Liz could still win that game show; perhaps she could still be a competitor, and reach for that dream. The picture-perfect image of herself with her child, up in lights at the top of whatever pyramid of steps she had to take to get there.

Maybe, even, there didn't have to be a game show. There didn't have to be a crazy number of steps to follow, or tasks to master in the pursuit of a child. Maybe she shouldn't think of it as such hard work. There were other options, like adoption or fostering, or even surrogacy. All of those options brought their own difficulties, sure, but she was up to those challenges.

And maybe that idealised picture she'd thought about so much could also change: maybe it wouldn't be just her and her baby in the picture now. She realised, all of a sudden, that Paul had never been in the picture when she'd imagined it before.

But she could imagine Ben standing next to her in the photo. He fit perfectly.

Liz, her hand in Ben's, followed him back down the mountain, and into their new life together. She knew that whatever came, they would face it together. And she was immensely happy and grateful for that.

EPILOGUE

EIGHTEEN MONTHS LATER

'It's going to snow. That's what it said on the forecast, anyway,' Liz called out to Ben, wrapping her cardigan around her shoulders as she stood warming herself in front of the log fire. 'We were going to go up the mountain. Do you still want to go?'

'No. It's too cold.' Ben came into the lounge of his manor house carrying two mugs of cocoa. 'Here. Get this down you.'

'We should go, in the snow. It would be romantic.' Liz smiled at him, taking the mug and sipping it. 'Mmmm. Thanks, that's perfect.'

'Don't be daft. I'm not taking you hiking up a mountain in sub-zero temperatures.' Ben set his cocoa down on the coffee table and wrapped his arms around her, carefully, so that she didn't spill her drink.

'It was quite cold when we went up last. It's cold every time, actually,' Liz giggled. 'That first time, even.'

'It wasn't this cold. And I was giddy with new love, that first time. Wasn't thinking straight,' he chuckled. 'Now, before you say it, I'm just as giddy now. But I'd rather stay next to a crackling log fire with you, if that's okay.'

'That's okay with me.' Liz put her mug down and turned to cuddle up to Ben, loving the feel of his body against hers. It still gave her the same feelings of safety and security, as well as being deeply arousing. 'You make me giddy every day.'

'Oh lord. Probably an inner ear problem.' Ben hugged her tight and kissed her head. 'Now, listen, you. In January, we've got the appointment with the new fertility doctor. Best in the country. You've got that in your diary, haven't you? Sally's primed to hold the fort while we're in London. I thought we could spend a few days in a nice hotel while we're there.'

'I've got it in my diary. Don't worry.' Liz checked her phone and showed the calendar to Ben. 'How many days? I like the thought of a hotel, for sure. But we can't be away long.'

'We're allowed to take time off now and again, babe,' Ben chuckled. 'I told you. Sally will be fine. She can get hold of us if it's urgent.'

'I suppose so,' Liz conceded.

Since they'd been together, Liz and Ben had agreed that if Liz hadn't got pregnant within a year without them doing anything other than not using contraception, then they'd start fertility treatments – at least once, just to give it a final go.

Ben wanted children. They wanted children together. That in itself was huge for Liz, but she trusted him completely. Ben had given her everything: half his business, and all of his heart. They hadn't got married, but they'd agreed that they would if a baby came along, or if they decided that they really wanted to.

It was strange. When she'd been with Paul, he'd always wanted her to give up work, and she'd always refused. Her work was so important to her, and she hated that he didn't understand that about her.

But Ben knew exactly how important her work was, and he thought so highly of her professional skills that he'd promoted her to joint CEO of the distillery. They'd been running it together for the past eighteen months, and it had been amazing. The Royal Warrant was in progress, the Old Maids range had launched to great acclaim, and the standard Loch Cameron Ten Year Old was stocked in two major supermarket chains.

And, because Liz knew that Ben respected her professionally, she was happy to try again for a baby. They'd try one round and see how it went. Possibly, she might feel that she wanted to give up after that, or she might not. Whatever she decided, Ben had made it clear that he was behind her a hundred per cent.

As well as that, Liz was at a place in her life where she was completely happy. She had great friends, she loved her job, and she loved Ben with all her heart. She remained hopeful that she might still win the baby game show she'd invested so much time into, but she also knew that she'd be happy, regardless. And that was a huge realisation.

'It feels like I've been on such a journey already,' she confessed, nestling into Ben's chest. 'You know? This is a new chapter, but unlike before, I don't feel as desperate about it. I'd love it to happen. But I don't feel that everything will fall apart if it doesn't.'

Ben's voice tickled her ear. 'I know exactly how you feel. Listen, if it doesn't work out – and you know that I hope it does as much as you do – then it's okay. Because I love you. And you're more than enough for me as you are. If a baby comes along, then so much the better. But I just want you to know that. Okay?'

He turned her around to face him, and she looked up into his eyes.

'I know that,' she murmured. 'And I love you. More than I've ever loved anyone.'

'Here's to us, then.' He leaned down, and kissed her softly. 'And a happy Christmas, Liz Parsons. I hope the new year is full of wonderful things.'

'It will be, because you're in it,' she replied. 'I know that sounds corny. But it really will. Baby or no baby.'

'I know. But I have a good feeling about it. Don't you?' Ben breathed.

'I do,' Liz replied, and wrapped her arms around his neck. 'I really do.'

A LETTER FROM KENNEDY

Dear reader,

I want to say a huge thank you for choosing to read *A Secret at the Cottage by the Loch*. If you did enjoy it, and want to keep up to date with all my latest releases, just sign up at the following link. Your email address will never be shared and you can unsubscribe at any time.

www.bookouture.com/kennedy-kerr

A Secret at the Cottage by the Loch is the second book in the Loch Cameron series; book one, *The Cottage by the Loch*, is out now!

In *A Secret at the Cottage by the Loch* I wanted to tackle the subject of infertility, which affects so many women and men. It was important to me to leave the reader with a hopeful feeling for Liz at the end of the book, but also to make it clear that Liz could be happy with or without a baby. In Loch Cameron, she finds a new life where she feels supported and valued, as well as a man who loves her, and she comes to realise that having a baby doesn't have to be her only goal. I definitely have my fingers crossed for Liz, though – she deserves to have all the good things.

I wish the same for all of my readers, too. It's important to me to write about the issues that affect women in my books, whether that be divorce, breast cancer, bereavement, stalking, family expectations and so many other things. I try to write about them sensitively and with empathy, and also prioritise writing about the way women help other women, from the supportive crochet coven in Loch Cameron to the wild swimmers of Magpie Cove and beyond.

Thank you as always for reading my books. Your faith in me means the world, and thank you for all the wonderful reviews. I'm so happy that you enjoy Magpie Cove and Loch Cameron – and I look forward to writing many more books for you to enjoy.

I hope you loved *A Secret at the Cottage by the Loch* and if you did I would be very grateful if you could write a review. I'd love to hear what you think, and it makes such a difference helping new readers to discover one of my books for the first time.

I love hearing from my readers – you can get in touch on my Facebook page, through Twitter, Goodreads or my website.

All my love,

Kennedy xxxx

facebook.com/kennedykerrauthor

twitter.com/kennedykerr5

instagram.com/kennedykerrauthor

AUTHOR'S NOTE

I based the site and descriptions of Loch Cameron Distillery on Glenturret Distillery in Crieff, the oldest whisky distillery in Scotland, and on the Lagavulin distillery on Islay. There are over 140 working whisky distilleries in Scotland at the time of writing, and it's well worth visiting some of them if you can. All are different and unique in their own way.

I was also greatly inspired by the Netflix documentary *The Amber Light* featuring presenter and whisky specialist Dave Broom, particularly the old legends regarding the Fairy Queen and her bestowing the knowledge of distillation to the locals on Islay.

Here are some interesting facts from the Scots Whisky Association Facts & Figures (scotch-whisky.org.uk) which helped me write this book – and appreciate how important distilleries are to Scotland.

- **44** bottles (70cl @40% ABV) of Scotch Whisky are shipped from Scotland to around **180** markets around the world each second, totalling over **1.3bn** every year

- Laid end to end those bottles would stretch about **377,000kms**
- In 2021, Scotch Whisky exports were worth **£4.5bn**
- In 2021, Scotch Whisky accounted for **75%** of Scottish food and drink exports, **22%** of all UK food and drink exports, and **1.4%** of all UK goods exports
- The Scotch Whisky industry provides **£5.5bn** to the UK economy
- More than **11,000** people are directly employed in the Scotch Whisky industry in Scotland and over **42,000** jobs across the UK are supported by the industry
- **7,000** of these jobs in rural areas of Scotland providing vital employment and investment to communities across the Highlands and Islands
- Around **90%** of barley requirements of the industry are sourced in Scotland
- In 2019, there were **2.2 million** visits to Scotch Whisky distilleries, making the industry the third most popular tourist attraction in Scotland
- Some **22 million** casks lie maturing in warehouses in Scotland waiting to be discovered - that is around **12bn** 70cl bottles
- To be called Scotch Whisky, the spirit must mature in oak casks in Scotland for at least **3** years.

Made in United States
North Haven, CT
26 July 2024

55492538R00182